A HAND IN THE BIRD

Iuti almost tripped as a feathered fern bush bustled into her path. "What?" It was not a bush, she saw, but a bird. The bird trembled and shook. A handful of feathers dropped away.

A human hand appeared at the tip of one wing. Iuti blinked, but the brown-skinned fingers retained their form—she wasn't dreaming. A long arm lifted away from the bird's wing; then the rest of Ma'eva's sleek, naked body emerged from the gull. The great seabird blinked its dark eyes as Ma'eva's face appeared, superimposed over beak and high, crowning feathers. The faces separated with a soft pop, and finally Ma'eva pulled free. There was one last struggle as he shook his toes loose from the bird's claws.

By Carol Severance
Published by Ballantine Books:

REEFSONG

DEMON DRUMS

DEMON
DRUMS

Carol Severance

A Del Rey Book

BALLANTINE BOOKS • NEW YORK

A Del Rey Book
Published by Ballantine Books

Copyright © 1992 by Carol Severance

All rights reserved under International and Pan-American Copyright Conventions. Published in the United States of America by Ballantine Books, a division of Random House, Inc., New York, and simultaneously in Canada by Random House of Canada Limited, Toronto.

Library of Congress Catalog Card Number: 91-92393

ISBN 0-345-37448-7

Manufactured in the United States of America

First Edition: July 1992

Acknowledgments

The author would like to thank Carolyn Inks Reed, Rhea Rose, Alan D. McNarie, Craig Severance, Annie Yu Brown, Shelly Shapiro, and the 1984 Clarion West follow-up crew for helping to bring the Island Warrior to life.

The story itself belongs to Linina and her gecko.

☙ Chapter 1 ☙

IUTI squatted motionless near the edge of the reef flat. Restless waves swept across her time after time, soaking her to her shoulders and leaving her shivering in the evening breeze. She wore a faded tan skirt, tucked carefully between her knees, and a long-sleeved man's tunic that blended perfectly with the tumble of coral stones and boulders.

Only her eyes moved as she searched the incoming swells.

"Come to me, brothers," she chanted softly. She didn't use a true beckoning spell—she only said the words in time with the shifting waves. "Come fill my nets before I turn into a cold stone here in the sea."

Flickering color caught her attention, and she shifted her gaze to follow the erratic paths of two blue-green parrot fish. They approached the reef in unison and began feeding on the living coral. Iuti watched patiently while they darted here and there among the colorful growths, turning and drifting together through the clear water as if they were one.

Then suddenly, she dashed forward, leapt a gap in the coral, and scooped the startled fish into her hand nets. As quickly as one touched and tangled itself in the left net, the other did the same in the right. Iuti struggled for footing in the wave's strong backwash while she lifted each of the fish to her mouth. She bit them just behind their eyes, killing them instantly and removing them forever from Pahulu's power.

The island sorceress was particularly dangerous near

1

and around the sea. Pahulu could send her soul into living fish and other sea-life, enchanting them so that their flesh caused terrible nightmares, even death, for those who ate it.

Iuti glanced back toward the beach. She saw only sunset-gilded coconut trees and distant firelight from the village, but she knew Pahulu was lurking somewhere in the shadows—watching, waiting for her to break her resolve never to use magic on this isle.

"It won't happen, witch," Iuti muttered. "Not tonight or on any other. You've had your last taste of my soul."

Iuti had faced many sorcerers during her years as a mainland warrior. Her personal bond with the shark god, Mano Niuhi, had provided her with both the physical and the magical strength to withstand them, even to defeat them. But never in all her travels had she met a witch quite so insidious as Fanape's self-proclaimed protector.

Iuti had come to Fanape Atoll five months before, tired and sick to death of the endless horrors of the Teronin War. Even with Mano at her side, she hadn't been able to move the southern army toward victory. As soon as one battle was won, the Teronin began another, each time employing ever-darker magic and a seemingly endless supply of empty-eyed warriors. Lately, they had even begun using the demon drums of Losan.

Finally, it had become too much even for Iuti Mano, the warrior the south depended on most to defend them from the invading Teronin. She had retreated alone to the distant island of Fanape, where she bargained with the island elders, and with their sorceress, for a time of peace far from the constant bloodshed and death.

During her early days on the island, Iuti had been exhausted; the simple acts of fishing and gathering food for each day's meal left her weak and shaking. Her sleep was restless and filled with dark dreams. At first, she thought her weakness was caused by her healing wounds and overall weariness. But after a time, even without

Mano's help, her war-trained senses detected something more.

She set a careful watch on her mind and discovered that each time she attempted a simple sleep or self-healing spell, each time she sang the fish into her nets instead of simply waiting for them to come near, Pahulu was using the opportunity to drain her strength away.

"A miscalculation, warrior," Pahulu had said when Iuti confronted her. "I sought only to test your intentions, to verify that the fish you provide the villagers aren't tainted by any mainland war sorcery."

"Aye," Iuti had replied, "a miscalculation," and from that day on, she had employed only her physical skills. She lived and fished as she had in her childhood before being bonded with Mano Niuhi and trained to the ways of power and war. She avoided all use of the magic that would give Pahulu entry to her soul. The nightmares had ceased and her strength had slowly returned.

As she disentangled the fish from her nets, Iuti wondered if the island's permanent residents knew that their sorceress gained her power by draining it from other living creatures. It might explain why so little magic was in evidence here.

Pahulu's power had surprised Iuti at first: the strength of it seemed out of proportion to the island's size and isolation, and to the sorceress's own lack of repute. The old woman carried the same name as the more notorious southern islands sorceress, but Iuti knew for certain they weren't the same. She had dealt with the southern Pahulu before. Still, this witch's sorcery had the same foul stench. Perhaps they were distant kin.

Iuti scanned the reef casually as she stuffed the parrot fish into her woven waist pouch and wiped the slickness from her hands. The sun had almost set, and the island's shadow stretched toward her across the rippling water. The tide was still low enough for her to make out the wavering shapes of the underlying coral, although their brilliant colors had faded in the dimming light. The ever-present surf on the outer reef edge rumbled quietly, and were it not for Pahulu's evil presence, the approaching night would have been a time of pleasant calm.

Iuti saw that the girl Tarawe had crept closer while she was busy with the fish, and that made her smile. Her unacknowledged apprentice was lying prone in the water now, with only her head above the shifting waves, no doubt thinking herself well hidden.

Iuti knew she would have to do something about Tarawe soon. Send her away. Make her angry or afraid enough to stop her spying before the others, especially Pahulu, decided to take notice. It was too bad, for the teenager showed great promise and was obviously interested in learning. Often, Iuti came upon her practicing some water or war skill learned only from distant watching.

Tarawe was alone among the island's youngsters in defying the elders' orders to ignore their mainland visitor. Iuti was relieved that the rest kept their distance—she had no wish to explain her daily actions to a gaggle of curious children—but she still found it odd that they didn't come. She had grown up on an isolated atoll much like Fanape, and remembered all too well the excitement any new visitor caused.

Her own brothers had left her stranded high in a breadfruit tree once, when the call came that an approaching canoe had been sighted. They had been catching birds, and Iuti was the only one light enough to climb in the upper branches where the birds could be snagged with a sap-tipped spear. Because she couldn't climb down alone, she had been forced to stay in the tree until her brothers came back for her many hours later.

The time had not been entirely lost. Iuti had made the acquaintance of many birds, catching them with the sticky breadfruit sap, then removing a few feathers from each before cleaning them carefully and setting them free. Still, she had been furious with her brothers, because she had missed the arrival of the southern army's envoy. Any distraction to the lonely island life was welcomed, and the story of her imprisonment in the tree had provided the islanders, and their mainland visitors, with laughter for days.

Until the shark god passed them all by and chose me to carry him onto the human battleground, she thought. There was no laughter then. They'd have been wiser if they'd left me in the tree.

A change in the air brought Iuti's full attention back to the sea. The rhythm of the waves had not changed, nor had the wind, but something was oddly different. She listened carefully above the rumbling surf, wishing she could call on Mano's power to amplify the sounds. She had lived so long under her family god's protection that now she distrusted her own natural senses.

Iuti grew taut as she recognized the soft splash of canoe paddles, accompanied by the barely audible cadence of a whispered war chant. Quickly she squatted again and turned her look toward the open sea.

No islander would be on the ocean at this hour. She herself had stayed out this late only to teach Tarawe a lesson—and to irritate Pahulu. She hoped the girl, at least, would have sense enough to remain hidden.

The chanting drifted off with the wind for a moment, then returned, just loud enough for Iuti to follow the boat's steady movement toward the island. Through squinted eyes she made out a shadow on the water, then the wavering silhouette of an outrigger paddling canoe. As it neared the breaking waves, the steersman dug his paddle deep into the sea and turned the canoe parallel to the reef's edge. The chanting stopped.

Then, abruptly, it began again—this time with a strong, powerful beat. Deep male voices rang out over the rumbling surf, and dread crept like mainland cold across Iuti's back.

"Mano, protect the girl," she whispered softly.

The song was a ghost chant, sung only by crews of the dead.

The canoe moved steadily closer. Iuti could see now that it carried only seven paddlers. The place before the steersman was empty. The ghost canoe would pass just a few arm lengths away from where Iuti hid. She braced herself as best she could against the surge and breathed sporadically between the sweep of deepening waves. The tide was reclaiming the reef.

The sudden thought that the canoe might have come for her made Iuti shiver again. She tasted brine through inadvertently parted lips. The great warrior Ser Iuti Mano, she thought, one of the Teronin War's bloodiest survivors, dead with a sackful of fish on her back. Now there's a joke to test the gods.

Iuti had faced death more times than she could count. She had once heard her southern companions boasting that for as long as the shark god swam in Iuti Mano's mind, her body was immune to death.

I'm not immune now, she thought. She sucked in a slow, deep breath, tucked her chin to her chest, and slid beneath the water.

As soon as the canoe had passed, she surfaced again. There was something familiar about the ghostly vessel. Iuti studied its shape carefully. Suddenly wood thunked on wood and a muffled curse reached Iuti's ears. She choked in surprise and quickly dropped underwater again.

That's no ghost canoe! she thought. Not unless dead men now curse in the gutter tongue of Teron. She shifted and peered again through the near darkness. The vessel appeared island-made from a distance—and certainly the death chant was authentic enough, it was being sung in Fanape's own dialect—but the decorative prow was slightly higher than the outer island style, and the outrigger was a good deal wider.

The men aboard that canoe, Iuti wagered, were as alive and warrior-wise as any she had faced on a mainland battlefield.

She was staring at a Teronin war canoe!

Iuti whispered a curse of her own, then settled low in the water again. She remained as still as the growing coral while the canoe completed its passage along the windward reef.

After it had turned back to sea, she slipped across the reef flat. She startled Tarawe from her hiding place and urged the soaking, shivering girl back to the village. Pahulu was already there, talking excitedly to the islanders who had gathered outside the main canoe house at the village center.

"You must all remain inside tonight," she called out as Iuti approached, "and for the next two nights, as well. No one should take any unnecessary chances until the ghost canoe completes its third passage. I'll set a protective spell against accidents and illness, and the canoe will be forced to seek elsewhere to fill its vacant seat."

Iuti stepped forward, still dripping from the sea. She was much taller than Pahulu and most of the others, and she did nothing to disguise her size. Even the sorceress sidled back as she approached.

"The only lives that vessel seeks are those too foolish to prepare a defense," Iuti said. "It's an old Teronin trick. They use some local superstition to frighten their intended victims into huddling together unarmed. Then they attack when you're most vulnerable."

"We have no quarrel with the Teronin," Tarawe's uncle said. He was chief of the leading clan, and in the absence of an elder sister, he spoke for all the others.

"If you insist on hiding in your homes to avoid a nonexistent ghost canoe," Iuti said, "Teronin warriors will walk ashore unchallenged two nights from now. They'll slaughter you in your own homes."

"These islands are neutral territory," Pahulu said. "They're more valuable left alone than destroyed by roving warriors. We pay regular tribute to the Teronin to leave us in peace."

Iuti wondered, not for the first time, what these small islands had to offer that kept the Teronin away. Perhaps it was only their isolation and their seeming poverty that provided their protection. The islanders owned little more than their thatched houses, a few coconut and breadfruit trees, and the small bit of land upon which they stood.

"I swear to you," she said. "Those were real men on a real canoe. If you will allow me, I can show you how to protect—"

"No, warrior," Tarawe's uncle said quickly. "That was a true ghost canoe. Pahulu saw it from shore. We all heard the death song right here in the village."

"But Pahulu was far up on the beach," Iuti insisted. "I was at the reef's edge, so close I could have reached out and touched the canoe." She explained again about the shape of the vessel and repeated the whispered war chant she had heard, and the Teronin curse. She implored them to aid her in preparing for the island's defense.

But they only murmured and whispered among themselves.

"Go back to your hut," Pahulu said finally, "before your foreign ways and tales of bloodshed corrupt our children." Her black teeth glistened and her eyes flashed triumph.

Iuti knew that further argument was useless. She could never convince the others while their own sorceress denied her warning.

"You gave your word not to bare your sword on our soil," one of the younger men said.

"Aye, and you killed your own family god to seal the bargain," another added. "How can you even think of taking up that blade again?"

Iuti lifted a hand to her neck, where she had once worn a strand of Mano's teeth to signify her shame. The necklace was gone now, but the feel of the shark's lost strength still burned against her skin.

"We're not interested in war here," Pahulu said. "Go away and don't speak about it further."

Iuti cursed—the islanders for their stubbornness, Pahulu for her duplicity, and herself for having so foolishly accepted the conditions of their peace. She was enraged by the casual reference to her disgrace. She dumped her pouch of fish at Tarawe's uncle's feet and stalked off, taking little satisfaction from the envious comments concerning the size and quality of her catch. She pointedly ignored Tarawe, who had entered the village canoe house and was measuring the height of the largest canoe's prow.

"Fools," she muttered.

"Shark-killer," she heard one of the women reply.

❧ Chapter 2 ❧

TARAWE came to Iuti early the next morning. She sat cross-legged just outside Iuti's small, thatched hut. Iuti had built the house herself, in the Western Islands style, with thatch made of woven coconut fronds and the floor raised several hands off the ground so air could flow freely underneath.

The islanders had thought the raised floor an extravagance, but in return for a portion of her daily catch on the reef, they had supplied the needed support posts and breadfruit planks for flooring. She had gathered the thatching materials herself, using discarded mangrove poles and coconut fronds that had fallen on their own to the jungle floor. The work of both the building and the fishing had brought a desperately needed quiet back into her mind.

Tarawe watched in silence while Iuti moved boiled breadfruit from the kettle to the wooden pounding board. Iuti slammed the heavy *po* down onto the mound of softened breadfruit.

"What are you going to do?" Tarawe asked after a time.

Iuti didn't look up. "You can see very well what I'm doing, preparing my breakfast." She crashed the stone pestle down again and again. Had this been an ordinary day, the sounds of similar pounding would have echoed across Fanape, for boiled and pounded breadfruit was a staple in the islanders' diets. But the residents of Fanape were performing only silent and safe duties today, those that could be done in or near their homes, and without any possibility of injury.

10

"I mean about the Teronin."

Iuti slammed the *po* down with enough force to spatter white breadfruit paste.

"If you keep swinging like that," Tarawe said dryly, "you'll bash yourself right in the head. Then a ghost canoe will come for sure."

Iuti bit back a sharp reply, then smiled slightly and lightened her strokes. "I'm not afraid of ghosts," she lied.

"Are you afraid of the Teronin?"

Iuti sighed. "Go away, girl. You know I can't talk to you about the Teronin."

Tarawe leaned her elbows on her knees, chin on crossed hands. "If they're going to kill us all tomorrow night anyway, what does it matter if you talk to me now?"

"It matters because I gave my word not to," Iuti said. She met the girl's frank stare. "I killed my own family's totem, gave up my right to his power and his protection, to prove my word was good and gain your elders' permission to live here in peace. Do you think I took that oath lightly?"

Tarawe's look dropped. Iuti returned to her pounding.

"If what you say is true, my uncle and the others might be eager for your sword arm tomorrow," Tarawe said after a time.

Iuti snorted, wondering why the girl was being so persistent. She had never encouraged Tarawe's interest in her warrior's skills—and certainly the islanders had not. More than once Iuti had seen Tarawe scolded for simply watching her while she did her daily chores.

"Even if I were released from my vow," she said, "my sword arm would be of little use after the entire Teronin fleet arrives. The Teronin don't engage in contests of honor. They won't stride across the reef one by one tomorrow night to meet your island champion."

Tarawe's hesitation was very slight. "Then you should face them tonight," she said, "when there are only a few."

Iuti blinked. She glanced around to be sure they

weren't being overheard. The girl was right, of course, that it no longer mattered, but her word had been given and the habit of caution was strong. She sucked a wad of breadfruit from the side of her hand.

"You could surprise them," Tarawe said. Her eyes sparked with sudden excitement. "They won't be expecting you on the reef tonight. You could kill them all before they even knew what was happening. My uncle said you once killed three men with a single stroke of your sword."

Iuti took a deep breath and resumed her pounding.

"I'll help you!" Tarawe cried. "I know the reef, and I know how to use a knife."

That made Iuti laugh. "You know how to slice breadfruit and gut fish, girl."

"I can cut the inner muscle of a giant clam with a single stroke!"

Iuti rested the *po* on the edge of the board. "Have you ever cut through *human* muscle? Killing one of your own kind is not the same as killing a shellfish, girl. It's not easy, nor can it be done with so little consequence."

Tarawe pulled back, and Iuti forced herself to speak more calmly.

"When you take the life of another person, even an enemy," she said, "you expose your own soul to the evil that surrounds all violent deaths. You become vulnerable to the darkness. Without careful training and the protection of your family gods, even the strongest warrior has little defense against the killing thrusts."

"But you've been trained," Tarawe said. "You've fought the Teronin before. You have a real metal sword and a—"

"I have a metal *sword* that I cannot *use*, girl." Iuti lifted the *po* and began pounding again, striking the breadfruit to the beat of her words. "A sword that I *will* not use even if your elders *ask*." A gob of sticky paste stuck to the pestle and flew off with the next downward stroke. It splatted on the ground near Tarawe.

The girl stared at the breadfruit for a moment, then angrily kicked sand over it.

"I thought you were different," she said. She stood and settled her fists on her hips. "They told me you weren't afraid of anything, but you're even worse than the others! You just sit here and take what comes. They at least had the excuse of being tricked into giving up their strength before the Teronin came. You're still whole and strong and—"

"What *others*?" Iuti demanded.

Tarawe hesitated again. Then she laughed. Her voice became a mocking parody of Pahulu's. "Did you think you were the first to be invited to Fanape, warrior woman? Oh, no, you're not that special despite your great reputation. We offer our hospitality to many—as many as it takes to keep the Teronin recruiting ships filled. They care nothing about prior loyalties, but they prefer those already trained to war."

"By the very gods!" Iuti breathed. "The tribute! You buy your freedom by selling human lives!"

"Not lives," Tarawe corrected. "*Souls!* Pahulu strips them of their power while they rest here in 'peace,' and then the elders sell their empty shells to the Teronin. Most are here for only a few weeks. You've stayed the longest."

Iuti straightened as a shadow, darker than the surrounding shadows, flickered near the edge of the clearing.

"Go away, girl," she said very softly.

"But—"

"Go away. Don't come near me again!"

Tarawe stood silently for a moment, then spun and ran off between the trees. Iuti lifted the *po* high.

Her next downward stroke split the wooden pounding board in two. The shadow disappeared.

Late that afternoon, Iuti closed herself inside her sleeping hut and opened her private box. The locking spell wasn't of her own devising, so it had remained safe from Pahulu's influence. Iuti removed her cold-weather cloak from the box. Powdery sprays of mildew blossomed on each of the leather clasps and on the torn leather boots that lay underneath. She sneezed and tossed them all outside.

Then she lifted her forbidden sword. Rust lined the edges of the scabbard. It pained her to see so ill-kept a weapon, but even if her oath had not been given, she wouldn't bare that blade again. She had used it to kill Mano Niuhi, the great gray shark, protector of her clan and family. It had been the price of her stay on this "neutral" island.

Iuti had been desperate for a time of peace, for a time away from the blood and horror of the never-ending war. She had fought so long, and killed so many, that the deaths had come to mean nothing to her. She simply fed the bloodied kills to the ever-ravenous Mano, and sealed the rest away at the back of her mind.

She had known it was a dangerous road she traveled. There was only a short distance between cold acceptance and that place where enjoyment in the killing began. But she had believed that with Mano's help, she would never step over the line.

A sluggish breeze rustled the thatch over Iuti's head. She glanced up to see a tiny gecko, newly hatched, wriggling through the woven fronds.

I crossed the line at Kugar Village, she thought. I heard the Teronin retreat whistles. She could admit that now. I heard the southern call to stand, as well—and she had chosen to ignore it.

Iuti remembered racing after the terrified Teronin warriors, thrilling along with Mano at the taste of their blood. A movement beside a burning hut had drawn her attention. A small, rag-clad figure had stumbled into view, stared at her, and then turned to run. Ignoring the cries of her comrades, Iuti had shouted Mano's name and followed.

One stroke! she remembered thinking. I will kill this coward with one stroke! A small sweet tidbit to please Mano's palate. She remembered laughing aloud, "Little Teronin, you haven't the strength of an infant compared to mine and my brother Mano's!"

She had lifted her sword high, plunged it down . . .

. . . and seen in that instant that it *was* an infant! A village child, who had run from her for no other reason than terror.

Iuti had tried to stay her blow. She tried to yank back her blade before it could touch that soft, smooth flesh. But even as she threw herself aside, tripping just as the child had over the body of what might well have been its mother, she felt her sword's tip catch and tear.

The child screamed sharply once, then began a steady, shrill wail. Mano had thrashed with frustration at the back of Iuti's mind, and she had cried, "Be silent!"

She whispered the words again, there in the hut on Fanape. "Be silent, brother. I cannot kill again!" But she knew now that she would have to.

I will never let it become what it was before, she promised.

A healer had come eventually and taken the bloody infant from Iuti's hands. "It will live, but the scar will mark it forever as a child of war," the healer said. She spoke in a voice so carefully neutral that Iuti was forced to turn away.

Later, Iuti sat apart from the others, feeling nothing but the cold touch of death all around. She refused the victory drafts that passed with increasing frequency among the southern warriors. They were celebrating a battle won, even though they all knew it for a hollow victory. Kugar Village remained under southern control, but the farms that had supported it were destroyed. The village would die when the army moved on.

Late in the night, the healer who had taken the child came back to sit beside Iuti. "You should go away for a time," she said.

Iuti sighed and rubbed her eyes. Her hands still smelled of blood. "I have nowhere to go," she replied. Word of her presence in any isolated place acted like a magnet for troublemakers and Teronin spies eager to test their skill against hers and Mano's.

"I know of a distant place," the healer said. "A place where you wouldn't be a danger for those around you.

For a small price, you could live there in secrecy and peace for as long as you wish.''

Now Iuti fingered the edges of her sword's rusty scabbard. "A small price," she muttered.

The islanders had demanded that she surrender her most prized possession, her personal bond with the shark god, and because she had known no other way to turn back from the cold evil sucking ever more strongly from her soul, she had agreed.

Iuti glanced again at the rusty sword, then around at the inside of her sleeping hut, thinking of the strange peace that Fanape had, in fact, brought. Until now . . .

She reached into her box again and took up a package wrapped in a finely woven mat. Inside was a wooden club and a shield. She lifted the club in both hands and carefully inspected the double row of shark's teeth that lined the weapon's jagged edges.

They were Mano's own teeth.

Iuti ran her fingers along the glistening, white surfaces, testing their settings in the twisted coconut fiber and fire-hardened wood, then laid the club aside and inspected the shield. It, too, was studded with Mano's power.

She had honored her pledge to set aside her mainland war tools while on Fanape, but no one had suggested she not create new ones with the island's own resources. They assumed that because there was no metal here, there was no way for her to do so—and, Iuti realized now, the islanders had expected her to be helpless under Pahulu's dark influence.

Iuti remembered how the healer who had told her about Fanape had spoken privately with other injured warriors. Iuti herself had remarked on the woman's kindness when she saw how much time she spent comforting the most seriously battle-scarred among them.

"Speaking to them as she did to me," Iuti muttered. "Judging the depth of their despair, and then offering them surcease in some far-off land.''

Iuti had no doubt there were other ''neutral'' havens like Fanape. It explained the strange defections of so many southern warriors, the hollow-eyed men she had seen in battle, and the never-diminishing strength of the Teronin army.

She struck her fist on the support post beside her. The strength of her anger shook the wall. "By the gods!" she promised. "I will bring this to an end."

Iuti caught her breath as a tiny gecko, the one she had seen before, dropped from the dry thatch onto the face of her shield. It lay stunned between a row of jutting shark's teeth. Then suddenly it moved. It wriggled through the maze of jagged teeth to the shield's edge where Iuti caught it in the cup of her hand.

"Tonight," she promised the tiny creature. "Tonight I will end it for Fanape. And tomorrow I will return to the mainland and finish the work Mano and I began so long ago. This time I will bring an end to it all." The soft, silent gecko lay like a small piece of magic in her palm. It watched her with jet-black eyes while she set it carefully back into the thatch.

Iuti hid Mano's weapons under her sleeping mats and set the box and its other contents out to air. Then she walked to Tarawe's uncle's house and, without revealing what she knew, tried again to explain the danger the Teronin canoe posed.

Pahulu arrived just behind her and whispered into the chieftain's ear. He nodded and whispered back and refused to listen to Iuti's warnings. She called him a fool, him and all his people, and then did what she had really come to do.

"Keep your niece away from me," she complained. "I'm tired of her following me everywhere, watching everything I do. She belongs inside with the rest of the children." It was cruel to shame the girl so, but this wasn't the time to have an untried teenager at her back. Besides, if Pahulu joined in the battle that night, as Iuti suspected she might, Tarawe was safer locked away with her siblings. The sorceress wouldn't hesitate to harm the girl if she thought she could gain power by doing so.

If by some chance I survive this night, Iuti promised Tarawe silently, I'll take you away from this place and find you a home among people who pay their debts honestly.

Returning to her own hut, Iuti twisted her long hair into a knot at the back of her neck. She donned her faded brown tunic and pulled on her trousers under the cumbersome skirt the islanders insisted she wear. Finally she hid the war club and shield within the bundle of her fishing nets and set off through the jungle.

Pahulu met her at the darkest point along the path. "So, warrior," she said, "you think to defy the gods and fish on the reef despite their clear warning."

"If it's only a warning as you claim, I'm in no danger until tomorrow," Iuti said.

"A ghost canoe rarely departs without filling its empty place," the sorceress replied. "You could be injured on the reef today and die on the morrow." She reached toward Iuti's nets. "Perhaps I can offer a small warding spell . . ."

"If you touch my nets, sorceress," Iuti said without moving, "it will be *you* for whom the ghost canoe comes."

Pahulu smiled tightly and refolded her arms across her chest. Her eyes and her very stance pleaded with Iuti to defy her, to use some small spell to set their personal battle in motion.

Iuti watched her for a moment, then stepped silently around her. She shivered as the old woman's cackling laughter followed her along the path.

✍ *Chapter 3* ✍

IUTI chose a place on the reef near where she had been the evening before. Squatting in waist-deep water, she freed herself of the skirt and anchored it along with the war club and shield beneath the waves. After setting her fish spear atop a coral stone, she dismantled the wooden frames of her hand nets and tied the two nets together. She tested them with a yank before draping them across one shoulder.

Finally she pulled a leaf-wrapped packet of dark paste from her waist pouch. The dye had been boiled down months earlier from the sack of a giant octopus, and she used it now to draw dark lines along her cheeks. The marks of Mano would provide her no magical protection during the coming battle, for even if the shark still acknowledged her, she dared not use his power while Pahulu was nearby. Still, the Teronin might not know she had forsaken her totem; the marks might slow them at least for an instant.

As the sun began to set, Iuti listened for the distant beat of the paddlers' chant. Several times she thought she heard it, then realized it was only the waves or the whispering wind. When the faint sound finally came, she was stiff from not moving, growing cold in the late-evening air. Shifting carefully, she stretched what muscles she could without revealing herself and adjusted her height to the rising tide.

The whispered war chant stopped sooner than it had the night before, as if the Teronin were taking more care this time not to be overheard. Iuti fingered her nets as the false ghost canoe turned to follow its parallel course

along the reef's edge. Even though she was waiting for
it, she started when the eerie ululation of the death chant
began. The sound was like winter ice slicing through her
soul.

The canoe moved steadily closer.

Something moved on the reef to Iuti's right.

Abruptly Iuti sank so that only her eyes and her ears
were above the water line. There was a thud and a startled cry from the canoe, then a splash as one of the Teronin toppled into the water.

The death chant stopped. A man's voice shouted from
the canoe, and an instant later, a shrill keening wail answered from the beach.

"Mano's teeth!" Iuti cursed. The call had been one of
question; the wail—Iuti recognized Pahulu's hated
voice—was an answering Teronin attack command. The
sorceress was giving Iuti's position away.

The canoe drifted for a moment. Then a frantic, whispered command brought it closer to the reef. Before the
Teronin could get near enough to leap directly onto the
coral, Iuti jumped up. With a great shout, she slung
the fish nets across the front of the canoe and the foremost Teronin. Timing her movements to catch the incoming surge, she yanked hard, bringing the entangled
bowman crashing headfirst into the prow and turning the
canoe itself into the reef.

As the canoe lifted on a swell and sped toward her,
Iuti threw her spear. Her aim was true, and thanks to
endless hours of pounding breadfruit, her arm proved as
steady as ever. The thin, wooden spear pierced the neck
of the nearest warrior and lodged in the shoulder of the
one behind. Two slivers of cold touched Iuti's soul, telling her that the bowman and the first of the speared warriors were dead.

Pahulu slipped a wedge of darkness into the opening
created by the death thrusts. It was a trick Iuti had not
thought her capable of. Without calling on her own
magic, and without Mano's protection, Iuti had little defense against the intrusion, so she sealed her mind as best
she could and scooped up her club and shield.

"I am Mano!" she cried, and flung herself at the two Teronin warriors now leaping onto the reef. One man stayed on the canoe, trying to save it from the waves. Iuti laughed aloud when the others hesitated before shrieking their own battle cries in reply.

Even in the growing darkness she read recognition and fear in their eyes. It was clear they hadn't expected a battle on this night, and certainly not one with a fully armed and aware warrior. It was clear, too, that they knew they were facing Iuti Mano.

She parried a blow from the nearest man's sword, twisting her shield as the blade turned so that Mano's teeth dug deeply into the Teronin's sword arm. He cried out, stumbled. A wave washed away his footing, and instantly Iuti brought him down with the war club. Blood from his arm and the back of his crushed skull stained the twilit water black.

Warmth swirled at Iuti's ankles while Pahulu's darkness and images of horror forced a deeper wedge into her consciousness.

The second warrior's blow caught Iuti as she turned, still disoriented by Pahulu's oily thrust. She deliberately collapsed under the blow to lessen its force, but the Teronin's wide metal blade slid across her shoulder like a branch of fire coral. She fell, rolled painfully, and crouched to meet him again. She called on the honest pain in her shoulder, the true pain of ripped skin and torn muscle, forcing it to take precedence over the growing chaos in her mind.

She met the Teronin's second thrust with Mano's shield. She raked it down along the man's arm and chest. Then she killed him with a sweeping blow of the mighty war club.

Iuti staggered under Pahulu's immediate, penetrating attack. Her mind squirmed away from the darkness like an eel tying itself in knots to escape a fisherwoman's hook. Gasping, she slid the back of her hand along her shield's jagged edge and focused on the pain to keep from calling out to Mano.

There was movement on the canoe. Iuti spun around,

loosening the shield so it could be thrown. The canoe had pulled off the coral and was drifting slowly just beyond the line of breaking waves. Two people were on the outrigger platform, facing each other with drawn swords.

Tarawe and one of the Teronin!

Of course, Iuti thought, and cursed herself for a fool. It was Tarawe who had downed the first Teronin! With a fish spear, no doubt, thrown from the edge of the reef. Iuti had seen the girl practice the move often enough. But how had Tarawe escaped her uncle's vigilance, and where had she gotten the sword?

The Teronin crept forward, balancing with practiced ease on the bobbing canoe. Iuti couldn't throw the shield for fear of hitting Tarawe. The girl crouched, waiting, sword arm close to her side. There was a movement behind her as the man Iuti had speared earlier tried to pull the wooden spike from his shoulder. He yanked it free just as the other Teronin lunged at Tarawe.

The girl dipped neatly beneath the warrior's sword arm, and Iuti sent her shield sailing, knocking the man with the spear into the sea. Again ice grabbed at her soul. Another death. Iuti pushed Pahulu back.

The last Teronin stumbled as he passed Tarawe, caught himself, then abruptly slumped forward across a blood-soaked hull. Tarawe had killed him, gutting him as neatly as if he were a tuna.

Tarawe stared at the dead warrior for a moment, then gave a ragged cry and bent to jump into the water. A swift, dark shape slid beneath the drifting vessel.

"Stay in the canoe!" Iuti cried.

Another dark form approached the canoe, and another. Mano had come for the taste of blood.

"Stay in the canoe!" Iuti called again. She could hear panic in her own voice, see it in Tarawe's stance. Pahulu continued ripping at her mind's raw edges.

Then abruptly the sorceress stopped. She pulled back from Iuti's mind. The darkness faded, disappeared, and the nightmare images ceased. Startled, Iuti turned back toward the beach.

Pahulu was standing in knee-deep water. As Iuti

watched, the sorceress lifted both hands to point at the Teronin canoe. The shrill keening began again, and Iuti heard Tarawe cry out, a long shuddering wail.

"No!" Iuti shouted. "Let the girl alone!" She turned back to see Tarawe drop her sword and clutch her head in both hands. The girl swayed, stumbled, and reached again for the side of the canoe.

The sharks circled, waiting.

"You may not have the girl!" Iuti shouted across the reef to Pahulu. The sorceress's black teeth shone wet in the twilight. She grinned and pointed, and Tarawe screamed again.

"The girl killed twice," Pahulu cried with a laugh. "She carries no warrior's training, and she has no family god to offer her protection. She is mine!"

Tarawe's scream filled the night air.

"No!" Iuti lifted her own arms and flung a powerful warding spell toward Tarawe. The strength of it knocked the girl back against one of the outrigger struts.

"Stay still, Tarawe," Iuti called. Above the rumbling surf, she heard the sorceress shriek with laughter. Inside her mind, rotten black teeth grinned in triumph. The nightmare images swarmed back, filling the gap Iuti's use of the power had provided. Pahulu's shrill voice lifted again over the waves, and Iuti poured more strength into the warding spell.

Pahulu used her power over the sea creatures then. Small fish thrashed at Iuti's feet, tearing away her trouser legs. Their sharp, poisonous spines raked against her bared skin. Eels and other dark things slid from their holes and sank their teeth into her ankles. Iuti battered them away with the war club, but for every one she killed, a dozen more appeared. The coral itself burned.

Iuti knew she couldn't maintain the warding spell around Tarawe and fight Pahulu at the same time, not without Mano's help. Her only chance was to swim to the canoe and paddle both Tarawe and herself beyond Pahulu's power.

Iuti stared at the blood-darkened sea. She had swum in this place before. As an honored member of Mano's clan, she had mingled unharmed among the lesser cousins while she conspired to slay the great Mano Niuhi himself. She knew that no family song or sword, however strong, could protect her from the sharks' vengeance now. The small cousins were already ripping at the Teronin, and Mano Niuhi himself had yet to appear.

The sucking tentacles of an octopus wrapped around her ankle, tugging her against the sweeping waves. She smashed the creature away. The blow struck Pahulu; Iuti felt a slight ripple in the sorceress's power. But it did little to diminish her attack. I cannot kill all the creatures of the sea, Iuti thought.

She glanced again at the canoe. Then, knowing she could never use it against the sharks, she threw her war club as far as she could into the sea. She dove into the next wave and began to swim.

Something bumped against her leg. She gasped and sank, choking on foul-tasting brine. After fighting back to the surface, she saw that it was only one of the Teronin, torn almost in half by the sharks. She pushed the ravaged body away and swam on.

Pahulu smashed at her mind, forcing her deeper into the water. A school of tiny needlefish swarmed around her face, making it impossible to see. In desperation, Iuti attempted an attack spell of her own, ripping in the manner of Mano at the sorceress's mind. She had a swift taste of acrid bile before Pahulu twisted away and jammed her own wedge of control deeper.

Time and again, the racing sharks startled Iuti into choking down yet more of the blood-slimed sea. "Take me quickly," she tried to sing, "before Pahulu sucks my soul dry." Her arms felt like stones; she could barely lift her head high enough to gasp in air.

Then suddenly a great gray shadow appeared beneath her. It rose to her side.

"Mano!" Iuti gasped, then caught her breath as Mano Niuhi bumped against her. He slid like crushed glass along her wounded shoulder. She thanked him for the pain.

Smaller sharks circled, darted close, then dashed away

to feed on the Teronin. They returned again and again, churning the water to a bloody froth. Would Mano Niuhi take her himself, she wondered, or would the smaller cousins tear away her soul piece by bloody piece? Pahulu's attack receded slightly in the great shark's presence.

"Mano," Iuti whispered through frigid, terror-tightened lips. The shark continued to swim beside her, watching her steadily with one shining eye. She had expected rage, but she saw only calm strength. She reached for Mano's mind, for the bond they had shared for so long. She felt nothing.

"Brother, I stole your power to gain a few months of peace." Iuti slipped unconsciously into the singsong of an ancient family chant. "But I did not steal your soul. I did not eat your flesh or share it with others on the land.

"I don't call on your protection now," Iuti sang to the shark. "But I beg you, take back my family's power. Take it all, quickly, before Pahulu steals it from me and uses it against the girl and later against all others who cross her will."

Tarawe's shout tore Iuti's attention from the shark. She lifted her head and gagged again on foul-tasting water. The Teronin canoe was still beyond her reach. But there was a second canoe floating just beyond it. Iuti thought for a moment that it must be another of Pahulu's illusions, for it flickered and wavered with the movement of the waves. But then she heard the cadence of the death chant and realized that a true ghost canoe had come at last. It had one empty place—the other seven were filled with the still-flickering images of the dead Teronin.

The last place is mine, Iuti thought in despair. I will spend the rest of eternity paddling empty seas with a crew full of my most hated enemies.

"By the gods!" she sighed. "I do not want to die in this place."

Without warning, Mano Niuhi veered away, scraping once again along her side. For an instant, Iuti thought the end had come, that Mano would kill her at last. But the great shark merely circled, then raced back toward the reef. As the distance between them grew, Iuti felt Pahulu's crippling attack return. She swallowed brine, coughed, and sank. She gagged her way back to the surface.

Tarawe cried out again and pointed.

Pahulu had moved farther onto the reef. She was standing now in water up to her waist, and waves were washing as high as her shoulders. Pahulu's arms were still lifted toward Iuti, her eyes squeezed shut. Iuti caught her breath as she recognized the phalanx of dark forms streaking through the water toward the unsuspecting sorceress.

Pahulu cried out when the first shark struck. The twisting darkness in Iuti's mind shivered, then steadied. A second small cousin raked its razor-sharp teeth across the sorceress's hip. A third ripped a strip of flesh from her side.

Suddenly Pahulu was thrown back into the water, screaming, shrieking in surprise and agony. The sea creatures she had ensorceled tore from her mental grasp and fled, abandoning her to the frenzied sharks. And the darkness in Iuti's mind shattered.

When Mano Niuhi struck, Iuti was with him just as he had been with her on so many battlefields before. She tasted the slick tartness of Pahulu's blood, twisted her head from side to side as she shredded the sorceress's flesh between her double rows of teeth. She thrilled with her brother at this momentary pause in his endless, ravaging hunger.

And then realized it was only the memory of enemy blood she tasted, only the memory of Mano's battle lust that made her heart pound. Iuti reached frantically for Mano Niuhi's mind, attempting to reestablish the bond. But again there was nothing. The tie was gone. Only emptiness and cold remained, and a feeling of terror that she had never before experienced in the sea.

She grabbed for the paddle that Tarawe thrust toward her and pulled herself hurriedly toward the canoe. Something stabbed her foot as she clambered aboard, and she almost collapsed in relief when she saw that it was only Mano's war club, bobbing in the waves beside her. She lifted it onto the outrigger.

Tarawe was still staring at the place where Pahulu had stood. The ghost canoe had drifted into the blood-smeared shallows, and the old woman's image was slowly re-forming in the vessel's final empty place. As the image solidified, the last of the nightmare visions dissolved from the back of Iuti's mind.

Iuti crossed to the canoe's bow and dumped the remaining Teronin warriors overboard, shuddering as the small cousins raced back to take the kill. Leaning over to inspect the damaged hull, she saw her shield tangled in the hanging fishnet. She brought it aboard and laid it carefully, teeth down, in the bottom of the canoe.

Then she picked up Tarawe's bloodied sword. Its broad blade was specked with rust. "Where did you get this?" she asked, turning back to the girl.

"Pahulu." Tarawe said. Her voice trembled. "She brought it to my uncle's house. She said she found it in the taro patch, but I knew it was your's. I waited until no one was watching and snuck out with it. I didn't realize until too late that Pahulu meant for me to come so she could use me against you."

Tarawe glanced away for a moment, then straightened and looked back. "But it wouldn't have mattered. I wanted to come. I would have found a way even if Pahulu hadn't brought your sword."

Iuti remained silent.

"I want to pay my own debts from now on," Tarawe said.

And then, almost, Iuti smiled. She rubbed her hand across her injured shoulder, glanced at the frenzied sea, then wiped the blood away on her wet trousers.

"Do you want to go back there?" she asked, nodding toward Fanape. The island lay still and dark behind them. Not a single light showed among the trees.

Tarawe shook her head emphatically, wincing slightly at the pain from which she obviously still suffered.

"I no longer carry the shark's protection and power,"

Iuti said. "I have only a warrior's natural skills now. Still, I have debts of my own that need to be settled."

She offered Tarawe the rusty blade's hilt. "You can come with me if you wish."

Tarawe's dark eyes flashed in triumph as she took Iuti's sword. Something flickered far below them, and then they were alone on the empty sea.

⊷ Chapter 4 ⊱

IUTI ordered Tarawe to a place near the bow, and after a quick check of the canoe's seaworthiness, she took her own place at the stern. With a quick twist of her paddle alongside the canoe, she turned them away from Fanape. She was relieved to discover that Tarawe was a seasoned paddler. The girl dipped her paddle deep in the water, using steady, even strokes, and when Iuti quickened the pace, she matched it without complaint.

They paddled in silence for a time. It was a quiet night; the sea was calm and the wind light out of the northeast. The air smelled of echoing distance and the fresh open sea. The only taint was the foul odor of Teronin blood, but Iuti waited until they were well away from Fanape and the sharks before splashing seawater across the bloody stains to wash them away.

The water brushed quietly along the sides of the canoe, and from time to time, the coir wrappings holding the outrigger platform to the hull creaked and flexed with their motion across the waves. Occasionally a fish or some other small sea creature splashed in the distance. Otherwise, the night remained still. Iuti set her course by the stars.

"Where will we go?" Tarawe asked.

"North first, to avoid being seen here in the islands," Iuti said. "Then east and south to Manara."

"Manara?" Tarawe glanced back over her shoulder, her eyes bright with interest. "On the mainland?"

Iuti nodded. "That's where the southern chieftains will be. They need to know how these islands are being used

29

by the Teronin. They'll send troops here to drive them out."

"I've never been to the mainland," Tarawe said. "I used to travel to the outer islands with my mother before . . ."

Tarawe's steady strokes faltered. It was the first time Iuti had heard her speak of her mother. The woman had died two years before, from some unknown poison encountered on the reef, if Tarawe's uncle could be believed. She had been a healer, and had experimented once too often with the dangerous toxins found in and around the coral.

Tarawe's shoulders straightened and she resumed the steady dip and pull of her paddle. "I've always wanted to see Manara," she said finally. The subject of her mother, then, was not one she wished to pursue. That suited Iuti, as the thought of her own mother's reaction to the events on Fanape left her with a sour taste at the back of her mouth. Her kinfolk would not be pleased when they discovered she had severed her special bond with Mano Niuhi.

"See it you shall," Iuti promised. "After this night's work and the long voyage to come, we'll deserve a few days' pleasure. We'll take the best room at the Wharfhound Inn and make full use of their fine kitchens. Then I'll show you the city's sites before we go to my kinswoman's farm."

Iuti found herself grinning at the thought of sizzling limefish and succulent water-mutton stew. Her mouth watered at the thought of sugared berries and goat's milk laced with spicy shemm. Island food was good; it was solid and filling, even tasty when there was time to prepare special dishes. But it in no way compared to the rich delicacies of the Wharfhound.

Good food, a soft bed, and a willing warrior, she thought with satisfaction. The warrior would have to wait, of course, until Tarawe was safely delivered into Nelina's hands, but that would surely not take long. Iuti knew her cousin would take Tarawe in. Neli and her bonded mate, Kirin, had been trying for seven years for a daughter. To date, they had produced only six strapping sons. Tarawe would find a good home among that boisterous, happy brood.

"I shall be glad of some good food," Tarawe said.

"Are you hungry now?" Iuti asked. "I can sing a butterfish into the boat if you'd like. Now that Pahulu is gone, I can use my water magic again."

"I . . ." Again there was a slight hesitation in Tarawe's steady strokes. "I don't think I could eat anything right now." She stopped paddling and turned around on her seat.

"Are you really the shark's sister?" she asked.

Iuti smiled. She had wondered how long it would be before Tarawe started asking the questions she had been forbidden to voice on the island.

"Aye," she said. "Mano and I are kin. Although not in the same way you and your brother . . . Do you have brothers, Tarawe, or sisters?"

Tarawe shook her head. "Only cousins." She frowned and pursed her lips. "And my uncle."

"Ah," Iuti said. That explained Tarawe's exclusion from the otherwise close family ties on Fanape. It was no doubt the reason for the girl's deliberate defiance. Iuti had seen her chucking stones at her cousins after they had teased her for her solitary ways. Iuti glanced up at the stars to check their course.

"Mano and my family became kin many generations ago," she said. "The legends say that the sharks were curious about the strange, two-legged creatures who inhabited the shores of their domain. They were befriended by a woman in the far-off Western Isles, and to repay her, as well as to learn more about humans, they formed a kinship bond with that woman's bloodline. From the beginning, the sharks proved a most powerful ally."

Tarawe shifted on her seat, and Iuti remembered that Pahulu had said the girl had no family god.

"When the Teronin War began," Iuti went on, "the southern war chiefs approached my family and asked our help. There are many warriors among my bloodkin. Each carries the shark's protection and can borrow his strength when the need is great, and each is trained in battle magic, as well. But to fight the Teronin, the mainlanders needed something more.''

A fish splashed in the distance. Iuti glanced that way, then back. Tarawe never moved. Her eyes had brightened, however, at the mention of magic. Iuti continued to paddle.

''My own mother walked into the sea to speak with the sharks,'' she said, ''and Mano Niuhi, the great gray shark and the leader among all the rest, answered. They struck a bargain. Mano agreed to bond personally with a single human warrior. He would lend all his strength and his cunning, and his magic, in return for being carried freely in the mind of that one human.

''My brothers and my cousins all vied for the honor of carrying Mano into battle,'' Iuti went on. ''They competed in every known warrior's skill, in the water and on the land.''

''But you won the contest,'' Tarawe said with a grin.

Iuti laughed. ''I never entered the contest. At least not directly. My brothers laughed when I suggested it. 'Who are you, little girl,' they said, 'that the great shark would want you for his personal friend? Why don't you go back and practice climbing trees?' I was much younger then, little older than you are now, and I didn't know how to fight with words, so I was shamed and left out of the competition altogether.''

Iuti checked their heading again and altered their course slightly. Tarawe was leaning forward, listening intently. She reminded Iuti of herself many years before. Intense, intrigued. Innocent. Don't let your curiosity lead you where you don't want to go, Iuti wanted to warn the girl. Don't let it take you beyond the world where you belong.

''On the morning of the day set aside for choosing, I swam alone off the back side of the reef,'' she said. ''I was angry, and I swam hard and fast with no thought for any but myself.

''A shadow came up beneath me. Then another and another. The small cousins streaked through the water at my sides. I wasn't afraid. The sharks were my kin, and I knew they wouldn't harm me. But then, all at once, they swept away. Just as suddenly Mano Niuhi was there.''

Iuti paused, remembering that instant of terror when Mano Niuhi had first touched her mind. And then the burst of joy when she realized the great shark had selected her as his companion.

''We swam together for a long time,'' she said, ''until I gained the courage to return and tell my kinfolk the shark had settled the contest in his own way. I was much more afraid of my mother and my brothers than I ever was of Mano Niuhi.''

She laughed at Tarawe's look of surprise.

''Are they still angry?'' Tarawe asked.

''Aye. Some of them.'' And every one of them will be enraged when they discover I've broken that special bond, she thought. She shifted her paddle to the opposite side of the canoe to favor her injured shoulder. It had been a long time since she had taken a wound without Mano to blunt the pain.

''My cousins said you taught the southern warriors new skills and led them to many victories,'' Tarawe said.

Iuti sighed. ''Aye. But it wasn't enough to stop the war. The Teronin magic has grown stronger in recent years. What they lack in fighting skill, they now make up for in sorcery and cunning, and they no longer fight just to gain more land. Their goal is to destroy all those whose lives differ from their own. Finally, the endless, mindless killing became too much even for me.''

''When I killed those two men,'' Tarawe said, her voice tight with tension, ''I thought—I thought my heart was going to stop. I thought my whole body was turning to cold stone. How did Pahulu . . .''

Iuti shook her head. ''That wasn't Pahulu's doing. Not the stab of cold you first felt. That was the killing thrust that rebounds against those who take life in violent ways. I felt it, too, when each of the other Teronin died. That is a pain far beyond human sorcery, although a sorcerer with evil intent can make it worse, as Pahulu did to us both.''

"You felt it?"

"Even the most powerful and practiced of warriors feels it,'' Iuti said, "unless they've turned entirely to evil. It's the reason we must all leave the battlefields at times. The damage the killing cold causes is a cumulative thing. After many killings, or after we've been weakened by injury or exhaustion, or disgust, the darkness and the cold become almost welcoming. It becomes too easy to accept the evil as inevitable and to embrace it.''

Iuti thought again of the tiny, disfigured child that had unknowingly driven her to Fanape's treacherous shores. "Freedom from evil can carry a heavy price,'' she said.

"Will you teach me how to control the killing thrusts?'' Tarawe asked. "You said warriors were trained to do that.''

Iuti smiled. "It's not a thing you can learn sitting out here on the open sea. For those who can learn it at all, it's a skill that must be gained over time. When we reach the mainland, I'll ask my cousin Neli to test you and give you the proper training if she finds you suited to the warrior's way. Until then, we'll try to avoid situations that might force you to kill again. Don't worry, two honest kills won't cause you lasting harm.''

There was a small silence. Then the girl said, "Ser Iuti?''

"Aye.''

Tarawe hesitated again before asking, "Why didn't the sharks kill you tonight? They must be very angry after what you did.''

Iuti lifted her paddle and brought it forward and down, digging it deep into the sea. She pulled steadily back and lifted again. "I don't know,'' she said softly.

Tarawe watched her for a moment more, then turned back to the work of pulling the heavy canoe through the sea.

Some time later, Iuti said, "You fought well tonight. How did you know to keep your sword low like that?''

She knew the girl had not learned sword skills from watching her.

"I learned it from one of the other mainland warriors, before you came," Tarawe said. "He used to talk to me sometimes before Pahulu took full control of him. I watched all the warriors, and practiced the things I saw them do."

"Weren't they all injured or ill?" Iuti asked.

"Yes," Tarawe replied easily, speaking over her shoulder. "I learned more healing songs from them than I did fighting skills, but sometimes they were well enough to do interesting things. One of them knew how to set a spell on grabber vines to make them move at his command. He made one slide out onto the path in front of Pahulu once. She fell right to the ground."

Tarawe paused for a moment, and when she spoke again, her voice had turned hard. Her paddle thunked against the side of the canoe. She quickly reestablished her rhythm. "Pahulu killed him, that very day. When the Teronin came for him, they were very angry and threatened to murder us all. My uncle stopped them by giving them one of the island women to fill the dead warrior's place. Pahulu spelled her and sucked away her strength, and then the Teronin took her away."

Tarawe grew silent after that and would say nothing more. They paddled on through the quiet, starlit night.

At dawn, Iuti turned the canoe toward the rising sun. The vessel was not heavily provisioned and carried no sail, so she knew there had to be at least one Teronin camp within close paddling distance. She threaded her way carefully through the widely scattered islands, remaining as far as she could from land so the canoe wouldn't be spotted by some alert lookout.

Iuti avoided even those places Tarawe claimed were inhabited by islanders who would be sympathetic to their escape. A full crew of paddlers could overtake them easily, should word of their passing reach the wrong ears, and they had little chance of surviving a battle on the open sea. Besides, it might be best for all concerned if the fabled Ser Iuti Mano was believed to be dead.

The Teronin's water barrel had been kicked overboard during the battle, and by midafternoon, both Iuti and Tarawe were suffering from its loss. Iuti licked her cracked lips, tasting salt and sorcery-soured sweat. The various poisons inflicted by the reef creatures under Pahulu's control were taking their toll, and she found herself growing dizzy from more than just the sun.

"Tarawe," she said softly. She did not alter the steady rhythm of her dipping paddle. "It's time to bail."

Tarawe wearily lifted her paddle from the water and glanced back along the canoe's length. The wooden hull was old and dry, cracked deeply in places. There were new cracks where the bow had slammed into the reef. During their many hours at sea, Tarawe had spent as much time dumping seawater overboard as she had paddling. The wood stank where the sun had baked the remaining Teronin blood into black, ugly crusts.

"Warriors should take better care of their canoes," Tarawe muttered as she turned around and began bailing from the deep, narrow hull.

"Those weren't ordinary warriors," Iuti replied. "They were trained as such, but they hadn't fought a true battle for a long time. Gathering soul-dead recruits from terrified islanders had led them to laziness and lack of caution. Don't expect any others we might meet to be so easily overcome." She thought of the empty-eyed Teronin who fought with no regard for their own or their comrades' safety. Once the battle order was given, they fought until ordered to stop or until their bodies were as fully dead as their minds.

Tarawe stared at her for a moment, looking startled and somewhat dismayed. No doubt she thought that last night's battle had tested her to her limits. It was a belief many first-time warriors held, until they faced their second battle. The mental advantage of innocence came only once. Tarawe blinked, lowered her gaze, and resumed tossing water back into the sea.

Iuti's shoulders ached with fatigue. The injured one, despite a hastily applied healing spell just before dawn, felt as if it were aflame.

Tarawe, fortunately, had sustained no serious physical injury, although by late afternoon she was complaining of a fierce headache. The girl feared some damage from Pahulu's attack, but Iuti, hoping she was right, suggested that the glare of sun and sea might be a more likely cause. Her own head felt as if someone were using her skull for a drum.

She glanced up. The only clouds were small and distant. There was no sign of land or of rain. She wished she had a way to speed the sun toward the western horizon and bring them sooner to the comparative safety and comfort of darkness. There were those who could do such a thing, but whatever magic they employed was far beyond Iuti's ken. She and Tarawe would have to rely on the luck of the winds and roving rain squalls, or take the dangerous chance of going ashore for water. They couldn't survive another day at sea without it.

"We'll come abreast of Karolaro Island near midnight," she said. "If a rain squall doesn't cross our path before then, we'll go ashore for water."

"I have a cousin on Karolaro," Tarawe replied hopefully.

"We will avoid your cousin."

Tarawe sighed, finished bailing, and returned to her paddling.

Finally the end of the burning day came. The sun flared into sudden, brief brilliance, then dropped swiftly and silently into the western sea. In the blessed coolness of twilight, Iuti called a halt. They needed time to rest and properly attend their wounds.

Tarawe finished bailing once again and jammed the wooden bailer between a loose seat and the hull so it couldn't be knocked overboard. She was a careful sailor, despite her obvious exhaustion. During the early hours of their voyage, she had been full of restless energy. Now she sat limp and silent.

Iuti laid her paddle across her lap and leaned forward, resting her forearms on her knees. She was spent. The gash in her shoulder was more serious than she had hoped, and her sweat stank of Pahulu's poisons. She must attend to her damaged body soon, or Tarawe would find herself alone here on the sea.

"Can you stay awake for a time longer?" Iuti said. "To watch while I sleep?"

Tarawe looked up in surprise. "Aye. I'll watch." There was a touch of pride in the girl's tired voice, a hint of satisfaction that she had weathered the long day at sea better than Iuti herself. Iuti was careful not to let the girl see her smile.

Metal rasped against wood as Tarawe lifted her sword to within easy reach.

⚜ Chapter 5 ⚜

IUTI woke to soft music. Tarawe was chanting in the darkness. Her song was one about wind and rain and swiftly moving storms. She sang in one of the more obscure island dialects, one rarely used in day-to-day conversation. The girl's accent was far from true, but her tempo was firm and even.

Iuti listened for a time, satisfying herself that Tarawe remained alert in the drifting night calm. Then she whispered a song of her own, to ease the ache of overused shoulder and back muscles and to reinforce the stronger healing spell she had set earlier. She missed Mano's underlying strength—it had been a long time since she'd had to rely on only her own. Still, the simple spell left her relaxed and sleepy, calmer than she had felt in many months.

She suspected that the freedom to use it once again was almost as useful as the spell itself.

In her dream, the wind rose. It came in gusts and starts, as if unsure of the direction it wished to take. Something dark and evil-smelling twisted through the confused currents. The sea ran rough, and the troughs between the swells deepened. The air tasted of salt spray. The darkness writhed closer, but then was suddenly sucked away as a squall hissed toward her across the waves.

Rain, Iuti thought. Yes, good. We need rain.

"Ser Iuti." The wind whispered her name.

She started to reply, but then caught sight of the squirming blackness again, creeping around the edge of the squall. Thin tendrils explored the wind, turning more and more often her way. She shivered and remained still.

"Ser Iuti, wake up." The call was louder this time. Insistent. Something bumped against the bottom of the canoe, and abruptly Iuti came awake. She shuddered at the heaviness of her dream and glanced quickly around. The wind and quickening swells weren't solely a part of her dream. There was a true scent of rain in the air. Iuti sent silent thanks to the night.

Tarawe, sword in hand, was kneeling on a seat beside the outrigger platform, peering over the side of the canoe. She must have cleaned and polished the blade, for it glinted in the moonlight. A gust of wind lifted the edges of her skirt.

"What is it?" Iuti had to say it twice before she could force sound past her parched throat. Without conscious thought, she lifted her club from the weapons' rack along the inside of the hull.

Tarawe pointed. "There's something in the water."

Iuti lifted her shield from beneath her feet. A dark form hovered beneath the outrigger, close to the forward strut. "Drifting weed?" she asked, knowing it was not.

Tarawe shook her head. "It's something alive. I thought it was a shark at first, but . . ."

The shadow beneath them moved. It was not a shark. Iuti motioned Tarawe to silence and then back to her place near the bow. Iuti climbed carefully onto the wide triangular platform. It was made of bamboo poles, lashed side by side. There was enough space between the poles to see the dark shadow's outlines.

It looked like a giant blowfish.

Iuti set Mano's weapons aside and pulled a short, shell-tipped fishing spear from her belt. She slid it through an opening in the bamboo. As its sharp tip touched the shadow, the ball of darkness abruptly uncurled. Water splashed as the mysterious creature thrashed to the surface.

Iuti grabbed for it with her free hand, and for an instant, she thought she had caught hold of a fish, so slick was the skin that met her reaching fingers. Then the thing yanked against her, and she felt the strength of solid bone beneath flesh. It was an arm, strong and muscular. She yanked upward, and a dark face, framed in thick, black curls, lifted from the waves.

A man? she thought. How can that be? She called to Tarawe, warning her to keep watch in case there were more.

Her captive spluttered and coughed and clung to the outrigger strut with his free hand, causing the canoe to tip precariously. "Let me come aboard," he gasped, choking on his own splash. "I'm drowning."

"Who are you?" Iuti demanded, pulling him closer to the hull to restore their balance. "What are you doing out here?"

"For the sake of the gods, woman . . ."

"Tarawe," Iuti called. "What do you see?"

"A school of small fish," Tarawe replied instantly. "Umula, I think. And a small ray. Nothing more." Her voice was as hoarse as Iuti's; the hoarseness did nothing to hide her fear. Iuti cursed herself for her own earlier weakness that now forced the girl to face this new threat, if threat it was, without proper rest.

"I'm alone," the man said. "Help me aboard."

Iuti touched the sharp tip of her spear to the side of his neck, and he went abruptly limp.

"Don't cut me, Ser Iuti," he murmured in a voice suddenly gone soft. "Don't call Mano to this place!"

At that, Iuti lifted him from the water in one swift move. She dropped him facedown onto the outrigger deck and stepped back into the main hull. Before he could rise, she plucked a strand of her wind-blown hair and looped it once, twice, three times and four around his left wrist.

He coughed and choked and finally pushed himself upright, rubbing his arm where Iuti had held it. "Oh, thank the gods," he said. "Another minute in that cold sea and—" His fingers touched the hair wrapped around his wrist. He snatched them back as if they had been burned.

"By the hairy spines of a thorny starfish!" he cried.

"Curse you for setting a binding spell when I wasn't looking. You don't play fair at all, Iuti Mano."

Iuti smiled slightly and leaned back, relieved that her guess as to this creature's identity had been correct. She kept her club close to hand, nevertheless.

"Ho'oma'eva," she said. "What brings you so far from home?" She appraised the naked body carefully. Dark, smooth skin, still wet from the sea, glistened across well-defined muscles. The shoulders were broad, the waist narrow. The thighs were those of a swimmer, and the only hair was that framing the beautiful face and a small black tuft surrounding the creature's manhood. Nothing about him resembled the darkness of her dream.

"And in the guise of so handsome a human male?" she added.

"Who is he?" Tarawe said. "How do you know him? How can a man be alone out here in the ocean?"

"Ho'oma'eva isn't a man," Iuti said. "He's a sea mimic. He changes his shape as easily as he changes his mind unless someone binds him to one form." She recalled many a frustrating game of hide-and-seek with Ma'eva and his kin before she had learned the secret to capturing and holding them. But that had been long ago, part of a childhood now best forgotten.

"I'm man enough, warrior woman," Ma'eva said. He shifted his position so that it appeared as if, indeed, he might be.

She laughed. "I think not tonight, my wet friend," she said. "I remember you too clearly as an overstuffed blowfish." She studied him again, unable to find a flaw in his human mimicry, unless it was perfection itself.

He returned her laugh, then slid his glance toward Tarawe.

"Don't even think it, Ma'eva," Iuti said, growing instantly serious again. "If you touch the girl, I'll return you to the deep in small pieces. One of them will be that manhood of which you seem so proud."

Ma'eva blew her a kiss and grinned. He took another long look at Tarawe, who blushed and held her skirts tightly down against the wind, then turned back to Iuti.

"You know you would never deny *me* my manhood," he said.

"Why are you here?" she asked.

He looked genuinely surprised by the question. "To get you to stop this storm, of course."

Iuti blinked and glanced around. The wind and the smell of approaching rain had grown stronger, but this was far from being a storm. "Stop this squall?" she said. "Even if I knew how, I wouldn't stop it. The coming rain is a gift from the gods. *True* humans need fresh water to survive, friend mimic, and we have long been without it."

"This isn't a squall. It's a full-force storm, called here by a badly sung wind chant," he snapped. Iuti heard Tarawe catch her breath.

"Pay attention to the winds, Iuti Mano," Ma'eva said. "They are gathering to this canoe. So far out of season, a major storm could destroy even more of my kin than your stupid battle last night. Tell the girl to sing these winds back where they came from, unless you want more death on your hands."

Iuti turned to Tarawe, suddenly remembering the music she had heard earlier—Tarawe's song of wind and rain and storm. By the very gods! "Did *you* call this—"

"I never meant to call a storm," Tarawe said quickly. Her eyes had gone wide again. She lifted a hand as if to ward Iuti away, then dropped it to clutch at her wind-blown skirt. "I was only trying to bring rain so we wouldn't have to go ashore for water."

"She has an abominable accent," Ma'eva said. "You really should have taught her better, Iuti. Sung winds aren't known for their keen attention to detail, not to mention their propensity for—"

"Where did *you* learn to sing the winds?" Iuti demanded.

"I—I watched Pahulu do it, back on the island," Tarawe said in a small voice. "I remembered the words and just thought . . ."

Iuti sank down onto the side of the canoe. She remembered the soft, comforting sounds of Tarawe's song, the

ancient dialect, Tarawe's awkward accent. Just awkward
enough to call the wrong winds, she thought. And only
the gods knew what kinds of evil Pahulu's spell could
pull from those winds.

"That sorcerous witch follows me even in death," she
muttered. She scanned the southeastern horizon, dark
now with gathering clouds. She wouldn't have been surprised to see a Teronin ghost canoe hovering there with
Pahulu at its helm. No wonder she had been suffering
nightmares.

"The sorceress follows you," Ma'eva agreed. "I can
taste her stench with even this poor human tongue."

"It's only her spell you taste," Iuti said. "Pahulu is
dead. Mano Niuhi killed her last night. I saw it done."

"Paagh." Ma'eva spat. "That old witch? I'm not talking about her. She was just one who'd sold her soul for
a taste of the true Pahulu's power. It's a very live sorceress who rides these winds, friend Iuti."

"What do you mean?"

Tarawe made a small sound. Iuti turned to her.

"Pahulu . . . she didn't always call herself by that
name." Tarawe's voice trembled. "She took it after the
Teronin first came."

"You thought you'd won the war, didn't you, warrior
woman?" Ma'eva said. He was mocking her, but Iuti
could see deep concern in his flashing eyes. "You thought
you'd found the secret to the Teronin's growing strength
and could now easily destroy it," he said. "Ah, friend
Iuti, you've lived the landbound ways too long. You've
forgotten how to watch with more than your eyes, how
to listen with more than your ears."

He turned to stare for a moment at the approaching
clouds. "Pahulu has been gnawing about the edges of
this sea for a long time, always trying to take greater
control over the folk who live here. Now she uses the
Teronin war-kills to feed her power. She's trading her
evil for theirs, and in the doing has made both more
dangerous."

He pointed. "She rides far to the rear of this storm.
She is cautious, confused, as is the wind itself, unsure

of the storm's purpose or destination. She's already ensorcled several of my weaker water brothers, sending them forth to seek the mysterious wind singer, because she knows it wasn't one of her own who sang the spell."

He turned to Tarawe. "She's angry. She wants to know who dares use her power without first begging her protection—and paying her price."

Tarawe pulled in a controlled but clearly audible breath.

"Sing the wind back home, young one," Ma'eva said. "Quickly, before she finds us here. Not that I intend waiting—"

Iuti lifted a hand for his silence. "Do you know how to disperse the wind?" she asked Tarawe.

"I know no such song," Tarawe said in her dry, whispery voice.

Ma'eva said quickly, "Friend Iuti, surely you . . ." When Iuti shook her head, he groaned and cursed and sat back with a thump. "Humans," he muttered.

"It's as well that we don't know such a spell," Iuti said. "If we did, we might be tempted to use it, and that would draw Pahulu directly to us now that she's on watch. As it is, she'll find this place soon enough. A sung storm gathers to the spot from which it was called, unless it's sent elsewhere by the original caller. We must leave before the winds start to circle and trap us here. Even if we could survive the storm, we'd have little defense here on this canoe against a sorceress of Pahulu's skill."

Ma'eva lifted his bound wrist to her. "I must go, as well, friend Iuti," he said.

She let her look slide again over his strong, muscular body. "You would make a powerful paddler, Ma'eva, and we'll need great speed to outrun the storm. Give me a reason why I shouldn't keep you with us."

"If the storm can't be stopped," he said, "then the seafolk must be warned. You're already responsible for the deaths of many of my small reef brothers. The taste of your battle last night soured the sea."

"I apologize for killing your kin," Iuti said. "If I'd had a choice I would not have done so. You know that."

"Nevertheless," he said, "you owe us a favor." He picked at the hair circling his wrist, but the spell held. He remained solidly human.

"Your kin know well enough to stay away from this storm," Iuti said. "Give me another reason. A true reason, one that will remain true even after you're no longer bound."

"Ah, unfair, Iuti Mano. You seek to bind me even after I return to the sea."

Iuti nodded slightly in acknowledgment. "A trick you taught me, friend mimic."

"If you don't hurry, you'll never get away in time," he said.

Tarawe started to speak, but Iuti waved her to silence.

"Oh, very well," Ma'eva snapped. "I don't like paddling! It's too—too human! There, I've spoken a truth to you, Iuti Mano. Now you have the right to call me back to this form. But only once. Only once, and I can't guarantee that I'll still like you as much then. You should have taken advantage of this body while you could. I'm already growing bored with it." He ran his palms along his perfectly shaped thighs.

Iuti chuckled. It was obvious Ma'eva was not tired of this latest human form he had assumed. If anything, he was fascinated by it. She wondered where he had gotten the model, or if it was simply a composite like most of his childhood human forms had been. "Give me your hand," she said, and he offered it without hesitation.

Iuti licked the fingers of her right hand and pressed the tips against the circle of her own dark hair. The strand loosened under her touch, and she unwrapped it carefully so it wouldn't break and bring them both bad luck. She was surprised when Ma'eva stood quietly after she freed the hair from his wrist. She had expected him to try to snatch it away. It was a matter of honor among the sea mimics to hide the physical embodiment of a binding spell deep under the sea, where it could never again be used against them.

"There are battles enough ahead," he said. "You and I have no need to squabble over so small a thing." He lifted a hand to touch her cheek. A strand of her wind-whipped hair twined around his fingers, and he snatched his hand back quickly.

"This war you humans have started is no longer a thing just among yourselves," he said, staring at his hand, then up at her. "This latest evil of Pahulu's has upset the balance between landfolk and those of the sea. My kin don't wish to become involved, but if we must, to protect our waters, we will."

"Aye," Iuti said. "I understand. I'll take your message to the southern chieftains. Go now. Warn your people that this storm will circle here until it's released, something Pahulu might not be able to do, even after finding its heart. These waters may remain dangerous for some time."

"It is always dangerous in the sea," Ho'oma'eva said. He shifted his look to Iuti's war club and her shield. Mano's teeth still glistened despite the deepening gloom. The sea mimic met Iuti's look again and smiled very slightly.

"Go," she said.

Ma'eva slid silently back into the sea.

❦ Chapter 6 ❧

Iuti watched until Ma'eva had disappeared, then quickly began stripping a length of decorative sennit from the gunwale. "Take off your skirt," she called to Tarawe. She had to shout over the rising wind.

"What?"

Iuti looked up. "Your skirt. Take it off."

Tarawe's eyes narrowed. Her grip tightened around the hilt of her sword, and she lifted its tip toward Iuti. The wind immediately tangled her skirt around her legs, but this time she let the voluminous folds fly as they would.

"I won't let you throw me naked into the sea," she said.

"Throw you—"

Suddenly Iuti understood. Tarawe expected to be punished for calling the storm. She thought Iuti was going to throw her to the mercy of the naked creature that had so recently left their deck. *What kind of stories was the girl told about me to expect such a thing?* Iuti wondered.

"I'm not going to throw you overboard," she said as reasonably as she could. "I need the fabric in your skirt to make a sail."

Tarawe blinked. The tip of the sword dipped.

"The winds will blow steadily this way until they reach the spot where they were called," Iuti said. She restrained a smile at Tarawe's sudden look of relief. "Then they'll turn and begin to circle. If we move quickly enough, we can use these early, steadier winds to escape this place, but if we wait until they're spinning, we'll be caught at the center. We'll never move the canoe fast enough with only two paddles. We need a sail."

Tarawe stared at her for a moment, then bent to step out of her skirt. She was wearing roughly made trousers underneath, similar in cut to Iuti's own.

Iuti laughed. "You're as much a mimic as Ma'eva, girl. Here, use that fine, shining sword of yours to remove the anchor from this line." She continued to smile as she ripped the shirred waist from Tarawe's skirt and began measuring lengths of the sturdy fabric along her arm. When the anchor was free, she set Tarawe to work stripping more line.

The wind gusted and swirled, snapping away the tips of the waves. Stinging spray chilled Iuti as she worked, but it was a welcome cold after the long day in the sun. Her skin felt blistered and raw.

She lashed the extra paddles together to create a mast and spar. Then, using the sennit to secure the fabric to them, Iuti rigged a V-shaped sail at the bow. It was much smaller than a canoe that size needed, and the mast was awkwardly rigid where it was tied to the high, narrow bow. But it was the best she could do in a hurry. She used one length of the anchor line to stabilize the mast and the other as a control for the sail.

At her command, Tarawe scrambled to the stern for the steering paddle.

"I'll handle the sail from here," Iuti shouted as she took a place just behind canoe center. The wind tore at her words. The canoe dipped and swung in the churning seas. "You sit right behind me. Keep the bow turned as far as you can into the wind."

Both the wind and the current would drive them steadily north, but by tacking into the wind they could travel east, as well. Iuti hoped to be close enough to the storm's edge by the time it started forcing them west and south again that they would be able to break free entirely.

Tarawe slid the steering paddle into the sea. She braced it firmly against the hull and began turning them into the oncoming swell. Carefully Iuti let the sail begin to fill. The fabric billowed and rippled. It flapped loose at a place where the bindings had not been fully secured. Quickly she luffed it to make the repair.

Then she began the slow, careful procedure again. This time the sail held. It caught the wind solidly, and the canoe surged forward. Tarawe let out a shout of approval as Iuti fed the rest of the sail to the wind, then pulled it taut to achieve the greatest possible speed. Tarawe laughed and called out a challenge to the wind she had summoned.

The sail was not an easy one. The rising wind grew steadier and stronger. The swells ran deep. Tarawe was hard put to keep even a slight easterly heading. Their struggle was made easier when the first of many rain squalls crossed their path. Iuti and Tarawe lifted their open mouths to catch the cool, fresh water and were rewarded with an almost immediate surge in strength and energy.

"For not knowing what you're doing, you sing up a mighty fine storm," Iuti called after the first rain had doused them and then raced away with the wind. The sail snapped as an errant gust caught it off-center. Iuti quickly brought it back to true, reestablishing its steady vibrating hum.

Tarawe met her look with a grin, then nodded toward Iuti's feet. The hull was calf-deep in water. "It's time to bail, warrior woman," she shouted, and laughed aloud at Iuti's curse of grudging agreement. Since Tarawe needed both hands to control the steering paddle, Iuti was forced to do the job of bailing. Tarawe obviously thought it a good joke after her own long day of bending and scooping.

Iuti braced the sheet with one hand and a foot while she bent to the task of emptying water from the hull. The waves were slopping as much over the sides as was leaking in through the cracks. Iuti caught her floating shield and tucked it carefully into the weapons' rack.

A sudden chill touched her mind. It was an icy cold not caused by the wind or rain. It was the cold she had felt in her dream. She glanced up quickly, but saw only scudding cloud and wind-torn sea. As quickly as she could, she returned her full attention to the sail.

Again and again, as they flew across the angry sea,

Iuti felt the icy touch of what could only be the seeking sorceress. She shivered, missing Mano's calm presence at the back of her mind. She had already warned the girl to use no further spells that might attract Pahulu's attention, and she knew of none herself that could make the canoe go faster than it was already going. She applied all the sea-skill she knew to keeping the canoe moving swiftly without being torn apart in the process.

She handled the sheet one-handed and added her own strength to Tarawe's, trying to keep the canoe turned into the wind. Even with her paddle wedged between the outrigger and the hull, it was difficult to twist it against the strong current.

Finally there came a time when they were no longer able to turn the canoe into the wind at all. Iuti tried to slow their speed to gain better control, but the canoe seemed to have a life of its own. It raced on, creaking and groaning as it sliced through the churning waves. Lashings loosened and set the whole vessel trembling. Tarawe shouted in time for Iuti to duck away from a length of bamboo, torn loose from the straining outrigger.

"The wind is circling well and good now," Iuti called. "We'll ride it awhile longer, then drop sail and try to break free using the paddles."

The sky was thick with clouds, and the only light came from the eerie phosphorescence of the sea. Again a touch of cold brought Iuti's look up and around. Tarawe must have noticed it this time, too. She nudged Iuti's back and nodded toward a place behind them where a coiling strand of something darker than the dark night twisted through the tumbling wind and waves. They exchanged silent looks before returning their full concentration to the canoe.

The wind's strength finally began to lessen. Judging by the current, Iuti reckoned them to have gone as far north as the storm would allow. She shouted a warning to Tarawe and luffed the sail. Immediately the canoe slowed and began drifting with the still-strong current. There was no time to dismantle the sail; Iuti merely lifted the outer spar and tied it and the sail cloth to the upright mast so it could no longer catch the wind. She bailed one last time. Then they both began to paddle.

Dig deep, pull and lift. Dig deep, pull and lift. A brief pause to control their direction with the paddle held firmly angled against the side of the hull. Then dig deep, pull and lift.

Iuti found herself singing the beat silently. A moment later, she realized with a start that she was not the only one singing. Tarawe was chanting aloud. Iuti spun around to confront her. "Have you no sense, girl! Pahulu is not deaf. She'll find us even here outside the storm if you sing more of her words."

Tarawe's surprised look turned quickly to anger. "I'm not singing one of Pahulu's songs," she snapped. "It was just a common sailor's chant. I learned it from my cousin on Karolaro two years ago."

Iuti stared at her, heart still racing from her instant of mistaken concern. Tarawe continued to paddle, maintaining a steady, although somewhat slower, beat than before. The canoe was much too heavy for one person to paddle easily alone. Especially for one who was as obviously exhausted as Tarawe.

"I will remain silent, if it makes you more comfortable, warrior woman," Tarawe said.

And Iuti was thoroughly shamed. "My apologies, able crew woman," she said with a rueful smile. "Your wits have outlasted mine on this long, rough voyage. I humbly return to my paddling."

Tarawe nodded once, coolly. But after Iuti had turned her back and dipped her paddle back into the sea, she heard what sounded like muffled laughter.

They paddled on through the night, veering ever eastward as the wind and swell dropped. At least Iuti hoped they were traveling east. The sky was still fully cloud-covered, so she could only guess at their general position. She wasn't concerned about being lost, because at daybreak, they had only to follow the rising sun until they could see the mainland's high, dark outline.

After the wind had been left behind and the swells

were running smooth again, Iuti felt Tarawe stop paddling. She glanced back to see the girl sound asleep in her seat. Iuti removed the paddle from Tarawe's limp hands, slid it into the bottom of the hull, then paddled on alone. For an untrained and untried child, Tarawe had proven better disciplined than many adults with whom Iuti had shared adventures. She was surprised that the girl had stayed awake as long as she had.

As dawn approached, turning the sky gray, then pink, and finally fully azure, Iuti saw that they were already well within sight of the mainland. They were so close they would have run into it had the night gone on much longer. That surprised Iuti, for it didn't seem possible they could have traveled so far east against the storm winds. The canoe must have been moving much faster than she had reckoned.

She didn't recognize the coastline ahead, but she could see the vague outlines of high mountains in the distance. Thick fog blanketed the north, but far to the south, a light flickered. It must be one of the guide lights marking the entrance to Kala Bay, she decided. They were fortunate indeed to have been carried so near their intended destination.

Iuti brought them as close to land as she could. It was clear that the battered canoe was not going to carry them all the way to the bay and up the Veke River. Even with Tarawe's help, Iuti doubted she could keep the dying canoe afloat much longer. They were going to have to make their way ashore and follow the coastline south on foot.

She called gently to wake Tarawe.

"We'll have to swim the rest of the way," she said as the girl blinked awake. Tarawe looked around in confusion, at the canoe, at the high, jungle-lined horizon of the mainland, at Iuti. "Our canoe is sinking under us," Iuti said. "Even your expert bailing couldn't keep it afloat much longer."

Suddenly Tarawe understood. She turned another startled look toward the coastline—Iuti could remember her own astonishment upon first seeing that great mass of land, something a lifetime spent on islands little higher

than the highest of high tides could not prepare a person
for. Then Tarawe turned back and asked what she should
do.

Iuti handed her her shield, wrapped now in protective
layers of fishnet, and directed her into the water. "Use
it to help keep yourself afloat," she said. She had already
lashed the sword and the wooden war club together so
she could carry them ashore herself.

"What about the canoe?" Tarawe asked.

"I'll sink it," Iuti said. "It would be too dangerous
to leave it afloat. It might drift ashore somewhere where
the Teronin could find it. I'll lay a weighting spell on it
so it can rest peacefully at the bottom of the sea."

"What about my skirt?" Tarawe asked when she saw
that Iuti intended to sink the sail along with the canoe.

"Where we're going, that mountain of cloth would
make us more conspicuous than my trousers ever did back
on Fanape," Iuti said with a smile. "Don't worry. No
one will think you improper, dressed as you are. There
are many who wear a good deal less."

Tarawe looked skeptical, but slid over the side without
argument. Iuti waited until the girl had drifted some ways
away, then lifted the sword and club high in the air. She
pointed them toward the bow and toward the stern, then
swung them in a slow, wide circle.

"Honor to you, fine canoe," she said. "You have
served us well. Rest heavily now in the safety and quiet
of the deep." She brought the paired weapons down onto
the joints that held the outrigger to the hull. The outrigger
platform split, and the whole of it fell away, sinking
instantly under the weighting spell.

Balancing on the suddenly precarious hull, Iuti swung
the combined weapons again, this time tearing a wide,
jagged hole in the bottom of the canoe. It immediately
began to sink. She rode it down until the high bow and
stern were submerged, then kicked away. By the time she
looked back, the tip of her makeshift mast had disappeared beneath the waves. Except for its faint taste in the
salty sea, it was as if the canoe had never existed.

"That was a good canoe," Tarawe said softly beside her. "Those Teronin should have taken better care of it."

"Aye," Iuti replied, pleased that the girl was wise enough to give honor to the vessel that had carried them so far. "Let's move now. It's a long way to shore." Pushing their weapons before them, they began to swim.

It was past midday by the time Iuti and Tarawe felt solid ground beneath their feet. Fully exhausted, they stumbled ashore and dragged themselves up the rocky beach until they reached a shallow freshwater stream. After drinking their fill, they collapsed under a canopy of heavy, dripping foliage. Tarawe fell instantly asleep.

Iuti tried to sit watch but after only a few moments knew it was impossible. Even if she was awake to see someone coming, she could do nothing to stop their approach, she was that tired. She sprawled beside Tarawe and set a simple hiding spell over them both. The spell wouldn't hide them if anyone guessed they were there and looked at them directly, and it would do nothing to protect them if they were discovered—but, like the makeshift sail, it was the best Iuti could do at the moment.

"Sometimes you have to take chances," she murmured, and here on this deserted stretch of southern coastline, she felt free to do so. They were far from both the islands and the Teronin now, and Pahulu had no way of knowing they were here. Iuti whispered a strong curative spell and sank into healing slumber.

It was dark when she woke. The sound of clicking palm fronds and gurgling water welcomed her gently back to consciousness. A gecko chirped somewhere back in the trees. It was the steady drumroll of breaking surf on the outer edge of the reef flat that reminded Iuti of where she was. She and Tarawe had swum through that surf on their way to shore, but Iuti remembered little about how they had managed it. Ragged tears in her shirt and trousers and the fading itch of spell-healed coral scratches indicated that the passage had not been entirely without incident.

Tarawe continued to sleep, totally relaxed, snoring softly with a small smile on her face. Her clothing was as torn as Iuti's, but Iuti saw no sign of injuries beneath the salt-encrusted fabric. The girl was either a better swimmer or had employed a healing spell as effective as Iuti's own.

Probably both, Iuti thought with wry humor. Gods, but traveling with this youngster is making me feel old.

After assuring herself that Tarawe was sleeping safely, Iuti waded into the deepest part of the stream to wash. She rinsed her clothes as best she could without removing them, knowing that even on the mainland, it was never wise to go naked until one knew the ways of the local inhabitants. This place showed no sign of human, or any other, occupation aside from scuttling land crabs and a few geckos and lizards in the trees, but that didn't mean no one was there.

Paranoia, she mused. The curse as often as the salvation, of a well-disciplined warrior. She splashed cool water over her face and sighed with blessed relief.

She woke Tarawe for just long enough to drink from a folded leaf, then took up a post where she could watch both the beach and the jungle. She listened to the steady roll of the breaking surf and watched the slowly shifting stars. The jungle whispered softly, and muscle by muscle, thought by thought, she relaxed.

And slept.

And woke with a start. *How* . . . She glanced quickly around but saw only the empty beach and the quiet jungle. How could she possibly have fallen asleep when she had set her mind to watch? She had never done such a thing. "I must have come to rely on Mano's vigilance more than I realized," she muttered. Frowning, she sat back to watch again.

And slept again—or nearly so. The surf and the softly clicking palm fronds lulled her, drawing her insidiously toward inattention; the sounds slowed and with them her heartbeat. She began to drift deeper, deeper, until . . .

Abruptly Iuti came full awake. This time she reached for her war club.

Disciplined warrior, she thought in disgust. *Dead* warrior if she had been any more careless. She turned in a defensive crouch to survey their starlit domain. It was not the ocean sounds lulling her to sleep. It was not the gentle quiet of the night. She listened carefully, while cold dread slid through her veins.

Drums!

The demon drums of Losan, without any doubt. She had heard them often enough on Teronin battlefields of late. But their sound had never been like this. The air vibrated with drumming so well disguised as natural sounds that even fully aware, she had difficulty separating the false sounds from the true. This was no small cadre of hired drummers such as the Teronin employed. The jungle was filled with their presence.

Losan, she thought. She and Tarawe must have landed on Losan Island itself, the very homeland of the dreaded drummers! The wind and current must have swept them far north of where she had thought them to be. No wonder they had reached the mainland so quickly. The light she had seen was not a guide to Kala Bay, but the warning light at the western tip of the northern peninsula. The fog bank had hidden the rugged cliffs of Teron to the north.

In her mind, Iuti formed a warding sign, though she knew it offered no protection against the drummers' power.

"Tarawe," she called. "Tarawe, wake up!" The girl remained silent, unmoving.

Iuti circled carefully toward her, watching all around as she moved. Shadows shifted deep in the jungle, leaves or drummers it was impossible to tell. None large enough to be a human was close to their small clearing. She reached out to shake Tarawe.

The girl's skin was icy cold, and she was as limp as if she were dead.

Iuti dropped to her knees beside her. "May Mano take them," she muttered as she bent forward to listen for Tarawe's breath. A barely perceptible movement of air

proved the girl was still alive. Iuti pressed her fingers
along the side of Tarawe's neck.

Nothing. No, there! A flutter. A single, soft beat. It
seemed forever before Iuti felt another.

Iuti realized suddenly that she was holding her own
breath. Her heartbeat was slowing again to match the
almost inaudible drumming that shivered through the
night. Deliberately she sucked in deep, strong breaths.
She began slapping Tarawe's cheeks, lightly but firmly.
"Wake up, Tarawe," she said. "Come on, girl. Come
back. Don't listen to them. Breathe."

Her light slaps grew softer; they took on a quieter,
slower rhythm. They became a caress.

Iuti snatched her hands back. She slapped her palms
together so that they stung. "No!" she shouted to the
jungle. "You won't control *me* with your damnable
noise." Quickly she ripped a length of cloth from the
bottom of her shirt. She stuffed pieces of it into her ears.
Then she did the same for Tarawe. It didn't stop the
drums' power, but it dulled it.

She grabbed Tarawe by the shoulders and shook her.
Tarawe's head lolled as Iuti pulled her upright. The girl
was barely alive.

"Come on, Tarawe," Iuti insisted. "Breathe. Set your
heart beating to its own rhythm, fast and hard. Think of
the ocean. Think of the wind, girl. *Your* wind. The storm
you called."

She shook Tarawe's limp body as she called to her.
She raised and lowered her voice, being careful not to
use any pattern or predictable cadence. Even through the
ear plugs she could feel the drummers trying to capture
her rhythms, so that they could match them and then
change them subtly to their own.

"Tarawe, think of Pahulu," she shouted close to Tarawe's ear. "Remember your fear. Remember how your
heart raced with terror at her touch."

A spot of color brightened Tarawe's pale cheeks. She
moved very slightly.

"Remember," Iuti said, hating the use of such bitter
memories but knowing no other way to set Tarawe's heart

free of the deadly slow tone of the deepest of the drums. "Remember how you felt as your blade slid through the Teronin's heart."

Tarawe shuddered. She pulled in a shallow, ragged breath, and Iuti sighed in relief. The drummers would not take this child tonight. The drummers recognized their attempt had failed, too. The tone of their pounding call changed instantly. Angry, rumbling vibrations spluttered through the jungle.

Tarawe's eyelids fluttered open. She lifted her hands to her ears.

"No, leave them," Iuti said. "We're not alone. We must leave this place quickly."

Tarawe either heard her or read her lips, because her eyes widened. She tensed and glanced rapidly around.

"Come," Iuti said as soon as she was sure Tarawe was fully awake and could stand on her own. The drums were still trying to control her emotions and movements, but she set her warrior's training in place and ignored them.

"What's wrong?" Tarawe asked. "Who's out there?" She touched her ears again, but Iuti stopped her from removing the cloth.

"Wait," she said. "I'll explain when it's safe." She took up her club and shield and waited while Tarawe strapped her sword to her waist. As she led the way to the water's edge, she freed the net wrapping from the shield. Mano's teeth glinted in the starlight.

Abruptly the drumming stopped. Even with her ears blocked, Iuti felt the sudden, hollow silence. She paused to survey the concealing jungle for a moment, then removed the cloth from her ears. The honest susurration of the surf was like cool, fresh water being poured over a fire.

"Keep them," Iuti said when Tarawe started to toss her own ear plugs away. "You might need them again before this night is finished."

"Why?" Tarawe asked. "Who's out there? What was that sound I heard before?"

"Drums," Iuti replied. She started walking again, toward the south. Tarawe stayed close to her side. "I was mistaken before. The storm pushed us much farther north than I thought. We are far from the safe southern lands. We've landed on the demon drummers' isle. They'll kill us if they get the chance."

Tarawe took an extra running step to keep up with Iuti's long stride. "Why? We've done no harm here. We didn't even take food from the trees."

"They care nothing for what we do or don't do," Iuti said. "They're only interested in our skins."

"Our *skins*!"

"For their drums."

Tarawe's choked response brought a quick glance from Iuti, to be sure the drummers hadn't managed to somehow affect her without either of them noticing. But the girl's expression merely showed horror at Iuti's remark.

"They cover their drums with human skin?" Tarawe said.

Iuti nodded.

"Are they sorcerers then?"

"Not sorcerers," Iuti replied. "At least not like any you've known. Although the magic they use is so powerful it's sometimes hard to tell the difference. They use their drums to control the natural body rhythms of other living creatures. The effect is all the more powerful when the drum head is made of the same species they wish to control. I suspect they're using human drums tonight."

Tarawe shivered visibly.

"They tried to take us in our sleep," Iuti said. "They almost succeeded. If they'd found us earlier, before I first woke, they would have."

"How do you know about these people? *Are* they people?"

Iuti nodded again. "The Teronin sometimes hire the drummers to help them influence a battle," she said. "They trade the skins of their dead comrades for the drummers' services."

Tarawe stepped closer to Iuti, and they walked in silence for a time. Iuti's look never left the dark edges of the jungle. Finally Tarawe asked, "Why are they letting us escape if they want us dead?"

"Their weapons are their drums and their secrecy," Iuti said. "Maybe, since they know we're aware of them and can't now be easily fooled, they've decided to let us go." Iuti didn't believe that, but their only option was to act on the assumption and keep moving.

"Ser Iuti."

Iuti stopped at the sudden tension in Tarawe's voice. Her hand tightened on her club.

Far up the beach a dark figure had stepped out from the jungle shadows. Another followed, then another, and another, until the entire treeline was alive with shifting movement.

Dark figures began moving slowly toward Iuti and Tarawe.

Faintly, far off, drums began to call.

☙ *Chapter 7* ☙

Tarawe moved closer to Iuti's side. "What are we going to do?" she asked. Her voice trembled.

"Just be still, Tarawe," Iuti replied. "Be calm. Try not to listen to the drums."

"We could go back in the water."

"We'd never make it out through the surf at this tide, and even if we did, we'd have to come back ashore sometime. They'd be waiting."

"Can't you do some magic? Frighten them away? Can't you—"

"Tarawe . . ."

"Look, Ser Iuti! They have spears! And clubs! They're going to kill us! You have to—"

Iuti grabbed Tarawe's shoulder and shook her, hard. "Tarawe. Stop listening to the drums."

Tarawe blinked, stiffened again. "But they . . ."

Iuti shook her again, being careful not to do it with any rhythm that the drummers could catch and follow.

A shudder ran through Tarawe's body—Iuti felt it clearly. More quickly than Iuti expected, the tension of uncontrolled terror left the girl. Tarawe shook herself slightly and looked down in surprise at the sword she had been about to drop.

"They're drumming to your fear," Iuti said. "They're amplifying it by making your heart race. I've seen it done before, on Teronin battlefields. If you panic and run, they'll kill you in an instant. Our only chance is to stay calm and to stay together."

Tarawe tightened her grip on her sword. She ran one hand across the flat of the blade as she looked up again at the approaching drummers. She whispered something Iuti couldn't hear and took a slow, deep breath. Calm settled over her like a visible thing.

"What you say must be true," she said. "I'm afraid, deep inside, but not nearly as afraid as when I faced the Teronin." Anger touched her voice. "I don't like being controlled by other people."

"Good," Iuti replied. "Remember that. It will help you resist them." How, she wondered, am I going to keep this untrained child from falling under the drummers' influence? At least Tarawe was female—the drums' power didn't usually affect women as strongly as it did men—but Iuti had seen even seasoned sisters succumb to the insidious sound. She wished she had left Tarawe back on Fanape.

The nearest of the drummers stopped about twenty paces from them. He was short, no more than a hand taller than Tarawe, and more than a head shorter than Iuti herself. He wore dark, patterned cloth wrapped tightly about his limbs and carried a short wooden spear in his left hand. The spear looked better suited to ceremonial use than to serious battle, but Iuti knew better than to judge a weapon's power by its outward appearance.

The fingers of the man's right hand fluttered against the skin of a fist-size drum strapped to his thigh. The others who quickly joined him were doing the same. All of them wore other drums, as well, strapped at hips and waist. Dark fingers flicked over the drumheads. Iuti couldn't tell which, if any of them, were actually making sound. A glance toward the trees showed men with larger drums at the edge of the forest.

The drummers formed a semicircle around Iuti and Tarawe. They didn't step into the water.

"They wear no clothes!" Tarawe exclaimed as the drummer who had approached them first stepped forward. Drumming fingertips shifted instantly as Tarawe spoke, and the cadence of her surprised cry shivered in breathless echoes across the beach. Tarawe was so startled by the sound that she gasped, and that sound, too, was copied. It joined the other in the vibrating night air. Tarawe became abruptly still.

"Tattoos," Iuti said. She had been as surprised as Tarawe when she realized that what she had thought was patterned cloth was actually pigmented skin. The drummers were as naked as Ma'eva, save for their drums and fighting sticks, but had not appeared so because of the intricate drawings that covered them from neck to toe. Even their hands and fingers were dark with circular patterns. Iuti was glad she had left on her clothes back at the stream.

Their leader, if that's who the spear carrier was, returned Iuti's stare coolly. Finally he spoke. Iuti understood not a word, but his gesture at the end of his short, sharp speech made it clear he wanted her to return with them to the jungle. Tarawe, he indicated, was to stay behind.

Iuti pointed him back to the jungle alone. "The girl and I will stay here," she said aloud.

The man's eyes narrowed. His drumming fingers never ceased their movement, although Iuti could detect no sound from his drum. Again he motioned her toward the jungle.

Again she motioned for him to go alone.

Abruptly he threw his spear.

Tarawe caught her breath, a sound instantly echoed by scattered drums, but Iuti knew a controlled spear-cast when she saw one and didn't bother to move. The shaft struck a patch of sand between her feet. It had not been intended to hit her. It was meant only to frighten her if she could be controlled by fear, or to insult her if she could not.

Iuti bent to pull the spear free. It was carved in circular patterns, like those on its owner's skin. She snapped it in half across her knee.

A soft hiss of excitement passed among the drummers.

"Why are they waiting?" Tarawe asked. "Why don't they attack?" She frowned as the drums again mimicked her words. "Why do they do that whenever I speak?"

"Because they know you listen," Iuti said.

"You listen, too, but they don't copy your words."
Again the echo.

"They can see that I'm a warrior. They know I'm
trained to disregard their mimicry. They're still testing
you." Iuti scanned the line of waiting drummers. They
were nervous, eager to move. They glanced around as if
they were afraid of standing there in the open. It was
rumored that the drummers were afraid of the night. Ap-
parently the rumors were true.

They were willing to face their fear, however, to take
Iuti alive. That had been made clear by their leader's
spear throw. It was also evident that whatever they wanted
her for did not include Tarawe. Iuti had no doubt the girl
would be killed if she was left behind.

Alone, Iuti would have fought the drummers there on
the beach, killed as many as she could, and then retreated to the sea. She preferred drowning in the surf to
submitting to the drummers' desires, whatever they might
be. Even with Tarawe at her side, she might have made
the attempt. But with Pahulu threatening the precarious
balance not only between the north and the south, but
between the land and the seafolk as well, she dared not.
She had to stay alive long enough to warn the southern
chieftains.

"Tarawe," she said. "By your right foot there is a
patch of small pebbles. Squat very carefully, slowly so
as not to startle them, and fill your pockets with stones.
Keep your sword in your hand."

"Aye," the girl said softly, almost eagerly. The drums
whispered the word as she knelt to do as Iuti asked.

When Tarawe was standing again, Iuti said, "We're
going to have to go with them, but we'll stay together.
Rattle the stones in your pockets whenever you think the
drums might be slipping past your guard. The random
cadence of their tapping will help break the drums' spell.
Rattle the stones from time to time even when you're sure
you're safe, so I'll know you're fully conscious and with
me."

"How will I know *you're* fully conscious?" Tarawe
asked.

The taunting echo of her words had barely begun when Tarawe shouted, "Keep your demon noise to yourself!" She stepped around Iuti, pulled a stone from her trousers pocket, and let it fly at one of the drummers. The man yelped as the stone bloodied his fingers and then thunked discordantly onto the drumhead beneath. The laughing echo disappeared abruptly.

Tarawe glared around at the other drummers, then returned to Iuti's side.

Iuti was as startled by Tarawe's unexpected attack as were the drummers, who stood in astonished silence. "How did you know which one was sounding your words?" she asked.

"I *listened*," Tarawe snapped. For the first time since the drummers had appeared at the edge of the jungle, her words met with dead silence.

"Mano's teeth, girl," Iuti muttered. "You have more surprises than a sea mimic in a tag game. I suppose you learned to throw like that from one of Fanape's visiting warriors?"

"Aye," Tarawe replied. "I practiced on my cousins. It was a good way to keep them away from me." Drumming, far off, shivered through the jungle. Tarawe rattled the stones in her pocket, then huffed in satisfaction as the nearby drummers rustled with unease. After a moment, the distant drumsound faded.

Finally the man who had spoken before barked a command. This time, Tarawe was included in his gesture toward the trees.

"That's better," Iuti muttered. She took a step away from the water, and the drummers parted to open a wide path. "Stay at my left," she told the girl, "or walk ahead if you must. Here, take my shield. I'll watch our backs. If they're after our skins, they won't want us cut up, so if they do anything, they'll probably try cracking our skulls with those staffs they're carrying."

Iuti wrapped her nets around her left arm and pointedly rested Mano's club on her right shoulder.

The beat of unseen drums described their progress across the beach and into the dark jungle—muffled, measured beats matched Iuti's stride. They walked through a shallow stream for a time, then moved onto a path just barely wide enough for Iuti and Tarawe to walk side by side. The drummers became shadows on the path ahead and behind. They moved like wind-blown smoke through the trees, always well out of reach.

"Where do you think they're taking us?" Tarawe asked. A nearby thrumming beat echoed the question. She glanced to her left with a frown and slapped her trousers to make the stones rattle. The nearby echo stopped, but the cadence of her question was repeated far back in the trees.

"I don't know," Iuti replied. "But they're in a hurry to either get us there or tire us out. That deep drum, the one matching our steps, has been gradually speeding up, and we've been following its lead. Let's avoid matching strides. There's no use making it easy for them."

"My uncle always complained that I couldn't keep a proper beat," Tarawe said. "Maybe I should try singing to them." She giggled at her own words and shouted "Ha!" as her silly laughter was drummed through the trees.

"This isn't a game, girl," Iuti muttered.

A shadow that Iuti recognized instantly was not a shadow at all flickered beside Tarawe. Iuti spun. Her war club met the attacking drummer in midlunge. Tarawe moved almost as fast. She dropped to her knees and swept Iuti's shield up to cover her head. The dead drummer's falling body landed on the shield's ragged face. It slid slowly, heavily to the ground.

There was an instant of total silence.

Then, all at once, the forest exploded with sound. Iuti yanked Tarawe back to her feet.

Dissonant drumsounds reverberated through the trees. Deep and sonorous, high and shrill, a cacophony great enough to raise the dead—or to make a sane person want to join them. Tarawe trembled under Iuti's hand. Her lips moved, but Iuti couldn't make out the words over the sound of the drums. She held herself poised for another attack.

The man ahead of them on the path, the one who had thrown the spear, walked back toward them. Iuti faced him, club at the ready, but he paid her no attention. He reached out to prod the fallen drummer. The body rolled over at the side of the path. Blood welled from the crushed skull and the deep, jagged gashes that Mano's teeth had torn through his patterned skin.

The lead drummer stiffened when he saw the damage the shield had done, then cursed and spat. He beat a quick, shrill cadence on one of his drums. The beat was picked up by others and repeated again and again until all other sounds stopped and that single cadence rang alone. The drummer spat again, on the body this time. He glared at Tarawe, then motioned for them to continue along the trail.

Tarawe began chanting softly as they began walking, and immediately, hidden drums began echoing the rhythm of her words.

"Tarawe," Iuti said, touching the girl's shoulder. "Sound your stones."

Tarawe looked up at her. Her eyes showed deep fear, but they looked to be entirely free of the drums' control. She didn't touch the stones in her pocket. "I know it isn't a game, Ser," she said. "I'm singing to keep their noise away from me. If they're going to kill me, let them do it to *my* beat." Without waiting for a response, she returned to her chanting and the path ahead.

They walked on and on, climbing ever higher into the jungle-laden hills. The night was bright enough that the path was always easy to see. It remained wide enough for them to continue abreast. From time to time, torch-light showed far back in the trees.

Tarawe sang sporadically, drawing the drummers to her cadence, then forcing them into confusion by shifting without warning to some wholly unrelated chant. She rattled her stones and tapped her sword along the edge of the shield or on an occasional tree trunk. She walked fast, then slow, skipped a step or stopped abruptly, then moved on again. The drums tried in vain to anticipate her moves and reestablish control.

"Your uncle was right." Iuti chuckled finally. Tarawe's clever defense had clearly turned into a challenge—a surprisingly successful challenge. The drummers had grown tentative; they now hesitated before attempting their vibrating echoes of Tarawe's moves.

Tarawe threw back her head and laughed, long and loud. "My uncle's never been right about anything in his life," she called into the resulting drumroll of her own mirth.

At that, Iuti laughed, too. Some of her own tension fled as she acknowledged the girl's unexpected skill at disregarding, even at controlling, the drummers' noise. Tarawe was right. If they were going to die at the drummers' hands, they might as well do it to their own tune. When Tarawe began singing again, Iuti joined her. She sang deliberately off-key and fractured the tempo at whim, a thing not difficult for her as she had never been noted for her musical skills. Her efforts drew first a grimace, then a grin from Tarawe.

The drums stopped beating altogether.

The sun was just rising when they reached a small village. The drums started beating again just as Iuti caught sight of a thatched roof ahead. "They're drumming to welcome the dawn," Iuti told Tarawe. "They always do that, even on the battlefield. More than one ambush has been averted because of their stubbornness and their early-morning noise."

The drummers' village was a simple clearing. Huts of grass and clicker tree fronds, looking more like great fat mushrooms than proper dwellings, were scattered across the open ground. The houses were surrounded by countless drums. They were of all sizes and shapes. Many were patterned in circles similar to those on the drummers' own skin.

As Iuti and Tarawe passed, women and children ran from the grassy shelters to peer at them. Iuti and Tarawe stared back. The women wore less even than the men. Iuti saw only one with more than a single drum at her waist. A few were as heavily tattooed as the men, but, with the exception of their well-patterned bellies, most bore large patches of unmarked skin. Only a few of the children, mostly boys, were marked.

They passed a roofed, but otherwise open, structure near the village center. It was filled with carved and polished hollow cylinders—they were clearly the makings of a great set of drums. At the center, dwarfing the others in size, rested a single, enormous drum body. Another, somewhat smaller, sat at its side. The two barrels looked as if they had been carved from the trunk of a single, gigantic tree. Iuti suspected the entire set of cylinders had been taken from the same tree.

On the far side of the clearing, surrounded by rough scaffolding, was a high, wide thicket of living thornvine. The spear thrower led them to it. He pointed to a low opening into the thicket and motioned for them to enter.

When Iuti hesitated, he barked what was clearly a warning. Drums boomed across the compound, and the gathered drummers crowded nearer. To Iuti's disgust, the children were pushed to the front, and behind them, the women. If she resisted, she would have to kill countless innocents before she could reach the weaponed men. Cursing, she motioned Tarawe into the thornvine. As they crept cautiously through the narrow gap, a plug of living vine was shoved into the hole after them.

''Welcome!'' a breathless voice greeted them as they neared the end of the passage. ''Welcome, warriors! Enter this abode and be at peace. Let our weapons rest as brothers.''

Iuti was so startled that she almost tripped over Tarawe. The words had been spoken in the purest of southern accents. The greeting was one used only between warriors of rank. She straightened quickly, taking in at a glance the high wall of thornvines that surrounded them. A most effective prison. The thorns were long and sharp and as hard as stone. Even a metal sword couldn't hack through such a barrier.

''Welcome, warrior sister,'' the wheezing voice went on. ''Ah. Ah, yes. I see now why the drummers treated you with such courtesy through this long night. They've waited a long time for one such as you.''

Iuti stared open-mouthed at the mound of flesh that greeted them from across the enclosure. The man—she judged him a man by his voice and the shape of the top-knot that secured his mass of ebony hair—was as enormous a human as she had ever seen. Standing, he would have been little taller than Iuti herself, but his girth was vast beyond measure.

His arms were like tree limbs. His shoulders like massive stones. Great pendulous breasts lay like half-empty waterbags across the enormous mound of his bloated belly. His manhood, if such he still had, was entirely hidden under folds of flesh. Flaccid wattles hung at his throat and from his massive arms and thighs. His dark eyes were almost lost in the swollen folds of his face.

And every inch of him was covered in drummers' tattoos.

"Mano's teeth," Iuti muttered. She lifted her gaze to meet his steady stare.

"Have I become that repulsive to look upon, fair warrior," he asked, "that you must refuse my honest welcome?" Infinite sadness touched his breathless voice.

Iuti found it difficult to speak. "Forgive me," she whispered at last. Then she said it again, loud enough for him to hear. "Forgive me, Ser. I—I did not expect to find a warrior's welcome here."

"Ser Iuti!"

Iuti caught movement in her peripheral vision at the same time that Tarawe spoke her warning. She spun back to face the wall through which they had entered. The purpose for the scaffolding outside became clear as she watched a dozen and more drummers appear above the wall.

"They come only to watch," their companion in the enclosure said. "They don't understand the southern tongues, and they won't come inside unless they're sure you're drugged or fully under the control of their drums. You're safe for the moment."

Iuti turned back. She matched the man's stare for a moment, then knelt and laid Mano's club and her nets on the ground. "Let our weapons rest as brothers," she said. He nodded with great dignity at her formal acceptance of his hospitality. He glanced at Tarawe, but she only gripped her sword the firmer.

He smiled. "The drummers don't like you, little Ser," he said. "You broke a messenger's fingers, and you ruined a ranking warrior's skin. You stole the soul of the drum he was intended to become. Ah, no. They do not like you at all."

"I don't like them, either," Tarawe replied. "They would steal *my* soul if they could."

"Aye," he agreed. "And I commend you for taking your revenge before that happens."

Tarawe lifted her chin.

"What is this place?" Iuti asked. "Are you a prisoner of these walls?"

He snuffed and hacked, then pulled a long string of mucous from his nose. He flicked it toward the watchers on the distant scaffolding. There was a murmur of discordant drumsound, then quiet again. "I am a prisoner of my own flesh," he said. The terrible sadness had returned to his voice.

"How did this happen?" Iuti asked. "You speak with a scholar's accent and offer the welcome of a ranking southern warrior. Yet you sit here . . ." She lifted a hand toward him, then let it fall back to her side. "Who are you, Ser?"

"I was once called Ser Kunan Iliawe," he replied.

Iuti caught her breath. Kunan Iliawe was one of the south's greatest war heroes. More than one of the southern chieftains owed his life and lands to Ser Kunan's diplomacy as well as to his sword arm. He was said to have been the greatest student of war tactics the south had ever known. His disappearance five years before had dealt a great blow to the southern war effort.

"I fought last at the battle of Garamain," the man who claimed Kunan's name said. "We turned back the Teronin forces at great cost, then regrouped in the Simiran hills to rest and celebrate. Only I didn't go with the rest. I had lost too many companions to Krugar and his Teronin scum. I followed him north into the Kaikane swamps seeking revenge." He paused to catch his breath. His knotted hair bobbled atop his head.

"I was a fool. I let myself be seen," he went on finally. "Krugar was waiting when I reached the bogs. He trapped me in a pit of disappearing sand. I never got the chance to kill even one of his many men." Kunan spat. "I was bound by chains and spells and then carried through the swamps like a trussed pig. At the southern waterway that borders Losan Island, I was sold to the Apuka traders, and by them to the demon drummers. I've been here ever since."

Tarawe came to stand beside Iuti. She placed Iuti's shield beside the war club, but kept her sword in her hand. "You don't look much like a warrior," she said.

Iuti nudged her shoulder—if they survived this imprisonment, she was clearly going to have to teach the girl some manners.

But Kunan only laughed. "Nor do you, youngster."

"Why didn't you try to escape?" Tarawe asked.

"I tried. Many times. They finally cut my hamstrings so I couldn't run," he said. "I reached as far as the inland waterway that last time. I still remember the sight of the great basalt cliffs stretching their promise of freedom into the sky. If I could have reached them, I would have escaped. I'm certain of it."

He sighed, a long rasping wheeze. "But the drummers had set a net of waryvine around the isle, and I found myself tangled in it before I even realized it was there."

"Why have they kept you alive so long?" Iuti asked. She had never heard of drummers being interested in any but the unmarked dead. "Are you some kind of totem to them?"

"I am a god to them," he returned. "Or as near as their twisted minds can perceive. They force me to eat so that my body grows, and they mark my skin as it expands. Do you see this great whorl on my belly, fair warrior? Another time I'll show you its twin on my back. And see here, on my arms and thighs. Matching sets.

Even the backs of my hands are mirrored, and my cheeks, my earlobes, my knees.''

Again he paused to move air through his labored lungs.

"It's not me they're keeping alive, friend warrior,'' he said at last. "It's my *skin*. The demon drummers are growing the mightiest set of war drums ever to give sound.'' He lifted a hand to his face.

"The small drum made from my cheeks will one day control an enemy's voice; those from my shoulders and hands, his sword arm. My feet will pace a listening warrior's steps, and my thighs determine the speed of his run. My back and my belly''—he ran his hand across his great stomach—"will speak to his heart and his soul.''

Iuti lifted her own hand to cover her mouth. She closed her eyes, picturing the carved cylinders she had seen in the covered house outside the thornvine. Then she opened them again to meet Kunan's steady look.

"They use the thorns from this prison to inject their designs,'' Kunan went on. "As my skin grows and the patterns spread, they add more designs, more color. The repeated scarring has made my skin as tough as leather. Oh, I'll make a fine set of drums, there's no doubt. They even plan to flay me while I still live in order to transfer as much power as possible into the eventual drums.''

"Ah, Ser Kunan,'' Iuti breathed.

Tarawe made a small, choking sound. She stumbled away to kneel and retch on the ground. A rumble of taunting drumbeats mimicked the sounds of her illness.

Kunan watched her for a moment. "It won't be much longer. The drum cylinders are ready, I'm told, and I can't grow much larger and still breathe. Already my heart and lungs are being crushed by this great weight.'' His labored breathing gave truth to his words.

"I tried to kill myself when I realized what they were doing. But they kept me alive, drugged and bound and drummed insensible. They tore the nails from my fingers and toes and pulled my teeth so I would have no way to mar my freshly patterned skin.''

"You are surrounded by thornvine,'' Iuti said, holding

tight to her anger. "Why don't you throw yourself onto it and ruin . . ."

"I can't reach it," he said. 'I can't even leave this mat without aid. My legs will no longer support my weight. The wall was grown there to protect me from any outside harm."

Iuti glanced up at the watching drummers. The sounds of Tarawe's sickness had faded away. She turned back and lifted Mano's club. "*I* am not outside the wall, brother," she said.

Kunan leaned as far forward as his bulk would allow. He stared down at Mano's club, and Iuti could see the longing in his dark eyes, his tremendous desire for release.

"If it were possible," he said, wheezing with the effort of his move, "I would welcome the touch of your weapon. I would bless you and your descendants to the ends of time for a single moment of your warrior's skill."

He blinked and looked back at her. "But you cannot reach me, sister. There is a net of waryvine between us. It's spelled into place, so even the girl's sword couldn't cut a way through."

Startled, Iuti stepped forward, and then, because she was looking for it, she saw the fine, shimmering web of woven waryvine. Like the simple hiding spell she had used the day before, the vine couldn't be seen unless the viewer knew it was there. She ran her hand across the net's finely knotted surface. She tested its strength and knew that Kunan spoke the truth.

"They'll protect you in this way, too," Kunan said. "As soon as your ritual patterning is begun."

Iuti looked up. "Patterning?"

Kunan straightened and settled again, eyeing her sadly. "You must have seen the empty cylinders waiting in the drum house. Didn't you notice that every drum had a smaller counterpart? Ah, the demon drummers have waited long for one such as you, Ser. Tall and strong, a warrior of obvious skill, and with skin marked only by the scars of honest battle. And a female! The Teronin will pay well for a way to control the south's warrior women.''

Iuti stepped back from the net.

Kunan nodded. ''Aye, warrior sister. We are to be mated, you and I. Your fair skin will soon be patterned and colored like mine. When it has grown great enough in size, it will be flayed and cured, and stretched across the face of the great Mother Drum.''

❧ Chapter 8 ❧

IUTI cursed. A *drum*, by the very gods. She would consent to be these demons' Mother Drum right after she had taken a turn as a Teronin whore! She turned and glared up at the watching drummers. When her look met with that of the spear thrower, she spat.

Following the flickering shape of the waryvine net, she traced the confines of their prison. She whispered a simple release spell, then tried the strongest such charm she knew. Neither affected the net. She studied the place where they had entered through the thornvine, but knew it offered no escape.

"How is it these less-than-men know the secret to spelling a waryvine net in place?" she asked Kunan. "I thought they used no magic but that of their drums."

"The nets and the manner of their setting were a gift from the Teronin," Kunan replied.

Iuti returned to where she had left her shield and the fishnets. She sat cross-legged and lifted Mano's club into her lap.

"Tarawe, come sit here beside me," she called. She tore another strip of cloth from her already torn shirt. "These weapons have soaked too long in a coward's blood. Come help me clean them."

She spat again, on the cloth this time, and used it to begin cleaning bits of hair and flesh from around Mano's teeth. The drummer's blood had stained the sennit wrappings, despite the dunkings she had given the club in each of the streams they had crossed following the killing.

Tarawe approached slowly, accompanied by a soft su-

77

surration of mimicking drumsound. She sat on her heels
at Iuti's side and laid her sword on the nets. Iuti handed
her the shield, and Tarawe tore off a shred of her own
shirt to clean it.

"Best you stain those weapons with your own blood,"
Kunan said. "Do it now, before the drummers take them
from you."

"My weapons won't be taken from me while I still
live," Iuti said.

"Be cautioned, warrior," Kunan returned. "The
drummers count the girl among the most dangerous of
your tools. I urge you for your own sake and that of all
the south to kill her cleanly, and yourself, as well, before
it's too late."

"You should have left me at Fanape." Tarawe spoke
so softly Iuti almost didn't hear. Neither did the drummers catch her words. They remained silent. "Then I
would never have called the storm, and you wouldn't be
here."

Iuti turned to her. She, too, wished she had left Tarawe
behind, but it would do no good to tell her that now. The
youngster needed encouragement if she was to survive.
"If I'd left you, I'd have paddled directly to Marama
believing Pahulu was dead. The southern generals would
have acted on my counsel and sent troops to drive what
they thought were unprotected Teronin from the isles.
Those fighters would surely have been lost, and Pahulu's
power made all the greater."

Tarawe glanced up at her. Her look flicked toward Kunan, then lowered again to the shield.

"If I'd left you behind," Iuti went on, "we wouldn't
have learned of this additional threat. The drummers
never make war directly. They'll sell their great war
drums' sound to the Teronin and through them to Pahulu.
We must find a way to stop them." Even as she said the
words, Iuti knew them to be true.

Tarawe's look came up again. Her breath was sour from
her earlier sickness.

Kunan harumphed, a flatulent wheeze, mimicked by
hidden drums. "So said I once. So said Risak when he

sat there in your place not a full year ago. Yet today I sit here unable to move, and young Risak twice weekly plays unwilling stud to the demon women. Our useless weapons rust somewhere there amid the thornvine.''

"Risak? There is another here?''

Kunan nodded. "A master swordsman from Ilimar. He was brought here wounded after a battle he swears was just outside Sandar City. He claimed the Teronin had reached that far south, though I find it hard to believe.''

"They held Sandar itself when I left the mainland five months ago,'' Iuti said. "Or at least all access to it. The Teronin fight with more than just the drummers' aid now. This swordsman. Is he healed? Is he whole?''

"Can he help you escape, do you mean?'' Kunan laughed. "Ser Risak escapes regularly, with the aid of the drummers themselves. They always recapture him, of course, but each run gives him the hope that the next might be successful. That and the exercise serve to keep him strong. They'll bring him back inside the thorn soon. The women refuse to lie with him in daylight. Warriors' sons can be conceived only at night, they say.''

Tarawe stirred. "Is that true?'' she asked.

"Throughout the wartorn lands, there are bastards aplenty to prove it false,'' Iuti said. "How do they make a man give up his seed if he's not willing?'' she asked Kunan.

"The drums,'' he replied. He spat again.

"Tell me about this patterning the drummers intend,'' Iuti said. "I presume you mean tattoos.''

Kunan nodded. "They'll mark your back first, then your belly. The experience is not pleasant, Ser.''

Iuti was sure it was not. She had once listened to a pair of Neisan spearsmen describing the tattooing ceremony performed at their initiation. If those powerful men could complain, the process was not likely to be pleasant at all.

"According to drummer legend,'' Kunan said, "they were once a strong and influential people, feared throughout the habitable lands.''

"Hmph," Iuti replied. "They and every other backwater tribe that has no strength today."

"Aye, the myth of past glory days is a common one," Kunan said. "But the drummers are attempting to bring those days back. They're selling their drumsound to the Teronin in an effort to eliminate at least one of their potential enemies. Once the southerners are under control, they intend to turn on the Teronin themselves."

"You speak as if you believe they might actually succeed," Iuti said.

"My skin will make a powerful set of war drums, Ser," Kunan replied. "And you . . ." He laughed softly. "Woman, if you ever walk the mating circle around the finished Father Drum and willingly strike its face with your full strength . . . Ah, ahh, yes. I believe the demon drummers may well achieve their goal."

A voice atop the wall spoke. Kunan snarled back a quick response. "They want you to set aside your weapons," he said.

Iuti continued buffing her well-soiled cloth over Mano's teeth, making them shine in the brightening sunlight.

Kunan laughed. "A warrior's response. It is good to see, Ser, even though I grieve at your presence."

It was quiet for a time. Iuti tried to order her thoughts, to devise some plan that would allow their escape. She could think of nothing. All she could do was wait and remain prepared for any opening that might appear. At least, Tarawe had regained her calm.

The creaking sound of a winch brought Iuti's look up and around.

"Risak," Kunan said. "They lift him over the thornvine in a sling. It's safer than keeping an opening cut through the wall. They drum him into submission before they lift him out, and he's always fully exhausted by the time they bring him back."

A basket, slung from a rickety-looking boom, appeared over the wall. It swung inward, then lowered almost to the ground. A latch released and the sides of the basket dropped, tumbling a man onto the ground. The basket jerked back together, then lifted swiftly, while the man groaned and stretched facedown on the bare soil. His upper back was unmarked, but his buttocks and inner thighs were circled with drummers' designs.

"Ser Risak," Kunan called. "We have visitors. Wake up and greet them."

"I've greeted enough visitors this night," Risak muttered without moving. "Be quiet and let me sleep."

"It's no longer night, warrior, and two fair sisters await your hospitality."

"Hunh. You've been here too long, Father Drum, if you claim any of these demon whores to be fair," Risak replied.

Iuti stood. Tarawe rose quickly beside her—bringing her sword with her.

"It matters not how fair you call me," Iuti called out. "But I'll take the tongue of a man who names me a demon whore."

Risak's head turned. His eyes opened and he scrambled to his feet. Iuti could see his start of recognition through the waryvine curtain stretched between them. "Iuti Mano," he breathed. "By the seven gods of Ilimar! How can it be?"

He walked as far toward her as the net would allow and spread his hands on the nearly invisible mesh. He stared.

"Do you know this . . . man?" Tarawe asked.

Iuti could sense the girl's horror at the sight of the patterns etched on and around Risak's manhood. She had to swallow her own. She hadn't considered what markings might be needed for drums meant to control sexual functions. Risak suddenly remembered his nudity. He turned quickly away.

There was a titter of laughter—drum, then human— from atop the scaffolding. Risak glared over his shoulder at the drummers.

"I've seen many a naked warrior," Iuti said, catching his look and holding it. "You seem little different from most. Your legs appear better worked than your shoulders, and you carry a bit more . . . color than I've seen before. But you have no reason to turn away with embarrassment."

"Embarrassment?" he cried. "I turn away with *shame*, Ser. How can I greet so noble a warrior as yourself while standing here a prisoner of such as these?"

Iuti recalled for just an instant those blessed months on Fanape when she had been free of the distracting courtesies her rank and reputation often commanded. She wasn't surprised that Risak had recognized her. Her face and form were well known to most of the southern warriors. "I'm their prisoner, too," she said, "and I haven't even the excuse of being caught during battle. Shall I, also, turn away?"

Risak turned partway back. For the first time, his look took in Tarawe, and the sword in her hand. His own hands curled into fists.

"These fair maids came to us direct from the sea, castaways so it appears," Kunan said. "The drummers found them on the beach late yesterday and think they came to Losan by choice. They consider the woman, of course, to be their long-dreamed-of Mother Drum, come willingly to their shores. They're not sure yet about the young one."

"I heard the drums," Risak said. "I wondered what had drawn the men out of the village after dark. They sounded to be in some disarray."

A drummer called out just as Risak spoke. Kunan raised his look to the scaffold, farted roundly, then returned his attention to Risak. "You were hearing their eventful passage through the forest. Our warrior sister killed a would-be assassin along the way—that was the celebration din you heard. But then the girl destroyed his skin. You recognized that beat, I'm sure."

The drummer shouted again, and suddenly Iuti and Tarawe were pelted with wads of sticky green paste. It was clearly Tarawe who was the target, so Iuti pulled her close to offer the protection of her body. The attack ceased.

"Let me go," Tarawe said. She pulled away and was immediately struck again. A gooey mass of gum sap

slapped against her shoulder and slid down her sleeve.
Tarawe reached into her trousers pocket with her left
hand. There was a pause, then a second wad of paste
came flying toward her.

As quickly as it was in the air, Tarawe flung a stone
in return. The drummer who had thrown the paste yelped
in pain while Tarawe turned neatly aside to avoid his
throw.

There was a flurry of drumsound and movement atop
the scaffolding. Suddenly three drummers stepped forward, one to each side of Tarawe, one directly forward.
To a drummed signal, they let loose their taunting missiles at the same instant.

Tarawe hit only one of them—the one on her right—
before they could duck away, but she hit that one squarely
in the face. He jerked his hands up to cover his bloodied
eye and staggered forward. Before his companions could
catch him, he tumbled over the edge of the scaffolding.
He landed on the jagged thornvine wall.

Iuti yanked Tarawe back against the waryvine and
stepped in front of her as the drums exploded into chaos.
Not only drumheads were beaten, but rims and wrappings, and only the gods knew what else. Women's shrill
shrieks and cries sounded from outside the wall. The
reverberating din all but drowned out the screams of the
fallen drummer. His thrashing served only to impale him
more securely upon the deadly thorns.

"Stay behind me," Iuti yelled when Tarawe tried to
squirm away. "Risak, watch our left." It was the one
thing he could do to help them from the other side of the
net.

"Aye," he said before the words were out of her
mouth.

"This is *my* battle!" Tarawe cried. "Let me go!"

Iuti held her pinned against the net. "This is *our* battle, youngster, and you've done your part. Done it well.
Now we stand together." She could see the tips of the
drummers' fighting sticks above the wall, but the drummers themselves had disappeared. She doubted they

would be throwing gum sap when they next showed their faces.

The fallen man's screams changed to a choking gurgle and then abruptly ceased. Iuti felt Tarawe's shudder clearly—the girl groaned and clung to Iuti's waist as the icy thrust of yet another violent death slid through her soul. Iuti was glad Pahulu was nowhere near. Tarawe's mind was still raw and vulnerable from her Teronin kills.

"Rest easy, child," Risak said from close behind. "It was an honest kill and needed doing."

The drumming shifted to the swift, staccato beat that had announced the ruin of the dead drummer's skin the night before. The cadence made Iuti's teeth ache.

Suddenly a different beat slid through the air. A message drum. Kunan shouted something in response and the noise, all but a chilling, underlying rumble, gradually ceased. A voice called from behind the wall.

"They want you to lay down your weapons," Kunan said.

"Two heads, far left and center," Risak said. "They're coming back up for a look."

"I see them," Iuti replied.

"That's quite a throwing arm your girl has," Risak added. "Is she as skilled with the blade?"

The lead drummer appeared above the scaffolding. He repeated the same demand. Iuti needed no translation this time. She shifted her club to her left hand and held out her right. "Tarawe, give me the sword."

Tarawe grew very still.

"Give it to me, girl," Iuti snapped, "unless you're prepared to run it through my back upon my order, and then across your own throat. That may be the only option we have left."

The sword slipped, trembling, into her outstretched hand.

The drummer called out again.

"He wants you to take her stones, too," Kunan said.

"If he wants her stones, he can take them himself and I'll dance at his funeral," Iuti said. "I'm not disarming

Tarawe, I'm arming myself. Tell him his Mother Drum wants her companion left unharmed.''

"He's afraid your *companion* is going to harm *you*," Kunan replied. "They want her away from you so they can begin their bloody ritual."

"Tarawe," Iuti warned, "I'm going to step forward to reach my shield. Stay with me."

They had no more than cleared the net, when Risak and Kunan both shouted. "Left!" But it was too late. Iuti had already spun to knock away a finger-thick drumstick hurled from the right. A thud and a grunt of pain told her Tarawe had been hit by something much heavier. Tarawe staggered and pressed her face against Iuti's back. Iuti felt the warmth and wetness of tears, proof that the girl had been hurt.

Before the drummers could strike again, Iuti lifted the sword's tip to her own left cheek and drew a line from her ear to her chin. The skin parted smoothly and blood flowed, thick and hot, down her face and neck.

The drummers, some with sticks and clubs already lifted to throw, froze.

"Tell them," Iuti shouted, "that for every hurt the girl takes, they will lose one of their cursed drums." The arm around her waist loosened, and Tarawe sagged to the ground behind her. A quick glance showed the girl's left hip to be smeared with blood. A carved wooden club lay nearby.

Meeting the drum leader's stare again, Iuti lifted Mano's club to her right cheek. The drummer shrieked in denial as Iuti yanked her weapon down, raking Mano's teeth through her skin. She sucked in her breath at the blinding pain.

The sword cut had been clean, little more than a scratch, but Mano's wounds were ragged and deep. Without thinking, Iuti called on the shark to help her control the fiery pain. It was a gift he had provided many times in the past. But this time, there was no response. Iuti almost cried out at the far greater pain of remembering that Mano was no longer there to call. Her mind filled with trembling, echoing emptiness.

She forced herself back to the physical pain and the danger of the present. The drummers had gone mad—drumming and screaming and shrieking atop their tenuous scaffolding, brandishing their weapons at one another and at Kunan and Risak. The latter two shouted back in derision. Tarawe moved, caught her breath, and was still again.

Iuti knew she was going to have to kill the girl. She knew she needed to do it now, quickly and cleanly, to remove her from this madness before more harm could be done. She would pierce Tarawe's heart with a single thrust of the sword and then score her own skin so that it could never be used for the demon drums. It was not the way she would have chosen to die, but it was better than having her strength turned against her own comrades.

She tightened her grip on the sword's hilt. It seemed not to fill her hand as perfectly as it once had. She knelt at Tarawe's side. The drummers shrieked and called, their drumsounds shaking the air, as Iuti laid the tip of the sword against Tarawe's chest.

Tarawe stared up at her. Her eyes were wide with terror, but she didn't lift her hand to stop Iuti's thrust.

The sword did not move.

Am I bespelled? Iuti thought in confusion. Why do I hesitate to do this thing that needs to be done? She listened to the drumsound. Had she somehow fallen under its control? But the drums offered only insistent encouragement to do the killing.

Iuti tried again to kill the girl, but still the sword would not move. The blade remained motionless, not even pricking Tarawe's skin.

It must be the sword, Iuti thought. It must be the sword that won't do the killing!

The cold metal Iuti had foresworn had slid easily enough through her own skin. It had drunk almost eagerly of her blood. Did it recognize her as Mano's kin? It had helped her slay the great shark with no hesitation. Why could she not now use it against the girl? Iuti glanced at Mano's club, but knew she could never use that weapon against a child.

What has happened to me, she thought, that I can't control my own weapons?

"Kunan," she called, forcing away her confusion. "Can you aid me by setting a warding spell over the girl?"

"Aye, but—"

"And you, Risak?"

"Aye," came the quick reply, "but to what purpose? It's better that you kill her now. A warding spell, even doubled, can't protect her long. They have but to separate us and—"

"What is the piece of me they treasure most?" Iuti asked.

"Your back and your belly," Kunan said. "Nothing else will grow large enough to stretch across the ends of the Mother Drum. Without those, the rest will be of only minor use. Ser, I beg you . . ."

Iuti reached out with the sword to pull her nets and shield within reach. She laid the sword at Tarawe's side. The drummers shrieked their protest. "Have you a healing spell that can deal with your injury?" Iuti asked.

Tarawe blinked away tears. Her lower lip was firmly caught between her teeth. She nodded.

"I think so," she whispered. She stared at Iuti's face.

"It's nothing," Iuti said quietly. "Just a little blood to scare the fool drummers. Kunan and Risak are going to lay a warding spell on you. Don't try to break it. Use the time and protection to heal yourself."

"What are you going to do?" Tarawe asked. She lifted a hand, but pulled it back quickly when she saw it was covered with blood. Iuti smiled at that small island courtesy. It was one of the few Tarawe had ever offered her. She laid Mano's club atop the nets and wiped her own palm across the cheek Mano had torn. Then she grasped Tarawe's bloody hand.

"I beg your forgiveness for being unable to kill you cleanly, little sister," she said. "But we will stand together through whatever comes. Our blood will flow as one."

Before Tarawe could resist, Iuti shifted her hand, smeared now with their mingled blood, to the girl's injured hip. Tarawe flinched at her touch. The skin was torn, but not deeply. Still, a great swelling had already begun. It was impossible to tell what damage might have been done to muscle or bone underneath. Iuti whispered a private spell, one known only to the women of her family, and Tarawe's eyes immediately began to close.

"Heal quickly," Iuti said. "We'll need to be strong to escape this place."

Carrying only her shield, Iuti stood and turned to face the drummers. Behind her, she felt a strong warding spell settle over the girl. The drummers felt it, too. Their damnable percussion split the air like invisible bludgeons. Iuti shook her head to clear her thoughts. Clotted blood broke loose and flowed hot and sticky down both cheeks. There was a collective intake of breath among the drummers, but the insidious drumming did not diminish.

A second layer of drumming began, deep and intense. It made Iuti's skin crawl. She felt at once excited and unutterably repulsed. Risak groaned, and Iuti felt the warding spell around Tarawe flicker.

"What is it?" she called. "Why can't you hold the spell?"

Risak said nothing, but Kunan cursed. "They're beating his blood song," he said. "What you hear is the sound of our brother's unwilling passion among the demon women. He can't resist. His conditioned response is something they did to him long ago." The screech of the winch hinted that Risak would soon be removed altogether from their presence.

"Tell them to stop," Iuti shouted above the din.

"They will not. They know they can't reach the girl now, but neither can she reach them—or you. That's their greatest concern."

"Then I will give them a greater one!" Iuti lifted the shield in both hands. She flashed Mano's teeth toward the watching drummers. Then she reversed the shield and rested its sharp face against her chest. The drum noise, all but that controlling Risak, abruptly ceased.

"Tell them to stop the rest, or I'll destroy their Mother Drum right now," she shouted.

"They won't—"

"Tell them I'll trade them my skin for their silence and the safety of the girl."

"Ser, you must not willingly give yourself to them! The war drums—"

"Tell them, Kunan Iliawe!"

❧ Chapter 9 ❧

NEITHER the drummers nor their tools of torture were clean. The tattoo artist used hollow thorns, taken from the prison walls, to inject their colors into Iuti's back. Each thorn was dipped into an inky paste before being jabbed through the skin. Then the artisan blew through the hollow thorn to force the ink deep beneath the surface.

Iuti set a strong healing spell as soon as the ordeal began, but by the third day, she could feel the growing sore on her back beginning to fester. She warned the drummers through Kunan that she could grow ill and even die if the festering grew out of control, but they seemed unconcerned. Stab by stab, thorn by thorn, they enlarged the Mother Drum's circular pattern.

Kunan suggested that they were deliberately trying to weaken her to the point where she could no longer hold her shield pressed to her chest. "They know most southern warriors are trained to control all but the worst of war wounds," he said. "If they can force you into unconsciousness, they can take the shield away while your body automatically repairs itself. After that . . ." He shrugged.

Iuti winced as the woman tending her jabbed another thorn into her back. She tried not to tense, knowing it only made the pain worse, but had little success in keeping her muscles relaxed. The artist spat the ink beneath her skin and stepped back to rinse black spittle from her lips.

Iuti could just see her from the corner of her left eye. The woman's hands and arms and the skin around her mouth were dark with circular patterns. The fingers of her left hand drummed nervously against her thigh as she waited for her assistants to prepare the next thorn.

Iuti had been surprised at first, when the tattoo artist turned out to be a woman, and when only women were lowered inside the thornvine to assist her. But then she decided it made a drummers' kind of sense, since they were preparing a female drum. She wondered if a woman would ever be allowed to bring sound from the war drums she was intended to be. She received only sullen silence when Kunan laughingly passed on her question.

"Save for the artist, women here rank well below the lowliest of their own drums," Kunan said. "Did the men push them to the front to force you in here?"

"Them and the children," Iuti replied. She recalled that it had been mostly women and girls and a few unmarked boys in that pressing crowd. She stiffened as cold water was splashed without warning across her back. She twisted around to grab the water bucket before it was empty. Blinking away the dizziness her quick move caused, she drained the bucket dry. From atop the wall, men cursed and shouted in derision. The women cowered.

"Well done," Kunan said. His swollen belly rippled with laughter, Iuti had repeatedly refused the food and drink the drummers offered. They stank of potions poorly prepared. Only the water they used periodically to rinse her back was pure, and she surprised it away from the women whenever she could. Her belly was knotted with hunger.

"Where were we?" Kunan said as Iuti tossed the bucket aside. She didn't aim directly at the artist, just close enough to make her duck away. "Ah, yes. Using unarmed women and children to stop an honorable warrior from killing. They learned that from me, I'm sorry to say. Now, if I had it to do over again . . ."

Kunan talked on and on, distracting her from the fiery pain. He paused only when his breath grew so labored he could no longer speak. Then Risak took over, and more and more often that third day, Tarawe.

The girl told the story of Fanape's treachery, then of
her and Iuti's escape and their sail through the storm.
She told the story well, but factually. She neither exaggerated nor was overly humble about her own part in the
adventure. When Risak asked about her swordwork, Tarawe admitted freely to her self-taught warrior's skills,
and when he expressed a willingness to answer, she began plying him with questions about his own.

"She moves that sword as if it had been made for her
own hand," Kunan commented once as they watched
Tarawe practice a defensive turn under Risak's guidance.
"Despite it being so much larger than her size war-
rants."

"Aye," Iuti said, sighing against the pain in her back
and the unease Tarawe's effortless learning brought. She
had only to be told something once to grasp its essence.
Then she practiced with a patience that belied her youth
until each move came as naturally as if she had been born
with it. She was right, Iuti thought. I should have left her
on Fanape. At least there she would have had a chance
to grow into the powerful woman she was so obviously
meant to be.

The only other distraction to Iuti's pain was the flock
of giant seabirds that began circling over the enclosure
the second day. The great gulls squawked and chattered.
They dived boldly into the prison dropping great splats
of pus-colored dung along their paths. They seemed to
have no difficulty seeing and avoiding the waryvine nets.

On the third afternoon, the largest of the birds—one
with a wingspan as wide as Tarawe's outstretched arms—
dived directly at the women tending Iuti. It dropped its
putrid load atop the tattoo artist's head.

"The birds must like you, warrior woman," Kunan
laughed as the cursing artisan screeched and screamed
and used the last of the clean water to wash the birdshit
from her eyes and mouth.

"I've rarely seen them so bold," Risak agreed.

The drummers kept to their word and stayed well away
from Tarawe. They threw food down to her, but made no
effort to strike her with it. And except for a brief dawn

greeting, a ritual both Kunan and Risak insisted the drummers would do regardless of Iuti's threats, the drums remained silent.

Like Iuti, Tarawe ignored the food after the first taste. She did drink sparingly from the water bag but always sat silent afterward, chanting some protective spell. It seemed to work, for Tarawe, despite her obvious hunger, continued sane and ever more healthy. Whatever charm she was using seemed effective against the drummers' poisons. Occasionally she stopped what she was doing and lifted a hand to her eyes. She shuddered sometimes, in pain or in fear Iuti had no way of knowing, but was otherwise as steadfastly strong as any seasoned warrior with whom Iuti had served.

The drummers had strung a waryvine net between Tarawe and Iuti, and others to keep Iuti from harming herself on the thornvine. It was a precaution they insisted upon when Iuti demanded she be left alone during the night. "I cannot sleep with their stench," she had Kunan translate, although in truth, she doubted they smelled any worse than she. None of them smelled worse than the odoriferous gifts of the gulls.

The women were more than happy to leave the prison, for as Kunan explained, their fear of the dark bordered on a supernatural thing. They believed the world was totally unsafe when the sun was not in the sky. Kunan assured Iuti that the men had made their nighttime trek through the jungle only because of her own great worth. Ordinarily they never left their huts after the sun went down. Even when they traveled in small groups with the Teronin, they insisted on remaining inside tightly closed tents at night.

After the drummers left on the third evening, Iuti crawled close to the net that separated her from Tarawe. She needed to sleep deeply to counteract the poisons in her back, and she trusted Tarawe's vigilance more than that of Kunan, who dozed at unexpected times, or Risak, who could at any time be taken over by the drums. She wondered why she bothered with vigilance anymore. There was no way out of the thornvine prison.

"Ser Iuti," Tarawe said very softly as Iuti settled herself. Iuti sighed, wincing against the pain even that slight movement brought to her back.

"Ser Iuti."

"I hear," Iuti replied. She wished the girl would leave her alone. She hadn't the energy to answer more of Tarawe's incessant questions. She longed for the peace and oblivion of deep, healing sleep, and she cursed herself for not doing what needed to be done, back when there had still been a way to do it.

Tarawe spoke again. "I've found a way through the waryvine."

Iuti didn't move. "What?" Could she have heard correctly? She was so tired, so hungry and hot. And the pain . . .

"Remember the spell I told you about?" Tarawe's insistent voice went on. "The one that warrior used to trip Pahulu? I've been experimenting with it, and I've found a way to make the waryvine move."

Excitement flickered. Hope rekindled at the back of Iuti's tired mind, then immediately died. No one just "experimented" with another person's spell to alter it safely for her own use.

"I can't move the net itself," Tarawe whispered. "But I can make the vines spread open wide enough for us to squeeze through."

Iuti pushed herself up onto her hands and knees. She jumped when Tarawe's hand met hers in the darkness. The girl had already come through the net! Tarawe closed Iuti's fingers around the haft of her war club.

"By the soul of Mano Niuhi, child," Iuti breathed. "You are a true gift from the gods!" She squeezed Tarawe's hand.

"You're hot," Tarawe said. "Fevered. You need to sleep now . . ."

"No," Iuti whispered, "we must go while we both still have the strength."

"I—I can't move the thornvine, Ser. It's too thick and strong," Tarawe replied.

Iuti looked up. The basket the drummers used to enter

and leave their prison hung several warriors' heights above them. "Can you spell the net open in more places than one?" she asked. "Could you make holes so we can climb the net?"

Tarawe nodded. "I think so. I have to touch each place first, but once it's open it stays that way until I tell it to close."

"Good," Iuti said. "First open a way to Kunan. Then get Risak, and the two of you climb up there." Iuti motioned toward the gently creaking boom. The basket swung slowly in the breeze above the wall. "Use the nets to pull the basket into reach. Risak will know what to do."

She stopped suddenly, remembering Tarawe's injury. "Your leg. Will you be able . . ."

"Able enough," Tarawe said, "to get out of here." Then she hesitated. She glanced at the dark mound that was Kunan. "He'll never be able to climb the net."

"I'll take care of Kunan," Iuti said. "Go now. Take the rest of the weapons. The drummer's club that hit you, too. Here, give me that broken drumstick. Let Risak carry the sword."

Again that slight hesitation.

"The sword is yours, girl. You earned it honorably. But the trained sword arm is Risak's. Let him carry it for tonight."

Tarawe hung the shield over her arm and stuck the club into her waistband, just as Iuti had done with the drumstick. Then she squatted to charm an opening through the net to Kunan. When she finished, Iuti touched her shoulder.

"Go quickly now," Iuti said. She pushed her toward the spot where Risak waited. There was enough light for him to see that Tarawe had broken free of her private prison, but he was waiting and watching in total silence. Iuti knew he would watch them escape without him if that was the only way it could be done, but his very stance in the quiet darkness displayed his desperate desire to join them.

She waited until Tarawe had reached him and explained their plan before ducking through the net to Kunan. She gasped as a loose strand of vine dragged across her tortured back.

Kunan was awake, waiting as silently as Risak. As Iuti approached, she saw that he had undone his topknot and braided his hair into a single, thick plait. It was draped over his massive shoulder and chest reaching almost to his waist. He had tied the end with a strand of fruit rind, and now his hands rested quietly on his wide knees.

"So," he said simply. "The drummers were right. The girl *is* your most dangerous weapon."

"So it would seem," Iuti replied. "I offer thanks to whatever gods stayed my blade from her heart." She reached out to touch his lifted hand. "I would take you with me if I could, brother."

"This great pile of blubber?" he replied. "You'd have to roll me like a boulder through the jungle." He lowered his hand and glanced down at Mano's club. Iuti's grip around its smooth haft tightened, but when she lifted it, he stiffened.

"No," he said. "Not with that."

Iuti frowned. "I can't leave you here alive, Ser."

Kunan ran one great palm over his patterned belly. "Do it another way," he said. "Do not mark my skin."

"But . . ."

"If my hide is ruined, they'll be after you in an instant. They might even follow you off the island if you get that far." He paused. "If my skin is left whole, they'll delay the search until it can be ritually flayed. They believe a warrior's soul lingers after death, so they'll try to capture as much of my power as they can. They've spent too much time growing me to do otherwise."

"But the war drums . . ."

"If you don't escape, the power of the drums will be doubled," he said. "All the warriors must assist in the skinning ritual, so you'll have at least an extra day to get off the island. They'll use the drums to call you, so beware, but only the women will follow directly until the skinning is complete."

He stopped to rest his overburdened lungs. "Take my hair. It will . . ." His strength gave out. "Ask Risak."

Iuti thought for a moment, then laid her club on the ground. The boom creaked. She looked up to see it swinging toward two dark shapes high above. Risak had snagged the basket with the nets and was pulling it slowly toward them. Clinging to the waryvine, he and Tarawe appeared to be hanging in midair.

Iuti reached out again. She laid a gentle hand on Kunan's cheek. His skin felt like leather under the circular tattoo. "You are a true warrior, Kunan," she said. "Were things not as they are, I would be honored to walk the mating circle with you."

"Listen for my heartbeat on the battlefield, fair warrior," Kunan whispered. "Beware my power."

"Our weapons have rested as brothers, Ser. I'll listen and gain strength from your voice." The boom creaked again. Iuti glanced up. Tarawe was in the basket now. Risak still clung to the net.

"Look at the stars, Ser," she said. "They shine with the light of our freedom."

Kunan held her look for a long moment—his eyes glistened in the darkness—then he lifted his great head to stare up at the stars. Iuti slid the broken drumstick from her waistband.

"Fair winds, brother," she whispered, and with a single, silent thrust, she plunged the stick's jagged end through Kunan's left eye. Something touched Iuti's soul. Ice or fire—she could not tell what it might be. "Fair winds, brother," she whispered again.

The huge body sagged so suddenly that Iuti was knocked off-balance. She broke her fall with her hands, grunting in protest to the jarring pain. As she pushed herself up, her hand brushed against something soft and sticky. A piece of limefruit. She stuffed it into her mouth, half gagging at the salty-sour taste.

She used Mano's teeth to saw away Kunan's hair, then used the heavy braid to tie the club to her waist. She glanced once more at the mound of Kunan's body before turning back toward the place where Tarawe and Risak had climbed. She found the first of Tarawe's spelled handholds and began to climb.

Iuti had thought the ruin of her back could become no more painful, but each stretch and pull as she felt her way up the invisible net was like liquid fire. She thought of the many injuries, large and small, that she had taken while in partnership with Mano. She shuddered at the quantity of pain the shark must have endured on her behalf. The liquid, she realized as she climbed, was her own blood, draining from torn-away scabs.

Risak was waiting at the top of the net. Tarawe had already reached the scaffolding. "It'll only hold one of us without creaking to wake the dead," Risak whispered. "You go first. I'll cut the lines behind us so it'll take the drummers longer to reach Kunan tomorrow."

He paused and looked down. "You did him a kindness, Ser. I wish it could have been my hand that did the deed."

Iuti accepted Risak's help into the basket. She was dizzy with pain and weak with hunger and over-spelled sleep. The limefruit lay like acid in her empty stomach. She had to force it to remain there while she climbed from the swaying basket to the wavering boom.

Tarawe took her arm as she reached the scaffold and supported her while they climbed down. Risak scrambled down the scaffolding behind them. He pointed, and the run began. Slowly at first. Carefully, because they were still within the drummers' village. But the night remained quiet and none save themselves moved. The drummers were safely inside their lamplit huts, hiding from the darkness they so feared.

Iuti trusted to Risak's direction. They stumbled through the jungle, on paths and tracks that carried both human and animal scents. They waded across streams and scrambled through thorny thickets, paying no attention to any trail they might leave behind. Iuti laughed at the puny barbs that snagged her as she passed. The drummers' tattooing needles had done more damage than any bramble bush could. She realized she was growing delirious.

They stopped once, when Risak tangled himself in a waryvine net that had been strung through the trees. Tarawe touched the vine and chanted her precious spell, and Risak pulled himself free. They stopped again, when Tarawe spied a fallen coconut. She took the sword from Risak. With one quick strike and twist of the blade, she cracked away the outer husk. She sliced off the top of the hard, inner nut and handed it to Iuti.

"Drink," she said as she passed the sword back to Risak. "All of it. You're falling over your own feet from hunger."

"As are you," Iuti managed to mutter before Tarawe tipped the slightly sour liquid into her throat. She swallowed eagerly. The nut was old and essentially tasteless—good drinking nuts didn't fall from the tree of their own accord—but it was the most welcome meal Iuti had ever tasted.

"You finish it," she said when she judged the nut half empty. "My stomach's too shrunken to take more."

Tarawe looked dubious, but drained the nut without arguing.

"Let's move," Risak said, and they ran on.

Twice more they were stopped by waryvine nets, and once by a wide trench covered with cut clicker-tree fronds. It wasn't a sophisticated trap, but it was one that Iuti and Tarawe might easily have stumbled into had they been traveling alone. Risak had obviously encountered such pits before: he spotted this one with plenty of time to stop. Rather than take the chance of leaping across into what might be additional traps, they made their slow, careful way around.

It was almost dawn when they reached a ridge overlooking the inland waterway. The cliffs Kunan had described rose dark and welcoming against the brightening sky. They scrambled down the steep embankment and ran eagerly toward the water just as the drummers began welcoming the rising run.

"Hurry!" Iuti shouted.

Suddenly the dawn song broke off. There was an instant of silence. Then the air exploded with percussive chaos.

Kunan had been found!

❧ Chapter 10 ❧

IUTI and the others splashed into the water with their hands pressed tightly over their ears.

The pronouncement of Kunan's death was deafening. The entire jungle thundered with discordant, echoing drumsound, amplified by means Iuti knew could not be natural. The distant cliffs sent the vibrating din back doubled.

Tarawe swam ahead, her fingers outspread for the first touch of waryvine. Iuti and Risak followed closely, watching behind them for any sign of pursuit. Suddenly a second cadence overlaid the chaos announcing Kunan's death. Risak gasped. His strokes slowed. After a moment he stopped swimming to press his hands over his ears.

"They call . . ." he cried when Iuti tried to pull his hands away and urged him to swim on. "I can't . . ."

The compelling cadence of Risak's song caught at Iuti, too. Her grip tightened on his arm. For an instant, their gazes met and locked. No! she thought. But he lifted a hand to her face. The drums throbbed.

A desire deeper than life itself shuddered through Iuti's loins. She pulled Risak close and their strength matched as they clung to each other in the warm, slick water.

"Yes!" she cried, abruptly blind to all but Risak's throbbing power. Now! Do it now! She tore at her trousers with her free hand.

Risak pressed his own hot, heavy hand against her left breast. His grin was dark and fierce as he brought his face close to hers. She tried to wrap her legs around his waist, then laughed when her move caused him to stumble in the shoulder-deep water. His grip loosened, and

101

his hands dropped to her waist, strong and hard. He slid one arm behind her . . .

Iuti screamed!

Risak's grasping fingers had ripped through the thick scab on her back. Iuti shuddered and gagged and tore herself away. "By the gods!" she cried. "By the very gods!"

Risak reached for her again, but Iuti understood it for what it was this time. She fought him away. The drums pounded Risak's song, Iuti's song. She thrust the noise away, focusing on the pain.

Risak's drum-controlled need turned to fury at her denial. He fought, panicked, desperate. His dark eyes blazed with desire, but his face was twisted with pain. Finally, when he could not overcome her, he turned back to the Losan shore.

"Oh, no!" Iuti cried over the drums. "Oh, no, friend Risak! I won't let you go back."

She grabbed him by the hair, and after another struggle, managed to shove his head under the water. She went under and held him there, struggling and fighting, in the blessed near silence of the inland sea until she thought her lungs would explode. Risak twisted and turned, trying to pull her hands from his hair.

Then, all at once, he stopped. Consciousness poured back into his tortured expression—a sudden realization of what had just happened. Iuti wished to weep at the shame and self-loathing that twisted the swordsman's fair features.

They had to go back up for air. As quickly as the breath was in him, Iuti pushed Risak under again. Even those few seconds of drumsound had brought confusion back to his eyes. She pointed him toward the opposite shore, urging him that way.

His eyes cleared. He nodded, and they swam underwater until once again they had to surface for air. Ahead, Tarawe waited, gesturing frantically. Another quick breath brought another brief struggle, then finally they reached Tarawe's side. She motioned them through a hole in a net they couldn't see.

There were two nets in the waterway. Tarawe tangled herself in the second before realizing it was there. Her eyes were bulging by the time she had mumbled whatever charm she used to control the fine mesh and burst back to the surface for air. But then they were all through and swimming strongly for the opposite shore.

When they reached shallow water, the struggle with Risak began anew. "Let me go," he begged as the drums forced him back and back again toward the drummers' isle.

And then, "Kill me! Don't let me go back!"

"We'll never get him up the cliff like this," Tarawe called.

"We can't leave him," Iuti shouted. She had to fight constantly against Risak's song herself. Not Risak's, she admitted with dread. They're playing my blood song, too! The drums were almost as loud on this side of the waterway as they had been on the island.

"Here," Tarawe said. She pulled two bits of cloth from her pocket—the plugs she had used their first night on the drummers' isle. She stuffed them into Risak's ears, and they both held his head underwater until comprehension returned. They cautiously let him up again. He shook his head, obviously still strongly affected by the pounding sound, but did not immediately begin fighting to return to Losan.

Iuti scooped up a handful of pebbles and broken shells and tied them loosely into what was left of her skirt, only rags now, dangling at her waist. She fastened small bags of stones over Risak's head, so that they hung beside his ears. Whenever he moved, the soft click of the stones sounded.

He frowned, but hope touched his eyes for the first time since the drums had begun. "Let's move," he whispered.

"Quickly," Iuti urged. They began climbing the rough face of the cliff, Tarawe in the lead, Iuti following an ever slower-moving Risak. Whenever he paused longer than the immediate terrain demanded, Iuti slapped his legs or whatever part of him she could reach. Then he would shake his head from side to side, his face rigid with concentration on the randomly rattling stones. Iuti had only to concentrate on the agony of her back to deny the pounding call.

The cliff wasn't as sheer as it had looked from a distance. Shelves of marginally level stone and gravel provided easy climbing surfaces up much of it. "Ah, Kunan," Iuti whispered. "I wish you could be climbing this wall of freedom at my side." Ahead, she heard Tarawe shout out her defiance of the drummers' din. She seemed entirely unaffected by the noise.

As they neared the top of the cliff, Risak gradually began climbing faster. Iuti no longer had to urge him along or stop him from turning back. She was so grateful for the reprieve that she had cleared the clifftop herself before realizing the difference in Risak's actions was due to a difference in the sound. The drummers' call was still strong, but it was no longer alone in the morning air. A beat with no discernible rhythm sounded from somewhere ahead.

After crossing a small rise, she saw row after row of coconut trees stretching inland and in both directions along the coast. The ground beneath the trees was clear of all but fallen copra nuts and dried fronds and a few small bushes and sprouting trees. Here and there, something dark and moving was strung between the trees.

Nets, she thought. Another trap!

But then a gust of wind, fresh with the smell of the open sea, brushed past. The clattering sound ahead grew louder. For an instant, it drowned out the drummers' call.

Windchimes! Iuti thought, and she laughed aloud. Windchimes! She recognized the hollow thud of empty gourds banging together, and the booming of giant bamboo pipes. She pushed Risak toward the trees. "Run! Get into the trees quickly! This grove is a barrier to the drummers' sound. Tarawe, make him go."

Once again she gave thanks for the girl's quick understanding. Iuti couldn't travel as fast as Tarawe and Risak—she was still breathless with pain and exhaustion from the run and the swim and the climb. But she had less need to reach the trees quickly. Tarawe gave her a calculating look, then grabbed Risak's arm and yanked him away from the cliff edge toward the coconut grove. Iuti stumbled as best as she could after them.

Tarawe stopped under the first of the great chimes, but Iuti waved her on. She paused only long enough herself to note the size and variety of the rattling gourds and swaying lengths of giant bamboo. They were attached to an intricately knotted web that was itself attached to the surrounding trees. Some of the calabashes had loose stones inside. Their sound in the gusting sea breeze, although much greater in volume, was not unlike that of the stones covering Risak's ears.

Kunan was right, she mused. Had he been able to cross the waterway all those years before, he might well have escaped. This noise-filled grove was here by design, set by someone long ago as a barrier against the demon drummers' power. Many of the trees were old, tall and graceful, their fronded peaks so high off the ground that they swung in great arcs in the wind. Others were smaller. Some, mere seedlings. They and the cleared ground beneath them proved that someone still actively maintained this place. Iuti offered their unknown benefactor silent thanks.

When the demon drumsound had faded into meaningless rumbles, Risak and Tarawe stopped to wait for Iuti. Risak removed the stones from over his ears and stood staring up at the clattering windchimes. Tarawe had climbed one of the shorter trees and was busy husking and opening fresh drinking nuts by the time Iuti reached them. She had obviously already drunk her fill of the nutritious fluids—her energy level had returned in remarkable measure, as had Risak's.

Iuti envied them their fast recovery. She collapsed onto her knees. It was going to take more than a quick meal to restore *her* health. It was all she could do to gag down the coconut water Tarawe and Risak forced upon her. Her back felt as if it were on fire. She wished she could just lie down on the bed of fronds and go to sleep. Overhead, a gull called out raucously.

The water had washed away the last of the torn scabs on Iuti's back and had soaked the raw sores as clean as could have been done by any other means. But now the scabs were hardening again. They pulled and tore with her every move. Her concern, though, was for the fevered sickness she could feel growing inside her body. Tarawe's grimace after a quick glance at her back did nothing to allay her fears.

"You'll die of the festering if you keep on like this," Tarawe said. "You should set a strong healing spell and sleep until it takes hold. I can teach you one if you want."

"I don't need your spells," Iuti said.

"Risak and I can keep watch. We can see anyone who comes into the trees."

"We can't stop now," Iuti objected. "We're still too close. If I set a spell deep enough to deal with this quickly, you won't be able to wake me if trouble comes." She leaned forward, resting her forearms on her knees, barely able to lift her head from exhaustion.

She shivered. Her fever had been cooled by the swim, but the climb and the run had returned her to her former aching misery. She would have to stop soon. But not yet. Not this close to Losan.

"If trouble comes, you're not going to be able to help anyway," Tarawe said. "You're already—"

"Forgive me, young Ser," Risak broke in, obviously offended by Tarawe's forwardness. "Ser Iuti is correct. We're still too near Losan."

Iuti looked up, but he refused to meet her gaze.

"You said before that they never leave the island except for those few who are hired by the Teronin," Tarawe argued. She stared boldly at the sword Risak had just picked up, reminding him with a look that he held it only by her grace.

He very deliberately lashed the weapon to a belt he had braided from fallen coconut fronds. "We've stolen their Mother Drum, girl," he said. "It's hard to tell what they might do. They won't follow until Kunan's skin is ready for drying, but they won't wait long after that to begin a search. When they don't find us on the island, they'll hire the Apuka traders to search this coastline for us. We must get away while we can.''

Iuti pushed herself back to her feet. ''We'll continue until dark. I can make it that long. Then I'll set a spell and sleep through the night while you two watch.''

Against the wishes of every aching muscle, she began walking again, using what she hoped was a strong, steady stride. In an instant, Risak and Tarawe flanked her, each offering a supportive arm. Iuti cursed her weakness and accepted them both.

They crossed the coconut grove as quickly as they could and continued their flight into the dense jungle beyond. They walked until they could no longer hear the echoing sounds of the windchimes, and then they walked on. Finally they reached a place where both Iuti and Risak agreed it would be safe to stop. Iuti immediately set as strong a healing spell as her weary mind allowed and slid into deep slumber.

She woke to the nutty fragrance of roasting breadfruit and the whispered singsong of an island healing chant. It was Tarawe, trying to speed the healing of Iuti's back with one of her odd assortment of spells. Iuti restrained a smile. She opened her eyes and the chanting stopped.

One night's healing, even with Tarawe's help, had not been enough. Iuti felt she could sleep another ten days and still be exhausted. But the fever was gone. Her back still hurt, but she could detect only lingering traces of the illness caused by the drummers' filth. She sat up stiffly.

Risak had built a small earth oven during the night, and he quickly brought her a cupped leaf filled with breadfruit and bananas baked in coconut cream. Tarawe sliced the top off a drinking nut and set it beside Iuti's knee.

''How did a swordsman from the highlands learn to cook like an islander?'' Iuti asked as she stuffed steaming breadfruit into her mouth. The taste was bland and solid, and perfectly suited to her empty stomach.

''He was instructed in very careful detail by one who hails from there,'' he said with a nod toward Tarawe. He didn't smile, but his eyes revealed a touch of humor. Iuti lifted a chunk of roasted breadfruit in toast to Tarawe.

"Did you sleep last night?" she asked the girl. "You were limping by the time we stopped. You look tired even now."

Tarawe nodded.

A glance at Risak brought an upward flick of his brows, verification that the girl had, in fact, rested.

Risak turned away then, to begin packing the remaining food for travel. He has not looked me fully in the eye since we climbed from the inland waterway, Iuti thought.

"Risak," she said.

He tensed.

"We must speak of it, Risak. We have too long a journey ahead to walk in silence."

He took a long, slow breath before turning back. He wore a loincloth now, made from Tarawe's leggings. The girl had wrapped herself in a skirt of woven vines and broad ti leaves. She was sitting to one side, cleaning her sword and seemingly paying them no attention. Risak said nothing.

"It was the drums," Iuti said.

He nodded and would have turned away again.

"No!" she said. "Listen to me, Risak. It was not you! Not *only* you! I was caught by them, too."

He lifted his startled look.

"If it had not been for the pain in my back," she said, wincing slightly in remembrance, "we two might be in that river still. I had no more control than you."

"But how . . ."

"Who knows what evil they do to capture the beat of a warrior's soul?" she said. "They held my blood in their filthy hands for three days, clearly long enough for them to do whatever it is they do. Let us not look on each other with shame, friend Risak. We were bespelled and we broke the spell. We are far beyond the drums' power now. And we are forewarned should they ever sound within our hearing again."

Risak watched her for a long moment. Then he nodded and straightened. She knew it was not finished. After a year spent servicing the demon women, it might never be finished for him. But he had regained his warrior's stance.

"If we move quickly, we can reach the Papali Hills by midday," he said. "We can travel through them to the singing bridge. We'll be safe once we cross the Veke River gorge and reach the high mountains, safe from the Teronin at least."

"The Teronin hold the bridge now," Iuti said. "They control the entire corridor south, except for a few isolated farms and villages."

"Is Sandar City still in truce territory?" he asked.

"It was still called neutral five months ago," she replied. "But the Teronin control both ferry crossings, and they have patrols in the surrounding river. There is nothing for us there. We'll have to follow the hills south all the way to the lower Veke River. We can swim across safely if we go far enough downstream from Sandar."

"We'll need clothing before we go much farther into inhabited lands," Risak said.

"Aye. We'll watch for unattended laundry at the outland farms. We can leave ragroot or drinking nuts in exchange." Or a silent blessing, if there is no other way to make unseen payment, she thought. Iuti retied the halter she had fashioned from what was left of her shirt, and wiped a gob of coconut sauce from her torn trousers. It left an oily smear. She stood very carefully and fastened her weapons to the woven belt Risak offered.

"I wouldn't have left you in the river," Tarawe said quietly to Iuti as they resumed their eastward journey.

Iuti measured her steps across the spongy ground so that the movement jarred her back as little as possible. She glanced at Tarawe.

"So you *were* listening? Did you understand what I told Risak?"

"I think so. I'm glad the drummers didn't play *my* blood song," Tarawe replied.

Iuti laughed. "So am I." It occurred to Iuti to wonder if Tarawe's blood had developed such a song yet. She was old enough, fifteen, perhaps sixteen years, but some girls entered full womanhood later than others. Tarawe might well still be virginal, which would explain some of her luck with borrowed magic.

"Will the drummers' picture stay in your skin?" Tarawe asked.

"Aye," Iuti said. "I might be able to make it fade if I had the time and the energy—and a healer nearby who knew what she was doing. But by the time I have all those things together, I suspect it will be too late. It doesn't matter."

"What about your face?" Tarawe said. "One of the warriors who came to Fanape knew how to make scars go away. If you want me to try to fix—"

"No," Iuti said quickly. "I do not want you to try to *fix* anything. It's *dangerous* to experiment with spells you know nothing about, Tarawe. Besides . . ." She traced the lines of Mano's teeth along her cheek. "I think it's best for me to keep these."

As a remembrance, she thought.

"As a disguise," she said.

"They make you look old," said Tarawe.

"Aye," Iuti replied, and they walked on in silence.

≈ Chapter 11 ≈

DURING the day's march, Iuti and the others kept as much as possible to streambeds and areas of lighter brush so their trail would remain hidden, and for much of the day made good time. Iuti's back, and her shoulder where the Teronin blade had struck, ached, but for the most part she managed to match Risak's rapid pace.

It was Tarawe who tired soonest. By midafternoon, she was pausing frequently along the trail. She would press her hands to her eyes and shudder, before steadying herself with an effort and moving on. Once she leaned against a tree trunk and Iuti thought she saw her wipe away tears.

The killing thrusts, Iuti thought. Tarawe had killed three times in as many days, and without any way to block the horror, her mind must be raw with remembrance. She might even be one of those who was never meant to kill at all. Iuti hoped the girl would not be forced to kill again before she could be touched by a healer. She set a warrior's warding spell around Tarawe's mind, but it had no obvious effect.

As the afternoon wore on, Iuti found herself growing uneasy with more than just Tarawe's increased exhaustion. She glanced back and around, searching the brush for some unseen presence. She saw nothing but natural jungle shadows, heard nothing but common jungle sounds. An awkwardly flying gull passed over them several times, but otherwise, they seemed to be traveling alone among the trees.

"I sense nothing," Risak said when she told him of her feeling, but he increased his own vigilance.

111

They stopped earlier than they had originally intended, when they came upon an easily defended clearing. They ate cold breadfruit and the last of the cooked bananas, then piled mounds of spongy moss to make their beds.

"I'll take the first watch," Risak said. "I'll wake you at midnight, Tarawe, and you can wake Ser Iuti several hours before dawn."

Tarawe grinned at being offered such a trust and immediately began settling herself for sleep. She laid her sword close to her hand. Iuti smiled, too, and nodded her thanks to Risak for setting a proper watch without offending Tarawe's pride. He had sandwiched the girl's watch between theirs so he could silently double it while Iuti slept through the night undisturbed. It was a precaution all seasoned warriors took when they traveled with inexperienced companions. Risak knew Iuti needed as much rest as she could get, and he could easily miss a few hours sleep to ensure their safety.

Iuti stretched out on the moss and whispered a deep healing spell. It was not so strong that she couldn't be wakened easily should the need arise, but it was designed to deal with the last of the sickness in her back and shoulder. She fell instantly asleep.

In the strange, fractured land of her spell-induced dreams, Iuti continued to sense the invisible presence that had disturbed her throughout the afternoon. She felt no menace from the persistent shade, but she came gratefully awake when, many hours later, Tarawe touched her shoulder and called her name.

From the speed with which Tarawe fell asleep, Iuti suspected the girl might have stayed awake to double Risak's watch just as he had hers. She smiled at Tarawe's protectiveness. The girl was strong-willed, but capable and eager to learn. She made a good companion.

Still, it would be a relief when Tarawe was safely in Iuti's cousin's hands outside Manara. Iuti was eager to turn her full attention to Pahulu and the Teronin, and to the coming threat of the demon war drums.

First, though, she must deal with the silent watcher. Iuti was certain now that someone was there. The watcher would not have touched her dreams if it hadn't wanted to be found. She waited until both Risak and Tarawe were snoring softly, then slipped quietly back into the trees. A short distance from the clearing, not so far that she couldn't hear any movement there, she stopped and made a small sign with her left hand.

"Friend or foe," she chanted softly. "Show yourself so I will know."

For an instant there was nothing. Then . . .

"Well, it's about time, Iuti Mano! I thought you were never going to wake up."

Iuti spun toward the sound, saw nothing, then almost tripped as feathered fern bush bustled into her path. "What?" It was not a bush, she saw, but a bird. A large gray-feathered gull like those that had overflown the thornvine prison and later followed them on their long trek. The bird trembled and shook. It tried to spread its wide wings in the narrow confines of the jungle brush. A handful of feathers dropped away.

"By the hairy spines of a—"

Iuti stepped back.

"Brrrrwarrk!"

"You idiot bird! Let go so I can—"

A human hand appeared at the tip of one wing. Iuti blinked, but the brown-skinned fingers retained their form—she wasn't dreaming. The slender fingers crawled along the wing from which they grew until they reached the bird's neck. They circled the feathered throat and began choking the squawking creature. The sight of the bird shaking itself by its own neck was so ludicrous that Iuti almost laughed.

"Be quiet, Iuti Mano. This is all your fault. I'm— ouch!"

"Ma'eva?" This time Iuti laughed out loud. "Ho'oma'eva? What are you—how in Mano's name did you get caught inside a seabird?" She squatted beside the struggling gull and tried to restrain its flailing wings. She pricd the dark fingers loose from the bird's neck and held them while she stroked the bird's back with her free hand.

"Be still now," she urged. "You're both going to get hurt if you keep on like this." The bird quieted quickly under her soothing caress.

"All right, Ma'eva," she said. "Come on out now. But do it with some care this time. Try not to scare the poor creature to death."

"Stupid egg layer" came Ma'eva's disgruntled reply. "I've never been so sick in my—"

A long, dark arm lifted away from the bird's wing. Iuti let go of Ma'eva's hand as the rest of his sleek, naked body emerged from the gull. The great seabird blinked its dark eyes as Ma'eva's face appeared, superimposed over beak and high, crowning feathers. The faces separated with a soft pop, and finally Ho'oma'eva pulled free. There was one last struggle as he shook his toes loose from the bird's claws.

"What are you doing here?" Iuti asked as he stretched to his full height. He had added a few inches, she noted, so that he stood just a bit taller than she. Otherwise, it looked to be the same body he had used on the canoe. The bird ruffed its feathers, then settled peacefully at Ma'eva's feet. They both smelled strongly of the sea.

"Looking for you," he said. He ran his fingers through his curly hair. "Just like the last time. You're going to be the death of me yet, Iuti Mano. And we've never even—"

"Why?" she said.

"*Why!* Because it's *dangerous* for a sea mimic to tackle a seabird that size. I could have been eaten! I wish I had been every time this miserable creature takes off. When we're in the air, my stomach churns like—"

"Why were you *looking for me*, Ma'eva?"

"Oh. That." Ma'eva walked to a fallen log, tested its moss-covered firmness, and sat. "Because there's big trouble out on the atolls. I was sent to bring you back to deal with Pahulu."

"What's she doing now?"

"Creating chaos," he said. "She's furious. She can't make that girl's wind stop, so she's deliberately making the storm worse, hoping to force the storm caller to return. She's created a tremendous whirlpool at storm's center and is sucking up strange dark creatures from the hidden depths. Creatures no decent seafolk wish to swim beside. The northern atolls are being battered by strong wind and high surf. All the seafolk who can have already fled.''

Iuti frowned. Storms on the low islands could be exceedingly dangerous. ''What of the humans?''

Ma'eva met her look. ''A fisherman from Kena Atoll drowned yesterday afternoon. His body was washed into the storm swirl before the seafolk could reach it and return it to land. What's happening ashore I can't say. The wind and water are so rough neither sea- nor airfolk can get near enough to see. The rest of the humans at Kena, if they still live, probably wish they were elsewhere.''

''But how can Pahulu create that much havoc when only her spirit rides the winds?'' Iuti said. ''Her lair is much too far away for her to have reached the atolls herself, and she'd have to be there in person to cause the damage you say. The journey by canoe would take a full ten days even with strong following winds.''

''Aye,'' Ma'eva said. ''In ordinary times. But Pahulu has made some pact with the forces that dwell in the murky depths. She's grown powerful enough to control almost any sea creature that falls into her spell-spun nets. She captured a pair of flying dolphins and bound them to her filthy war canoe with strands of her own hair, then forced them to carry her across the sea to Fanape. She's there now.''

He blinked rapidly and his fingers trembled. His distress was as real as any Iuti had ever seen. ''She did terrible things to those kind creatures, Iuti Mano. Things that cannot—'' He shook his head and grew silent.

''What of the humans on Fanape?'' Iuti asked quietly.

''Dead,'' he said. ''But not by Pahulu's hand. The Teronin, searching for their lost comrades, reached the island first and killed them all.''

''*All?*'' Iuti stared at him.

He nodded. ''Pahulu is furious about that, too, because she wanted to question them about the storm. And she wanted to kill them herself so she could steal the power from their dying souls. She tortured the reef folk until they told her of your battle with the old healer and your escape on the Teronin canoe. Now Pahulu thinks it was you who called the wind.''

"The reef folk know that Mano killed the healer," Iuti said. "Why did they credit *me* with the deed?"

"Well . . ." Ma'eva said. A hint of humor returned to his dark eyes. "They didn't, exactly. They just did nothing to remind Pahulu that you and the shark god are kin. To a human witch, your water spoor tastes the same, so they let her draw her own conclusions. It was safer to let her think you had done the killing than to have Mano called back onto the reef."

Iuti started to lean back against a tree, remembered her back, and straightened again. "Does Pahulu know Tarawe is with me?"

He shook his head. "She thinks you fought the healer alone." He hesitated. "Friend Iuti . . . about that girl. I don't know if she carries some strange power of her own or if it's only the land god's own good luck that plagues her steps, but I think it would be a mistake to let her fall into Pahulu's hands."

"Aye," Iuti replied. "I'm taking her now to a safe place in the south. I have a cousin there who will take her in. She and her mate and six sons live on a taro farm far inland from all the fighting zones. Tarawe will be comfortable there, and Pahulu need never know of her existence."

"Let the man take her south," Ma'eva urged. "You come back to the sea with me."

"I must contact the war chiefs in Manara first," Iuti said. "Then I'll go directly to Fanape."

"That'll take too long! You humans move like sea slugs when you're on land. Come back with me now. I can guide you through the inland waterway around the drummers' isle. They'll never catch us. The birds will keep them busy elsewhere on the island while we pass. They've already forced those noisy humans to delay searching for you long enough to build a shelter over that great mound of meat you left behind. Stupid creatures. Don't they know that the great gulls never eat anything that doesn't come from the sea?''

''Probably not,'' Iuti said. ''I think they're almost as afraid of the water as they are of the night.'' She suddenly remembered the persistent flock of seabirds that had tormented the drummers during her imprisonment. ''Was that you who shat on the tattoo artist's head?''

Ma'eva grinned and glanced down at the sleeping bird. ''It took some practice, but we finally got it right.''

''How did you know I was there?'' she asked.

''I followed the canoe's taste to where you buried it in the sea. Then, after Pahulu went to Fanape, I convinced the seabirds to follow you ashore. I was surprised when they said you'd stopped so close to the water, so I—'' He glanced down again. ''—accepted a ride to see for myself.''

''Accepted?'' Iuti laughed. ''What did you have to promise to get her help?'' She knew any alliance between a sea creature and one from the air would involve high payment. Long ago a pact had been made forbidding the sea mimics from actually taking the forms of birds. They could ride in the air only in tandem with true birds, and only as invited guests.

Ma'eva shrugged. ''Nothing of importance. Come. We can leave right now. I'll even walk a ways with you. Much as I dislike human transport, at least it doesn't make my guts churn.'' He rubbed his stomach, and Iuti smiled inwardly at the thought of a sea creature who suffered from motion sickness.

''I can't leave the others to travel alone through these dangerous lands,'' she said.

''Let the man take the girl to safety,'' Ma'eva suggested again. ''He's a warrior, too, isn't he? Although I've never seen one so intricately colored. I think I might . . .''

A shadow of circular patterns began forming around Ma'eva's manhood.

''Don't!'' Iuti said quickly. ''Don't do that!''

He eyed her curiously. "You have such a mark on your own back," he said. "Why shouldn't I?"

"It's not there by my choice," she replied. "Don't mimic the man's tattoos, Ma'eva. It would be an evil thing to do, and most unkind."

Ma'eva's brows lifted in surprise. He had always been very curious and *very* cautious about the things Iuti named evil. And he always paid attention when she said a thing was unkind. He blinked, and when Iuti looked down again, his skin color had returned to unblemished brown.

"I'll travel with Risak and the girl as far as the lower Veke River," Iuti said. "Once they're safely across, they can go on without me. Risak can take my message to the war council and deliver Tarawe to my cousin. I'll come back to the sea by way of the river." She lifted a hand. "It's decided, my friend. Don't waste your breath trying to change my mind."

"Hmph. You're as stubborn as a human, Iuti Mano," Ma'eva said. Iuti grinned because it was an honest and truly meant compliment. Ma'eva didn't often offer her those.

"I must return to the others now," she said. "Will you and the bird follow us a time more? A skyborne lookout would add safety to our journey."

"And speed?" he asked, standing so abruptly that the seabird tumbled away from his feet.

"Aye." She laughed. "And speed, my good friend. Without a doubt." She reached up to brush his cheek with her fingertips. His beardless skin was warm, and as smooth as a babe's.

Ma'eva's eyes sparked with curiosity as he glanced down at her hand. Very tentatively, he lifted his own fingers to touch her face. "Mano's marks make you look different," he said.

"I'll look even more different soon," she said. "It's best if no one knows Iuti Mano is traveling so near Teron. But don't worry, good friend . . ." She leaned forward to kiss him lightly on the lips. "I'll still taste the same when next we meet. You'll know me when the time comes." She grinned at his look of surprise and delight. She hadn't kissed him without being dared since they were children.

"Do not tease my small cousins during these troubled times," she said, still smiling. "I wouldn't want to see you eaten by my kin after having survived the clutches of this mighty gull."

Ma'eva arched a perfect brow. "Ahh, you mock me so kindly," he said softly. His look drifted down her body, then lifted again to her face. "I wonder if you are woman enough yet, Iuti Mano, to help me harvest the Great Pearl?"

He grinned at her startled response, then bent to scoop up the sleeping gull. "I must let this great lug fly home to eat," he said as he turned back into the shadows. "I'll find you again tomorrow." Then he was gone.

Iuti stared after him for a moment, then shook her head and turned back to the clearing. She was surprised to see that Tarawe had moved from her place beside Risak. Iuti glanced around, but the girl was nowhere to be seen.

"Mano's teeth," she muttered. "Tarawe must have wakened and gone looking for me in the trees. How could she have moved so quietly that I didn't hear?"

Tarawe had taken the sword, of course. She kept it with her always now that Risak had relinquished its use. Iuti hoped Tarawe and Ma'eva wouldn't meet up in the near dark. If they didn't run each other through with the blade, they would likely scare each other to death. She wasn't worried about Tarawe getting lost—the youngster had enough sense not to go far on her own. Still, Iuti was uncomfortable with the girl out of sight.

Suddenly a chill slid along Iuti's arms. The woven scabbard Tarawe had made that evening was gone, too, and the pack basket she had made to carry her share of the food. Iuti quickly bent to touch Risak's shoulder. He came awake in the way of warriors—all at once and with his hand on his weapon, the drummer's carved club.

"Tarawe's gone," Iuti said. She told him quickly of her meeting with Ma'eva and her return to find the girl missing.

"How far did you go?" he asked, obviously startled that anything could go wrong during Iuti's watch. Maybe this would convince him that she was still only human and as prone to mistakes as he, or any other. Even their encounter in the river had not done that.

"Not far enough that she could have gotten away without using one of her damn spells," she said. "Help me look for her. There's no telling what she's up to, and we can't afford to be separated now."

They searched the edges of the clearing for a long time before finally finding a sign of Tarawe's passing. Like everything else, the girl had learned jungle stealth quickly and well. "I wish Ma'eva and that idiot bird were here to help," Iuti muttered.

"Why would she run away?" Risak asked.

"I have no idea," Iuti replied. "Here. She went this way. Why in Mano's name is she going *north*?"

Risak stopped. "Ser, we can't follow her north. We're practically inside Teronin territory already. If we're seen . . ."

"I can't let her go on alone," Iuti said.

Risak took Iuti's arm—a bold move from a man who followed the formal manners of the south, and from one who still had trouble meeting her gaze. "I wish no harm upon the girl," he said. "I owe her my freedom—my life, if it comes to that. But if the Teronin capture her, they capture only a child. If they capture you, they capture the key to a complete takeover of the south. We must carry warning to the southern war council. You've said it yourself. The warning is our first and most vital duty."

"I cannot leave the girl behind," Iuti said.

"But—"

"I am tied to her," Iuti said. "Bound. I've felt it, and tried to deny it, since the night she helped me defeat the Teronin on their false ghost canoe."

"You could have defeated those men yourself," he said.

"Of course I could have. I could probably have defeated the old healer, as well, and the drummers down on the beach that first night, if I'd been alone. But I wasn't. Tarawe was with me each time. Each time I had to protect her, and each time I was led to the discovery of an ever greater danger to the south. Protecting her is what led me to you, Ser.''

"I don't *want* to leave her behind," Risak said. "I know better than you what I owe her, but—''

"I tried to *kill* her, Risak! I, Ser Iuti Mano, the scourge of the Teronin War, lifted my weapon to an honest kill and I could not do the deed.'' A chill ran along her arms as she recalled the alien touch of the sword on that strange day.

"It wasn't because of any softness in me,'' she went on. "I felt no hesitation about killing her or myself— only regret. But something stopped my hand. Something forced me to protect her just as I had each time before.''

"Something protected *you*!'' Risak said. "The girl was spared so *you* could escape the drummers' prison and carry warning to the southern warchiefs.''

Iuti shook her head. She glanced down at Risak's strong hand, still gripping her arm.

He cursed and let her go. "You can't leave her, and I can't leave you,'' he said. "You aren't the only one bound, Iuti Mano. Come on. Let's find her before the Teronin border guards find us and send us back to Losan.''

The eastern sky was beginning to brighten by the time they caught up with Tarawe. She was threading her way through a brambleberry thicket, eating handfuls of berries as she eased through the thorny vines. As Iuti and Risak watched, she stopped to rub a hand across her eyes, then jerked back to attention as a thorn pricked her elbow.

Iuti motioned Risak around the thicket to the left, and she crept carefully to the right. They were waiting when Tarawe pushed her way back into the open.

When she saw them, Tarawe spun and tried to duck back into the brambles. Risak caught her from behind, and Iuti reached over her shoulder to slide Tarawe's sword from the scabbard on her back. She didn't want the girl attacking them blindly.

"Give me that! It's mine!"

Risak pulled Tarawe tight, and Iuti placed a firm hand over her mouth. "Be quiet unless you want to bring every Teronin lookout in the jungle down on us," she said. "Didn't you see the feathered warnings tied to the trees? You've led us right into their home territory. Where were you going? Why did you leave us?"

Tarawe shook Iuti's hand away, but Risak kept a firm hold on both of her arms. "I'm not going to any stupid taro farm!" she hissed.

Iuti stared at her, dumbfounded. "Taro farm! What—" Then she remembered her talk with Ma'eva. Tarawe must have overheard them. But why should that have upset her so? "You don't have to go to that farm if you don't want to," she said. "There are other safe—"

"I don't—"

Iuti lifted a hand in warning and Tarawe lowered her voice.

"I don't want to go anywhere that's *safe*. I want to stay with—" She shook herself free of Risak. "I want to stay here and fight the Teronin."

Iuti met Risak's look of astonishment before returning her attention to Tarawe. "You can't fight the Teronin, Tarawe. You have no training, no skill. You're still a child."

"I'm not a child! I've already killed three men." Her voice caught as she said the words. "And I escaped unmarked from the demon drummers, which is more than you can say. I can fight as well as any, and you have no right to stop me."

"I am honor bound to stop you from killing yourself," Iuti said. She was completely confused by the girl's insistence on so foolish a course. A twig snapped not far off, and Iuti glanced quickly that way. A series of rustling crackles traced the fall of some heavy, overripe fruit as it crashed through the foliage to the ground.

"We must leave here quickly," Risak said softly.

Iuti nodded. She could taste the danger in the steamy jungle air. "Tarawe," she said. "Why? Is it revenge for the Teronin killing your people on Fanape?"

To Iuti's astonishment, Tarawe spat. "Those lying thieves? I would have killed them myself if I'd been able." Her face softened for just an instant. "Maybe not the children, but the others."

"*Why?*"

"Because they stood by when my uncle gave my mother to the Teronin," Tarawe cried. "After Pahulu killed that warrior, the one who tripped her with the vine, the Teronin chief said he would kill everyone on the island unless we gave him someone of greater value than the warrior who was lost. So Pahulu and my uncle gave him my mother. She was the island's *real* healer, and she'd been trying to stop what Pahulu was doing to the visiting warriors."

"Mano's sweet breath," Iuti muttered. So that was why Tarawe had been so intent on learning all she could from the warrior victims, and why she had been so eager to take this dangerous journey. Another fruit fell in the jungle. A bird called shrilly, making Iuti jump. Risak's eyes were in constant motion, searching the surrounding brush for hidden enemies.

"Tarawe," Iuti said. "We have to leave this place. It grows more and more dangerous. I won't take you south against your will, but come with us now, away from here. We can decide what to do once we've—"

She saw the flash of warning in Risak's eyes before it reached his lips. She spun, Tarawe's sword firm in her hand—and stepped directly into the arms of a grinning Teronin.

❦ Chapter 12 ❧

THE Teronin's breath stank like rotten ragroot—a tooth gone bad if the condition of those he flashed at Iuti was any indication. She tried to follow through with the sword strike she had begun with her turn, but his huge arms clamped around her like a vise. Behind her she heard Risak's war call, a scuffle, and a fall. She tried to knee her captor, then cursed as he turned easily away.

The man laughed loudly.

Iuti repeated the curse in Teronin, and abruptly the humor drained from his expression. He tried to knee her in return.

It was the mistake she had hoped for. She hooked her left leg around his right ankle and yanked him off-balance. His grip loosened as they struck the ground, and before he could roll off his side, Iuti twisted the sword to rake its sharp blade against his hip. He swore at her, and this time it was Iuti who laughed. She needed no translation of *his* gutter tongue.

The struggle ended quickly, because his rage made him careless. Iuti yanked her arm free and had the blade in his side before he had time to squirm out of her reach. She jumped up, snapped Mano's club from its waist strap, and swung back to where Tarawe and Risak had been.

Risak was circling with two Teronin, parrying their strikes with Iuti's shield and the drummer's carved club. Tarawe was being held to one side by another of their attackers. Iuti called a warning to Risak and tossed him Tarawe's sword. The hilt barely touched his palm before the blade drank of a second Teronin's life blood. The

124

Ilimar swordsman's year in captivity had not dulled his skill.

Iuti turned her attention to the border guard holding Tarawe. A subchief's band was tied around his right arm, proclaiming him the leader of this patrol. As she met his look, the smirk with which he had been watching the lopsided fight slid from his face. He pulled Tarawe closer and lifted his weapon.

"Put it down," Iuti said. "Call your man off, unless you want more trouble than you've already found."

His look shifted from her eyes to the scars on her cheek, and back to her eyes. She took a step to his left, but he turned to keep Tarawe fully between them. He held the girl wrapped in one arm, close to his chest. Tarawe was ashen. She trembled visibly. She was doing nothing to fight the Teronin's grip.

"You've entered forbidden territory, southerner," the man snarled. "*You're* the one with trouble."

"I carry a message for Krugar," Iuti said, "from the Losan drummers." She could think of no better time to test the depth of the Teronin's dependence on the drummers.

"You're no drummer!"

The measured rasp of metal on metal behind her hinted that Risak was holding back, postponing a finish to his fight until Iuti could get Tarawe safely away from the Teronin's hands. She had no doubt he had his opponent under firm control.

"A keen observation," she said. "One I appreciate since I have no wish to be mistaken for that filth. But I carry a message from Losan nevertheless. The mark on my back is proof enough that I come from there."

The Teronin glanced beyond Iuti at the ongoing battle, then back. He eyed her suspiciously. He didn't want to believe her, but he was clearly afraid not to.

"What message?" he said. "Give it to me."

Iuti made a show of relaxing. She rested the club on her shoulder and settled her opposite hand on her hip. "I'm not a fool that I would give away my only protection here in the land of Teron. Call your man off and we'll deliver the message together. Our only reason for traveling this perimeter openly was to find a border guard to escort us the rest of the way.''

"From what I heard a few minutes ago, you crossed the border only to retrieve *this* tidbit.'' Tarawe gasped as he tightened his hold, but otherwise remained still. There were tears on her cheeks, and her eyes kept fluttering closed. Iuti was surprised at her reaction, but judged this a good lesson for the girl who had been prepared to face the Teronin armies alone—if she lived to learn from it.

Iuti gestured toward the girl. "We'd have met you a lot sooner if we hadn't had to keep chasing that drummers' offal every time we turned around.'' Even that didn't bring a response from the girl. What was wrong with her? "She's been more trouble than she's worth this whole journey long.''

"Ha, and why would two southerners be traveling with a demon whore?'' the Teronin demanded. "It's widely known the drummers consider their women of little value, so don't say it's *she* who carries the message.''

"My companion''—Iuti nodded back toward Risak—"insisted we bring her after the drummers offered her services as partial payment for ours. A man needs a steady diet of meat, so he claims, and mine's not to his taste. How any man could take pleasure in a drummer is beyond me.''

The Teronin's lip curled back into a smirk. "One piece of meat's as good as another,'' he said. He called an order, and the clang and scrape of steel on steel abruptly ceased.

The Teronin fighter circled quickly to join his commander. He was breathing hard and his look kept shifting from Risak and Iuti to his two dead comrades. Risak moved to just within Iuti's line of vision.

"I don't believe you carry any drummers' message, warrior woman,'' the patrol leader said. "But it's clear enough you've had contact with the filthy beasts. Krugar will reward me well for the chance to question you.''

"You can be certain of that,'' Iuti said truthfully. "I

would pay well myself for the chance to share my story with that man.''

He motioned with his sword. ''You two walk ahead until we reach the perimeter road. We'll pick up a horse patrol there.'' He shoved Tarawe toward his underling. ''Tie this bitch to your—''

Iuti was on him the instant Tarawe left the protection of his arm. She shoved the girl aside while swinging Mano's club over and down. The Teronin's skull cracked as neatly as if it had been a drinking nut—and ice touched Iuti's soul. Risak drove the other Teronin away from where Tarawe had fallen and, before the man could raise his sword to defend himself, ran Tarawe's blade through his exposed chest.

''Border patrols travel in fives,'' he said immediately. ''The fifth one is usually a messenger. He's probably already on his way with news of our discovery.''

Iuti kicked the Teronin chief over and began stripping off his tunic. ''We'll have to go after him. We can't afford to have our presence known this far from the ford. Take what weapons you can use and whatever clothing fits but won't label us too obviously as Teronin. If they carry anything of value, take that, too. We may need it, and it'll make this look more like a bandits' ambush. Tarawe, come help me get these boots off.''

There was no response. Iuti looked up.

''Tarawe?''

Tarawe lay where she had fallen. She was folded in on herself, her knees clutched tightly to her chest. Her body shook as if she were sobbing, but she made no sound. Iuti frowned and moved to her side. There was no obvious sign of injury.

''Tarawe,'' she said. ''It's finished. There's no need to be afraid now. The Teronin are dead.''

She laid a hand on Tarawe's shoulder. There was still no response. ''What can be wrong with her?''

''Terror,'' Risak suggested. ''It happens sometimes.''

''She was in much greater danger in the drummers' hands,'' Iuti said, ''and while she was under attack from the Fanape healer. She never reacted like this.''

Risak slid the Teronin sword he had been examining into its scabbard and belted it on as he crossed to Iuti's side. "It was probably the Teronin's touch. She's likely never been held so by a man before. A young woman's fear of—"

"Mano's teeth!" Iuti breathed as she lifted Tarawe's face and brushed her hair back from her forehead. The girl's eyes had rolled upward so that only the whites showed. Her face was a mask of terror, and her lower lip bled where it was clamped between her teeth. She moaned softly and suddenly went limp.

Quickly Iuti said a word and ran her hand in a circle around Tarawe's head. She felt no evidence of outside sorcery affecting the girl, yet she could not believe that after all Tarawe had been through before, she would faint now from simple fear. Iuti looked up in confusion.

Risak reached out to touch Tarawe's cheek lightly. "She looks like . . ."

"Like what? We have to go, Risak. We can't delay here."

Risak pulled his hand back and said slowly, "Like one who's killed too often without taking proper care to protect her mind."

"But Tarawe's done no killing. It was you and I who—" She stopped. "The sword." She looked quickly around. "Tarawe's sword. Where is it?"

Risak reached behind him to where he had lain the bloody blade on the grass. He fumbled and almost dropped it before handing it to Iuti. Iuti, too, had difficulty holding the hilt firmly. They stared at each other, then back at the blade. Iuti placed it carefully at Tarawe's side. She wiped her palm on her trousers.

"Did you feel the death thrust when you killed those two men?" she asked.

"I—" He looked confused for an instant. Then he shook his head. "No, I felt nothing. But it's been a long time since I . . ."

"I felt it," Iuti said, "but only once—when I killed with my war club. They must be linked somehow, Tarawe and this sword."

"But . . ."

"You said yourself you were uncomfortable carrying the blade once we were well away from Losan," Iuti said. "We've both been able to use it to protect Tarawe, but not for anything more, not even to open drinking nuts. Remember how you cut your hand that first morning. That blade has been trying to get and stay in Tarawe's hand since we left Fanape. Can it be that the sword's kills become hers regardless of who strikes the actual blow?"

"I've heard of swords that choose their true owners," Risak said, "but didn't you say you had that blade forged for yourself?"

"Aye," Iuti said. "And until the night we faced the Teronin ghost canoe, it fit my hand as if it had been grown there." She stared at the bloody blade that was clearly no longer her own.

Risak pushed back. "Well, even if it's so, three deaths shouldn't be enough to do this." He motioned toward Tarawe's slack body.

"She's killed six now," Iuti said. "And she's never been trained to protect herself. Her mind is as open to death's touch as it is to life's, and who knows what she might have done to herself with all her borrowed magic? For all we know, she's the one who spelled the sword to her side. You heard what she said about her mother. She's been nursing *that* grudge for a long time."

Iuti glanced around. "We must get her away from here quickly. We'll go after the messenger, then head straight south until we're outside the forbidden zone."

"We're doubling her danger by staying inside Teronin territory as long as that." Risak began pulling clothing and weapons from the dead Teronin.

Iuti shrugged into the Teronin chief's tunic. "And tripling it if word of our presence in these parts travels before us." The rough cloth made her back itch, but the drummers' wound was almost healed. Only a few thin scabs remained. She tried the man's boots but found them too small.

As she twisted a boot from the first Teronin she had

killed, a rustle of leaves and snapping twigs sounded in the nearby jungle. It came from high in the trees, where only birds and small animals could climb, but she reached for Mano's club. She set a quick protective spell over Tarawe and motioned Risak away from that side of the clearing.

Something large struck the ground with a thump, something more than just overripe fruit.

"Teronin." Risak mouthed the word. He held a Teronin sword in each hand, facing the place from which the sounds had come.

Iuti shook her head. Not even a Teronin was stupid enough to approach a battle site where four of his comrades lay dead and the enemy still bore weapons.

She called softly, "Ma'eva! Is that you? Come out if it is. We need you."

A cautious voice sounded from the brush. "Don't let that big male kill me, Iuti Mano."

Iuti breathed a sigh of relief and waved Risak back. "You're safe here," she said. "You were wise to approach with care, though. These are dangerous lands."

Ma'eva stepped into the open, naked and glistening, as perfect as before. He glanced around. "So it appears," he said. His look stopped when it reached Tarawe. His expression softened. He walked to where she lay, squatted, and rested a palm on her forehead. Iuti withdrew her protective spell, and he caught his breath.

"The storm caller pays a heavy price for her deed," Ma'eva said.

Iuti frowned. "What do you mean? What has the storm to do with this?"

Ma'eva looked surprised. "She has the killing sickness. Surely you can see that. It's probably because of the storm. Another human was killed early this morning at Kena Atoll, and countless reef folk are being lost. Waves are sweeping the islands even now. The humans foolish enough to have stayed have tied themselves into the trees above the water line. We learned it from the dead woman. The tree she was in snapped off in the wind and was washed into the sea."

He looked down again at Tarawe. "I fear many more will be lost to her wind before this storm is finished."

"Sweet mother of Mano," Iuti said. "Are you saying she's suffering from the storm deaths as well as the lives taken here?"

"It is her storm," Ma'eva said matter-of-factly. He looked around again. When he met Risak's look he smiled his perfect smile. Risak's expression didn't change.

"What happened here?" Ma'eva asked, turning back to Iuti.

She told him quickly, then asked if he had seen any other humans nearby.

"Just one," he said. He pointed south. "No." He turned in a circle and pointed northeast. "That way, I think."

Iuti took his hand. "That man has gone to bring others here to kill us. We must stop him, Ma'eva. Can you get back into the bird and find him for us?"

Ma'eva pulled his hand away. "You know I can't kill a human on land, Iuti Mano. I have no wish to stay in this form forever." His expression changed. "Not unless you . . ."

"Risak and I will take care of any killing that needs doing," she said. "Just find him for us. Quickly. We must get the girl to safety so we can help her."

When he still hesitated, she said, "If Tarawe dies, or if she stops fighting and accepts the cold, we may never be able to find a way to stop the storm."

Ma'eva's eyes widened. "Aye," he said softly. "Of course. We must take the girl back with us to stop the storm. I should have thought of that myself."

"Ma'eva, that's not what I—"

But he was already on his feet and calling to the gull. He had to shake the sleeping bird awake before he could slip back into its body. "Stupid bird," Iuti heard him mutter as his shadow disappeared into the iridescent gray feathers. "Fly evenly this time or I'll choke . . ."

Iuti and Risak stared after the struggling bird as it made its clumsy way back into the sky. "Get the rest of what we need," Iuti said as soon as it was aloft. "Leave nothing of ours." She yanked on the larger Teronin's boots, disliking their feel but knowing the way would be safer with them on. She ripped the Teronin chief's badge of office off her tunic sleeve and stuffed it into a pocket.

Risak, too, was soon fully dressed and shod, with a Teronin sword strapped to each hip. He offered her the remaining two. She took one and hooked it to her belt. He slung the other over his shoulder, as Iuti did with her shield. She hesitated before lifting Tarawe's blade, but it rested easily enough in her hand while she slid it back into the scabbard on Tarawe's back.

A shrill call brought their looks up. The gull circled, dipped, then flew due east. Iuti lifted Tarawe to her shoulder. "Let's move," she said.

"You go south with the girl," Risak said. "We don't both need to follow the Teronin. I can handle him, and I can move faster alone. I'll catch up with you later. If the bird won't lead me directly, I'll follow your trail."

He smiled slightly at her quickly lifted brow. "You're good at jungle stealth, Ser, but you aren't perfect. Besides, this time you'll be carrying the girl. I'll find you. Go."

Iuti knew he was right. Tarawe had to be removed from Teronin territory as quickly as possible, and the messenger could be caught only by a fleet-footed pursuer. Still, she was loath to separate from Risak—for his own sake, as well as hers and Tarawe's. She touched his arm.

"You honor me with your continued aid, Ser," she said.

He stepped back from her touch. "I will find you," he said. Then he was gone. Iuti hefted Tarawe higher on her shoulder and began walking south.

They were well past the feathered warning signs marking the Teronin border when Ma'eva found them again. Iuti had turned east and was walking steadily along a dry creek bed when the gull swooped low and came to a skidding, stumbling halt on a nearby pile of stones. The pile shifted, sending the creature sprawling. Whatever grace the bird might have possessed on its own was lost under Ma'eva's guiding hand.

"Do you want that big male to find you?" the mimic asked without coming fully out of the bird. One or the other of them blinked.

"Aye," Iuti replied. "Is the other human dead?"

Ma'eva's half-formed face frowned. "That's a distasteful habit you humans have. Killing one another when you don't need the meat. Yes, he's dead."

A great weight lifted from Iuti's shoulders.

"I see the girl is walking again," Ma'eva said.

Iuti glanced at Tarawe. It was true she was on her feet, but her eyes were still dull with pain and confusion. Tarawe had regained consciousness some hours before. She had remained passive as Iuti dressed her in Teronin trousers and tunic and restrapped the sword to her back. She walked quickly enough now, at Iuti's command, but from time to time she shuddered and moaned, and then Iuti lifted her in her arms and held her close. The protective spells she tried did nothing to ease the obvious chaos in Tarawe's mind.

"I need to get her to Sandar City," Iuti said. "She won't survive if I don't get her to help soon. Bring Risak to us as quickly as you can."

Ma'eva and the gull both blinked this time.

When Ma'eva next appeared, Risak was with him. The sun had long set, and Iuti had grown concerned about Ma'eva finding them in the dark. But then suddenly there they were, striding into the clearing where she had made camp, chatting together easily and leading—Iuti almost wept in relief—a pair of fat, gray ponies. The gull rode on one of pony's backs.

"You came farther than I expected," Risak said. He glanced toward Tarawe. "Is she . . ."

"Sleeping," Iuti replied. "There must be a lull in the storm, or at least in the damage it's doing. She's much calmer tonight. Where did you get those?"

Risak patted the nearest animal's nose. "At a farm just outside Teronin territory. It had been raided months ago

and little was left. There was some women's clothing. I
brought that, along with a good wool traveling cape.
Ma'eva spotted these two beauties in a back pasture, out
of sight from the farmhouse and outbuildings.''

He glanced at the sea mimic. Ma'eva was now wearing
a pair of Teronin trousers and a necklace of polished
nuts. ''He claims to prefer riding the ponies to flying
with the bird.''

''It's bumpy, but it doesn't make my stomach churn,''
Ma'eva said. He stroked the bird. ''I must take this one
back to the sea to feed now, though. She's done a full
day's work and she's hungry. Which direction will you
take tomorrow, so I can find you?''

''Southeast,'' Iuti said. ''In a direct line to Sandar
City. The healer Ho'ola is there, if the Teronin haven't
killed her, and I doubt they could. She can help Tarawe,
if anyone can. She might be able to help us enlist the
services of a true storm caller, too, although that's going
to be costly. It's a three-day journey at most—two, now
that we have the horses.''

''How can we get into the city if the Teronin control
the ferries?'' Risak asked. ''They're not likely to let a
couple of southern warriors, especially ones arriving
from the *north*, pass their guard without question. We'd
be better to avoid Sandar altogether and go downriver as
we'd planned. It would only be another day before we
could cross the Veke into safe territory.''

Iuti shook her head. ''Tarawe's sickness struck much
more rapidly than it should have, and it grows worse at
an ever-quicker pace. This is only a lull in its intensity.
It won't last. Is there enough clothing for both Tarawe
and me?''

''Aye,'' he said. ''But . . .''

''Then you can go directly to Manara,'' she said. ''I'll
take Tarawe into the city, and we'll meet you again as
soon as she can travel safely.''

''How?'' he demanded. ''The Teronin will know
you . . .''

''I'll disguise myself as an outland farm woman,'' she
said. ''I'll darken my skin with ashberry and bleach my

hair white. In skirts, I can walk so my height doesn't show. I know the outland accent well enough, and with my face scarred as it is, they'll never even guess we're not what we seem.''

She turned to Ma'eva. ''Can you transform into a freshwater fish strong enough to reach Sandar from the sea?''

''With much greater ease than getting in and out of that stupid bird,'' said he.

She smiled. ''Good. You can be our messenger, then. You and Risak can arrange a place to meet along the riverbank, and I'll watch for you at the Sandar Lowtown dock—the old one that smells like rotting cheese. Don't come out of the water unless I'm there.''

Ma'eva flicked her the watersign for an overstuffed blowfish. ''I am your humble servant, mighty warrior woman.''

''Go feed the bird.'' Iuti laughed. ''You are a good friend, Ho'oma'eva. I will repay you for this, if ever I can.''

Ma'eva arched a perfect brow. He stepped out of the Teronin trousers and dropped the string of polished nuts into her hands. ''You know what I want, Iuti Mano,'' he said. A moment later, he was back in the bird and on his way to the sea.

Risak was still frowning when Iuti turned back. He had no better plan to offer, however, so after the ponies were set to graze, and Risak was fed, they set to the task of mapping the safest routes to their separate destinations.

❧ *Chapter 13* ❧

IUTI woke to Tarawe's scream. She rolled to her feet, sword in hand, but stopped when she saw it was only the ponies that had frightened the girl. Risak quickly calmed the animals while Iuti tried to convince Tarawe that they were not the spawn of some evil mainland sorcery.

Tarawe was almost as terrified of Iuti as she was of the ponies. Iuti had rubbed greenwort paste through her hair before she slept, and the color had already begun to fade. Mottled splotches of gray marred the thick, ebony mass, and her hair's usual sheen was fast disappearing.

"It's only a disguise," she assured Tarawe. "It's just a way to make us safer from the Teronin. My true face and form are too well known here on the mainland for me to travel openly."

Tarawe eventually calmed. She helped disassemble their camp, but balked when it came time to mount the ponies. Nothing Iuti or Risak said could convince her of the beasts' safety. She insisted on walking behind while the others rode.

It was midday before she finally consented to join Iuti on the back of her mount, and then it was only because she had been struck again by some far-off storm death. She clung to Iuti with trembling arms, as afraid of the demons within her mind as of those without.

Ma'eva joined them shortly after daybreak and warned them away from a nearby farm. He stayed in the bird, except to speak, and when he wasn't acting as lookout, they perched on the travel cape that Risak had draped over his pony's hindquarters. With their help, they made better time than Iuti had hoped.

Tarawe collapsed again on the second day. She didn't even react when they took her sword from her so that Risak could take it to the river crossing with the rest of their weapons and the Teronin gear.

Only the bird's presence seemed to give the girl comfort. She carried it in her lap and stroked its full plumage as she rode semiconscious through the afternoon and evening.

"She has the taste of an air creature," Ma'eva told Iuti the next morning. Risak had left them, and they were approaching the road that led to the main Sandar City ferry crossing. The temperature had dropped during the night and the morning air was cold. Iuti loosed the tangled mass of her now snow-white hair to hang about her shoulders. It added little warmth to the chill, damp air.

"That might explain how she called the wind so easily," Iuti said. "But if she's not a sea person, why are the deaths of your kin affecting her so strongly?"

Ma'eva and the gull shrugged. "Maybe she's both."

Iuti frowned at the thought of that much potential power being available to one individual. Humans akin to the sea were unusual enough, but those who could claim natural ties to the air were rare indeed. It was fortunate that so little magic had been used on Fanape. Had Tarawe practiced her borrowed spells there, the old sorceress would surely have noticed her and taken steps to make the girl's power her own.

The rattle of wagon wheels sounded ahead, and the curse of a disgruntled driver. "We're coming near the road," Iuti said. "Go aloft now, before you're seen." She lifted Tarawe down from the pony. She had already loaded the patient creature's back with a bag of ragroot and bundles of fresh drinking nuts. "We'll follow along with the others to the ferry crossing."

Ma'eva and the gull wriggled free of Tarawe's reluctant arms and lifted with more than their usual grace into the sky.

It was raining by the time Iuti and Tarawe reached the guarded gates at the ferry crossing. Iuti kept the heavy travel cape wrapped around them both as they walked

side by side leading the pony. Their full skirts were
soaked at the hems and thick with mud. Iuti's wrapped
clamily about her ankles with every step.

A seemingly endless column of muddy, muttering travelers was making its way toward the Teronin checkpoint
and the crowded ferry ramps. Most were women and
girls, or men too old or crippled to be of value to the
Teronin war effort. Many appeared to be farmers bringing their goods to market.

They carried their loads on their backs or balanced on
their heads, or in a few cases in handcarts piled high.
Iuti led one of the few horses. She was certain the Teronin would confiscate the animal, but as she had nothing
else with which to bribe the crossing guards, it seemed
bargain enough if it got them across the channel safely.

"I wish you no harm, little sister," she had apolo-
gized to the pony earlier. "The Teronin will surely send
you into war, but perhaps they'll use you only as a pack
animal and you'll live to run free again in some warm
southern pasture."

Iuti knew the day's rain and cold should be taken as a
blessing. The Teronin guards were less likely to search
every passenger thoroughly if it meant they had to stand
outside. Ma'eva had assured her before he and the gull
took to the sky that this storm was not connected to that
circling in the far off islands. Still, it made her uneasy.

Ahead, a young man—little more than a boy—was ordered roughly away from his elderly female companion.
By their clothing and demeanor, Iuti judged the pair to
be straight in from the outlands, farmfolk like those she
and Tarawe were mimicking, no doubt making their first
visit to the city since the Teronin takeover of the access
way.

When the old woman objected to the separation, one
of the guards slapped a weighted glove across her face.
She fell motionless into the mud and was kicked roughly
aside. Two other Teronin dragged the kicking, screaming
boy away. Their trade goods were quickly dispersed
among the laughing guards.

". . . fool should have known better than to bring a

healthy son near Teronin hands,'' a woman near Iuti mut- tered.

''He'll have a bloody sword in his own hands inside the month,'' a second agreed.

''Or one in his back if he keeps resisting,'' said the first. ''Uh-oh. Careful of the big one in black. Kindel told me he was a sorcerer, set here to watch for con- cealment spells. He feels demeaned by the job, so he likes to hurt people in repayment.''

''He's doin' some black sorcery right now. Look. He isn't even wet. I wish . . .''

Tarawe stumbled. Iuti caught at her, stumbling herself over the cumbersome skirt. The pony shied.

''Hai! You there! Clear the road if you can't keep that beast under control!'' The gate guard's shout brought the traffic to a momentary halt. Then, quickly, those near Iuti moved on, disassociating themselves from one so foolish as to draw the Teronin's attention. Iuti held Tar- awe close and calmed the horse as best she could with only one hand.

''What's that you're hiding under your cape, Grand- mama?''

Iuti started at the unexpected voice and almost dropped into a fighting stance. She recovered by faking another stumble over her rain-soaked skirt. Fear was not a diffi- cult emotion to display as she looked up to meet the Teronin sorcerer's stare. He was as old as Iuti now looked. His skin was lined with age. A sickly, gray film clouded one of his pale-blue eyes.

The other eye, however, was all too clear. Iuti could feel the tingle of the search spell he sent through her clothing. She was glad she had used greenwort paste to bleach the color from her hair instead of employing the spell Risak had suggested. She remained carefully hunched to hide her true height.

She hurriedly pulled the cape away from Tarawe's face. ''J—jus 'm' gran'babe,'' she stammered. ''Jus' m' gran'babe here wi' m'. She be cold ina rain, Sar.''

''Take it off,'' he said.

Iuti blinked. "Off, Sar?" The passersby were once again giving them a wide berth.

"Off," he repeated. "Quickly. I don't want to stand here all day." He leaned closer. "Or are you hiding something else under there? A weapon perhaps, or—"

"Oh, no, Sar. No." Iuti quickly undid the neck-ties and pulled the heavy cape from around their shoulders. Instantly the rest of their clothing was soaked through. The rain slid like ice across Iuti's bare arms. Tarawe caught her breath, and Iuti pulled her close, turning her face into her chest so she wouldn't speak.

No spells, Tarawe, she begged silently. No spells now. We're meat on this Teronin's platter if you play with your stolen magic now.

The sorcerer yanked the cape from her hand and threw it into the mud. "Phagh! You two smell worse than the sewage canal. No wonder you keep yourselves so tightly wrapped. Get on with you, before you make me vomit. Hai! You there!" He turned abruptly toward another of the wary travelers.

Iuti scooped up the cape and hurried toward the checkpoint as fast as the press of travelers and Tarawe's faltering steps would allow. Her heart was still pounding when she reached it. The guard who met her was wet and angry. As she had expected, he ordered the pony unloaded and led away. The drinking nuts disappeared into the guardhouse, and half the load of ragroot was added to an already overflowing cart of confiscated foodstuffs.

"That's your fee for using the ferry," the angry guard said. "If you smelled better, I might not have taken so much."

The ferry ride was blessedly uneventful. Because of their smell, Iuti and Tarawe were not overcrowded by their fellow passengers. When they reached the city dock, Iuti hefted the half-filled ragroot bag in one hand and supported Tarawe with the other. Tarawe trembled against her side, but otherwise made no move to either help or to resist.

Just a short way farther, she promised the girl silently. Just a few more steps. She made their way carefully across the crowded dock and sighed in relief when they finally entered the maze of narrow alleys that gave access to Sandar's lesser-traveled streets. She heard a shrill call and glanced up. Ma'eva acknowledged their safe crossing with a clumsy dip of the gull's wing before disappearing over the rooftops.

They passed more Teronin than Iuti cared to see in one place and without a weapon in her hand, but fewer than she had expected would be roaming the city's back streets. Most of them were easy to avoid. It galled her to scuttle out of the way of her hated enemies, but in her guise as an outland farm woman, she dared not do otherwise.

She moved aside even for the townsfolk who happened near. She pressed her back against the dank walls as they strode past and wished a pox on those who deliberately bumped up against her and Tarawe or splashed her with their heavy booted steps.

At last she reached the bridge across the Lowtown sewer canal. The healer Ho'ola could be anywhere in the city, if she was in the city at all, but the Lowtown docks were the place to start looking. Ho'ola maintained several houses here, and it was only a matter of asking the right questions of the right people to gain admittance to those who could locate her.

Iuti started across the arched bridge, then quickly backed off when two Teronin warriors stepped onto the narrow span on the opposite side of the canal. A pair of dockside whores hung on their arms, simpering and cooing, urging the soldiers' swift return to the delights of Lowtown.

The guards stumbled with drunkenness, and for a moment Iuti thought at least one of them was going to slip over the low stone rail into the fetid drainway. The larger of the whores caught him in time to prevent the accident and playfully pushed him on his way.

"Hoi, Grandmama!" one of the warriors called as they stepped off the bridge.

Iuti remained silent. Tarawe's steady shivering under the soaked cape was the only evidence that she was alive.

Iuti carried the girl's full weight with her left arm. She tightened her grip on the sack of ragroot as the Teronin stopped in front of them.

"Lemme get a look at you, Grandma," the shorter of the Teronin said. 'Maybe you can give us a little more play. Outlanders give their services for free, ain't that right, Tilin?"

"Right enough," his companion laughed. "But this one's ugly as a butcher and stinks worse than that ditch. Look at the scars on her face. I doubt she's worth even a free ride . . .

"Eh? What's this?"

Tarawe had shifted against Iuti's side.

The Teronin yanked the concealing cape away from Tarawe's face and lifted her chin in a dirty hand.

"Hoi," he said softly. "This one'll do. Come on, Grandma. Leggo your girl so we can show her a good time."

"'M' gran'babe be sick," Iuti said quickly.

The man pulled back slightly. "Sick?"

Iuti looked all around and then leaned forward as if fearing to be overheard. "Aye, Sar. She be—" She gave another exaggerated glance around, then said in a loud whisper "—woman sick, Sar. It's her blood time an' she be slow, ya see, an' don' unnerstan', so she's scart. She won't leave the rags alone. It's a terr'ble mess, I warn ya. Best I clean 'er up a bit afore ye go stickin' yer manhood in thar."

She pushed Tarawe to the ground and yanked up her skirt. A pair of groundrats had given their lives to provide the blood that now smeared Tarawe's thighs, but the Teronin had no way of knowing that. He cursed and stumbled back, gagging. His companion kicked Iuti hard in the side. The ragroot took the strength of the blow, but Iuti sprawled as if it hadn't.

"You're a pig, woman!" the man shouted. "We want no cursed idiot's blood." He spat and kicked her again before pulling his retching companion away. Iuti remained prone on the wet, stinking pavement, forcing her breathing to slow and thanking the gods for the Teronin's stupidity. Finally the two men stumbled out of sight. Across the bridge, the whores giggled.

Tarawe had come half conscious again, although she still couldn't stand without Iuti's full support. It was as if the only energy she had left was centered in her ravaged mind. Iuti lifted her and the ragroot and carried them across the bridge.

As quickly as she stepped from it, the two whores flanked her.

"That was a good trick, Grandmama," the taller of them said. "I've never seen it played so well. Here, you look tired. Let us help you with these."

Iuti met his look and said very softly, "Touch either the girl or the food, friend milimili, and your days of dock fun will end right here."

The whore's painted brows twitched in surprise, as much at her use of a southern warrior's term of endearment for a pair of high-class Lowtown whores as at her warning. His hand slid off the ragroot. He flashed a finger signal at his partner, and she moved ahead. She, too, looked surprised, but hid it behind a coy grin as she danced lightly backward ahead of them. She flicked a signal indicating that no one was in sight behind them.

"Is there some other service we can render, good mother?" she purred.

Iuti motioned them forward until they reached an alley she knew. When she was certain they were alone, she dropped the ragroot. Her back and shoulders burned with fatigue from the many hours of carrying first Tarawe and then both her and the heavy food sack, all the while maintaining her hunched posture. She didn't stand straight even yet.

"I seek the healer Ho'ola," she said.

Again the dual looks of surprise and quick recovery. "There are less expensive healers in Lowtown, Mother," the male said.

"Ho'ola's not taking new clients right now," said the woman. "Except from among the most wealthy, of course."

"Can you help me find her?" Iuti asked.

They glanced at each other—a calculating look. They were deciding whether this doubtful farm woman was worth aiding. Iuti did nothing to urge them, only lifted the ragroot again and resumed walking. There was a murmured exchange behind her, then the whores joined her again.

"We can take you to one of her houses," the male said.

"I can find her houses without you," Iuti replied. "I want Ho'ola herself."

He shook his head. "She'll never even talk to you. Begging your pardon, Grandmama, but your appearance isn't exactly upper class. Or are you a chieftain's dam in disguise?" They were still trying to assess her worth.

"I bring a child in need," she said. "We've traveled a long distance and time is vital. Will you aid me or not?"

"How did you know to call us milimili?" the woman asked.

Iuti smiled and relaxed. She had judged these two right. Their curiosity alone would be enough to convince them to help her now. "I had a southern lover once," she said, which was true enough. "He told me the most trustworthy whores in the settled world were to be found here in Sandar Lowtown. He said a true milimili pair always knew what was happening in the city and could be trusted if they were treated properly."

Iuti didn't see the signal exchanged, but it must have been done, because the pair of them suddenly straightened. They had decided she was worth at least a little more of their time.

"Come on then, Mama," one or the other of them said. "Ho'ola's not far. Or at least she wasn't two hours ago. If she's moved on, you'll be back on your own. Begging your pardon again, but you smell even more of trouble than you do of skagrat oil."

Iuti grinned. This pair was experienced indeed to recognize her use of the fetid oil to assure her and Tarawe's growing stench. Like most successful paired prostitutes, they no doubt ran a smuggling business on the side. They had clearly recognized from the beginning that she was in disguise. They would keep her secret, but they expected to be paid well for their services. She lifted the foodbag and followed them.

The gate before which they finally stopped was unfamiliar to Iuti, but Ho'ola was noted for changing the entries as well as the sites of her various homes. The male mili rapped four times on the metal knocker and pushed the gate open. It was unlocked. He motioned Iuti inside.

Iuti peered cautiously into the narrow walkway. Stone walls lifted on each side, several unclimbable stories high. There was a heavy wooden door at the far end of the corridor, topped by narrow, open windows. A perfect ambush site—and a trademark of Ho'ola's personal residences. There would be archers behind the windows.

"You two first," Iuti said. If they refused, there was nothing in the world that would make her enter such an obvious trap. The whores exchanged looks, then shrugged and walked into the corridor.

"She's not going to talk to you," the female said. "She's not even going to open the door."

"What do you two want?" a voice called from one of the windows. Female, or a neuter. Knowing Ho'ola, Iuti suspected the latter. "Who's the mama?"

"She's looking for Ho'ola," the male mili replied. "The young one is sick."

"The healer's not looking for new clients. Particularly not for such as these. Tell her to go elsewhere."

The mili met Iuti's look, then turned back. "I don't think she's going to leave," he said.

"Ola's not here."

"If you're here, she's here," Iuti called out. "Open the door, half-man. This child doesn't have much time."

The two whores sucked in their breaths and glanced fearfully up at the windows. "Don't you have any sense, woman? You should never call—"

They both jumped as the door swung silently open, then quickly stepped back from the massive eunuch that stood inside. He motioned the milis back to the street.

"Wait," Iuti said before they could go. She dropped the ragroot bag. "Take the two largest. As a gift. Not a payment. You've done me a kindness." She was suddenly so tired, she found it difficult to keep standing. Tarawe's hands felt like ice. The whores stared at her until the eunuch growled another low order for them to go. Then they scrabbled quickly through the bag, lifted two of the smallest roots, and squeezed back past Iuti and Tarawe.

The eunuch motioned Iuti inside.

❧ Chapter 14 ❧

IUTI lifted Tarawe and carried her past the huge eunuch, and away from the vulnerability of the overhead archers. As soon as she was inside, she stopped. They were in a small antechamber, bare except for a low bench along one wall. A beaded doorway led to whatever other rooms the warren held.

"I'll care for the girl," the eunuch said. "Put her on the bench."

Iuti turned slowly to face him. She straightened to her full height. The movement brought a stab of pain to her knees and her back. "She has the killing sickness," she said. "You can't help her any more than I can. Call Ola."

"Ola's not—"

"Call her, or I'll do it myself."

The beads rattled behind her. "You never change, Iuti Mano," a familiar voice said. "You're still as arrogant as ever. Give that child to Mapa before you drop her."

Iuti slumped again, this time in overwhelming relief. She released Tarawe into the eunuch's waiting hands. "I had a good teacher, Auntie Ola," she muttered. The eunuch gave her a curious look, but as she turned, she saw that Ho'ola was grinning.

"You look terrible," Ho'ola said, "and you smell worse. There'll be a bath ready shortly. Are you injured? What happened to your face?"

Iuti shook her head. "It's the girl. She has—"

"I heard." Ho'ola motioned Mapa to bring Tarawe to her. Even unconscious, Tarawe grimaced and groaned with her internal torture. Ola flicked her fingers before Tarawe's face, then swung them in a quick circle around

147

her head. "What in the world did she do? Murder her mother?"

"No," Iuti said sharply.

Ola looked up. "This couldn't have been caused by an honest kill."

"It was caused by many," Iuti said, "and she's had no training in dealing with death, honest or otherwise. I think she might be one of those never meant to kill at all."

Ho'ola cursed softly and returned her attention to Tarawe. "How many deaths?"

"Thirteen humans that we're certain of, probably more by now, and uncountable sea- and reef folk. She killed three by her own hand, and three more by way of a sword with which she's become bound. Most of the rest are the result of a storm she mistakenly called near the northern islands. Those deaths continue."

"A storm?" Ola's brows lifted high. "This young thing is a wind caller?"

Iuti sighed. She was shivering uncontrollably in the unheated room. She wanted nothing more than to collapse. Tarawe twitched in Mapa's arms. "It's a long story, Aunt."

Ola stared at her for a moment, then harumphed. "Yours usually are. Come on then. You can tell me while Mapa cleans her up. I can't work through the skagrat stench without doing more damage than good. You're a damn fool for coming into Sandar now. I hope you know that." She swept back through the beads without waiting for an answer.

"Aye," Iuti replied to the scented air of her passing.

A bath and warm clothing, a full meal in her belly, and the knowledge that Tarawe was in the best possible hands made it possible for Iuti to relax just a little. She told their story privately to Ho'ola, and after seeing the tattoo on her back, the healer agreed that her discretion was wise.

Mapa and the others of her household were trustworthy, Ola said, but since the blockade, anyone with knowledge of the drummers was in great danger. Lowtowners had learned quickly to avoid all reference to them, even in their curses, lest they be called in for questioning and conscripted into the Teronin army. The Teronin obviously hoped to keep the knowledge of their growing depen- dence on the drummers from reaching the southern armies.

"If the drummers ever make alliance with Pahulu," Iuti said, "the Teronin will wish they'd never heard of either of them."

Later, she showed Ola the braid of Kunan's hair. Risak had explained that the drummers had intended weaving the long strands into the ropes that would bind the war- rior's skin to the great war drums.

Without it, they would be forced to use what short ends they could salvage from Kunan's shorn scalp. The ropes would take longer to prepare, Risak had said, and the resulting bond between the drumfaces wouldn't be as strong as the drummers had originally planned.

"Risak says the drum tones won't be as perfect as if they had the longer lengths of hair," Iuti said, "but I doubt if any but the drummers themselves will be able to detect the fault. Kunan's drums will carry great power regardless."

"Aye," Ola said. "Kunan Iliawe was a man of great strength."

"You knew him?"

Ola didn't look up from where she was stroking Tar- awe's forehead. "I know all the great southern warriors, sharkwoman." Iuti grew silent then, because she had not told Ho'ola of her break with Mano Niuhi.

"Deep wounds heal slowly," Ola said softly.

Iuti wasn't sure whether the healer spoke to her or to Tarawe.

Four nerve-wracking days passed before Iuti met Ma'eva beneath one of the Lowtown piers. Ola had or- dered her away from Tarawe, claiming her nervousness only added to the chaos in Tarawe's mind. Iuti ate and rested, and rested and ate, and paced the narrow halls of Ola's warren until she was ready to tear the cold stones down with her bare hands. Finally she redonned her farm woman's disguise and went outside.

She chose a deserted portion of the most dilapidated pier. She squatted behind a refuse pile and dangled a weighted line in the water below. The water was dirty and not all the fish she caught were healthy—she spoke kindly to the damaged ones before throwing them back— but the solitary exercise in patience calmed her nerves.

The milimilis found her on the second day. They listened in grinning disbelief while she explained that she was fishing to repay the healer for taking in her and her girl. They knew she lied. Ho'ola would never eat, or serve, fish like these, but it gave them a story to tell others who might be curious about the silent newcomer on their dock.

It also let them know that Iuti and the very influential Ho'ola were on good terms, which meant that their investment in time might one day yield profitable results. Iuti offered them a generous portion of her catch that day and on each of the days that followed, but they never took more than a small share. They didn't want her paying off her debt in fish, however welcome the free meals might be.

Periodically, when Iuti was sure she was alone, she climbed down a rickety ladder to the waterline to gather bait crabs from the submerged pilings or to untangle her line from some bit of floating garbage. Finally Ma'eva appeared.

At first Iuti dismissed the sluggish redfish as not being worth the small effort it would take to scoop it up. The poor creature was so old and worm-ridden, not even a hungry Teronin would use it for food. But as she turned back to the ladder, the fish followed. It flickered and began to change color. Mottled, muddy-orange melted to iridescent gold, then glimmered into silver. Oozing lesions dissolved and disappeared.

The fish grew larger and sleeker, strong and virile in the way of the sea. It was Ma'eva, there was no doubt about it. He was showing off. For just an instant, he took on the vague shape of a nurse shark, and that made Iuti fear for him. Ma'eva knew better than to mimic Mano in any of his many forms.

She led the fish back into the crisscrossing maze of rotting timber that supported the pier, then flashed him the underwater sign to take his human form. With a splash, dark hair and bright eyes appeared above the water. He resumed his former human shape from the waist up. The half of him that remained in the water retained its fish form.

"That white hair makes you look strange, Iuti Mano," he said in greeting.

She laughed. "Not half as strange as that tail does you, friend Ma'eva."

He grinned and twined his tail sinuously around her ankles. He snatched a scuttling crab from a nearby piling. He popped it into his mouth, chewed, and swallowed, then grimaced. "Those taste better when I'm a bonefish," he said.

"Did Risak make it across the river?" she asked.

"Oh, aye. He swims very well for a land person."

"The weapons?"

"Hidden in a cave downstream," he said. "Shall I bring your club? It's easier to carry than the metal pieces, but I'm not sure it's a good idea for me to be carrying Mano's teeth through the river. Your kinsman has a long nose."

"Leave it," Iuti replied. "If I had it here, I'd be tempted to use it and that would be the end of us all. How far has Risak gotten?"

"He went straight to Manara and then to the river mouth where the southern fleet is gathering. I'm glad of that, because now I can talk to him from the water. No more flying. He said to tell you there are reports the Teronin are planning a seaborne attack along that coast. There are many Teronin war canoes amassed just north of the river mouth, so—" He shrugged. "—maybe the reports are true."

"Why do you hesitate?"

Ma'eva frowned. The action sent a trickle of water down his forehead and the length of his nose. His eyes crossed as he watched it drain away. He shook off the drip and met her look again. "The gulls told me this morning that those Teronin canoes aren't what they seem. From a distance they look ready to sail, but up close most of them look too old and broken to be useful in the water.

"The good canoes, the big, strong ones, are hidden along the coast north of Losan Island. Before the storm, some of them were traveling frequently between there and the atolls."

"Mano's teeth," Iuti muttered. "The canoes at the river mouth must be a diversion then, to draw the southern armies north. In the meantime, Pahulu will help the Teronin take over the atolls, and from there they can attack from both the north and the south. That explains why the security is so tight around Sandar, and why so few Teronin soldiers are here in the city. Have you told Risak about this?"

"Not yet. I decided I'd better come here first."

It had started to rain. A drip smelling of the refuse pile splashed on Iuti's cheek. "What news is there of the storm? Does it continue to grow?"

Ma'eva pursed his lips. "Haven't you looked at the sky today, Iuti Mano? Haven't you felt the cold rain? The storm is throwing off squalls in all directions now. This is one of them. The northern atolls are almost all underwater; many of the reefs are scoured of life. Storm surge is battering the mainland coast already. It won't be long before the direct winds reach even here."

"How can that be?" Iuti said. "Surely Tarawe's call was not that strong . . ."

"It's that other one's doing. That evil one who paces the beaches at Fanape," Ma'eva said. "She keeps calling up more winds and using them to twist the waves into monsters, which she then sends to look for you. She wants the original storm brought under control, so she can start her war. She still thinks you're the one who can do that."

Iuti frowned and wiped another sour-smelling drip from her cheek. The ridges of Mano's scars made her fingertips itch.

"The seafolk are very angry, friend Iuti," Ma'eva said. "They are tired of humans intruding on their world. If the storm isn't stopped soon, and the sorceress isn't removed from her place of power, the seafolk have sworn to drive all humans from the sea. They say they'll go back to the old days when the land and the sea were enemies. Already they've threatened to destroy any human vessel that dares enter their waters unasked."

"Surely the seafolk don't blame all humans for the actions of only a few," Iuti said.

"The sea people don't understand human affairs," he said. 'They don't understand that humans act independently of each other and oftentimes without conscious regard for the world around them. I confess, I don't understand it myself, but I've come to believe it."

"But there are many innocent humans dependent on the sea!" Iuti said. "Those who go there to gather food, those who must travel from place to place. You can't mean to kill them indiscriminately . . ."

He shrugged. "It's a thing we learned by watching how humans treat us."

"Ayii, Ma'eva. If this happens," Iuti said, "the humans will fight back. It might even be enough to draw the southerners and the Teronin together against you. There would be chaos both on land and at sea." She slapped her hand against the slime-covered piling. "That damnable Pahulu. It is she who is causing this useless conflict."

"There are those who say it is you," Ma'eva said carefully.

"Me! How could I—?"

"There are few secrets in the sea, Iuti Mano. We all know it was you who slayed the shark. Mano's fury at your betrayal has soured our waters for months now."

Iuti caught her breath. "Mano? What has he to do with this? He rarely even acknowledges the rest of the seafolk except to eat them."

"Friend Iuti," Ho'oma'eva said. "It's not just Pahulu who seeks revenge upon you. My kin are being urged to war by Mano Niuhi himself. He knows you won't stay away from such a conflict. He waits more eagerly than the sorceress for your return to Fanape.''

☙ *Chapter 15* ☙

"IF the storm is going to be stopped," Ho'ola insisted when Iuti returned with Ma'eva's news, "the girl is going to have to stop it herself. There is no other way." She sighed and leaned back against the embroidered cushion Mapa quickly slid into place.

She lifted a hand to stop Iuti's objection. "I told you before, warrior. The Teronin collected all the wind callers in the days before you came and took them downriver on one of their war canoes. There is only one left in the city, and he's so senile he can't remember his name much less how to control a major storm. I can teach Tarawe the basic calling and canceling chants, but she'll have to do the rest on her own—if she can do anything at all. I've never seen such a strange assortment of abilities bundled into one human."

"If you can teach her the spells, why can't *you* control the wind?" Iuti asked. "You're a sorceress to match Pahulu's skills. Even the Teronin fear you."

"Only a true air person can make wind spells work," Ola replied. "That's why there are so few who can do it. I am a woman of the land. All I can do is say the words. We're lucky I can at least do that."

Iuti recalled what Ma'eva had said about Tarawe being an air person, but she still found it hard to believe. There was no question now that she was, in fact, a child of the sea. Her reaction to the seafolk's deaths proved that. Iuti glanced toward the curtained doorway that led to Tarawe's room.

"How can I take her back to the site of so much killing?" she asked. "I don't want her death on my hands,

Ola. Not now, after she's been through so much. And if Pahulu should gain control of her . . ."

"You'll never even reach the islands with the wind as strong as it is now," Ola said. "Tarawe might never be able to control the entire storm, but with enough practice, she should at least be able to calm a path through it. She's been experimenting—"

"Mano's teeth! You're not letting her practice here in your house, are you? The girl is bright, Ola. And powerful beyond a doubt. But she's wholly undisciplined. She'll try anything!"

Ho'ola's thin brows lifted. "Shall I send her outside then? To be overseen by your friend, the Teronin sorcerer?"

"He's not *my*—"

"I know. I know, youngster." Ola waved Iuti back to her seat. "He's not seeking you in your guise as farm woman, but I'll warrant it *is* you he seeks. Pahulu's net stretches wide, and he has that witch's smell about him."

Iuti frowned. "Aye. He was on the pier again this morning. The milis said he asked where you were living now."

Ola gave a dismissive flick of her wrist. "He knows where I am. He was just trying to catch your sweet friends in a lie. Those two are favorites among the off-duty Teronin, and the Teronin chiefs are looking for an excuse to take them along on their next march."

"I'm surprised they haven't taken them already," Iuti said.

"The city is still nominally neutral territory," Ola said. "I suspect even the Teronin are smart enough to know the milis wouldn't remain so sweet if they were conscripted illegally. I hope you have a way to repay them for their continued vigilance, not to mention their silence, on your behalf."

Iuti pulled a small woven bag from inside the folds of her skirt. She poured a handful of gems into Ola's lap. Pearls as white as her own bleached hair, and ebony beads of black coral. "Will a pair of these do?"

Ola sucked in her breath. She blinked and touched the

glinting beads with trembling fingers. "Where did you get these? You have a fortune here!"

Iuti laughed. "Just a small one. Ma'eva brought them."

Ola lifted a pearl the size of a powderberry.

"Those are from the rock oyster beds off the lee side of Tana Atoll," Iuti said. "Ma'eva and I started seeding them back when we were kids. He still does it from time to time, so that when I ask, he can bring them to me."

"They're stunning," Ola said. She rubbed her thumb across the pearl's gleaming surface.

"The coral is from the deep sea," Iuti said. "Ma'eva carries pieces of it into the side eddies of the Great Gravel Banks, and the constant maelstrom grinds them into beads. We've tried it with more precious corals, but the black is the easiest to market discreetly."

Ola shook her head and began placing the beads back into the bag one by one. "I've always wondered how you could be so generous and still maintain your reputation for not looting." She handed the bag up to Iuti. "I should think one of each would more than cover your debt to the whores."

Iuti nodded but did not take the bag. "Keep them," she said, then added quickly, "As a gift, Auntie. I would not insult you by offering payment for simple hospitality. You know that."

Ola shook her head again and laughed softly. "You never change, Iuti Mano. I presume that when the time's right, you'd like me to pay the milis for you, too. As part of my simple hospitality."

Iuti shrugged and smiled. "If you don't mind, Auntie."

"Tana Atoll," Ola said. "Is that where the Great Pearl is?"

Iuti started. "How do you know about the Great Pearl?"

Ola smiled. "Tarawe heard Ma'eva ask if you were woman enough to harvest it with him. She wanted to know what that meant." Her brows lifted in question.

Iuti glanced awkwardly away. Then she looked back,

irritated that a childhood dare to a sea mimic could cause her shyness now. "It's none of *her* business," she said.

Ho'ola laughed. "I'll warrant it's a mating challenge," she whispered loudly to Mapa. "And I'll double the bet she's going to take it one day. The warrior woman is fond of that mimic, so she is. See how she blushes and turns away?"

That made Iuti laugh and turn back again.

"So, warrior," Ola asked. "Just what kind of bargain have you made with this man of the sea?"

"When we were children, Ma'eva and I sealed our friendship by seeding the largest of the giant clams at Kala," Iuti said with a grin. "I promised Ma'eva I'd bear him a child if he could someday trick me into agreeing to help him harvest the resulting pearl."

"A child!" Ola said. "You?"

"The promise was made a long time ago, Auntie."

A sudden gust of warm wind lifted the curtain to Tarawe's room. A quick call of delight followed the breeze.

"Oh, gods," Iuti groaned.

"I did it!"

The curtain swirled again as Tarawe swept it to one side. Her grin was as wide as it had been the night she called the storm. "Ser Iuti! I can make the wind come when I call!"

"I know you can make it *come*, girl," Iuti said. "What we need to find out is, can you make it *go*?"

Tarawe's grin tipped slightly. Dark circles still shadowed her eyes, but her look had grown bright again. "I— well, not yet."

"Oh, gods," Iuti sighed again.

The weather worsened.

The rain came sporadically at first, but as the days passed, the sky grew darker and heavier. The rain began falling in solid, heavy sheets. The Lowtown streets and alleys flooded. At least it's washing away the stench, Iuti mused as she plodded through puddles and potholes and ever-deepening streams to reach her place on the dock.

The wind was as cold as any she had experienced outside the high mountains.

Most days she sat cold and miserable, baiting and dangling her fishlines with no sign of Ma'eva's presence in the wind-whipped water below. When he did come, he tugged a signal on her line so she would know to climb down to meet him under the protection of the rotting timbers.

They would exchange brief messages, then Ma'eva would return to his downriver spying and Iuti to the interminable waiting. To pass the time, she braided Kunan's hair into dozens of long, thin strands. She braided the strands together, and then together again, until she had formed them into a pair of thick, heavy necklaces— one for herself, one for Risak. He, more than anyone, deserved this small piece of Kunan's strength.

She saw the sorcerer from time to time—he was the same one-eyed Teronin who had stopped her at the ferry landing. Once she recognized him in time to avoid being seen herself. Another time the milis warned her away from an alley in which the sorcerer lurked.

The few Lowtowners who traveled the cold, wet streets avoided the Teronin as carefully as she did. It was common gossip that his silent watching was centering more and more closely on the area near Ho'ola's home. Iuti heard her own true name whispered among those for whom the sorcerer had offered huge rewards for finding.

Inside Ho'ola's home, the weather was also growing increasingly stormy. Tarawe's attempts to control the wind kept the household in a constant state of wariness and, at times, in complete chaos. The air movements she caused were small compared to those outside, but they gusted and swirled and caught even Ho'ola off-guard at odd moments of the day and night.

Iuti's temper grew short as she became more and more concerned about the passing time. "We must go," she would say, and Ola would insist that Tarawe's training could not be hurried.

"That Teronin circles closer every day," Iuti said. "If he's any kind of sorcerer at all, he knows that something out of the ordinary is going on here. I saw him wave a discovery spell over the north entrance just this morning. He'll find an excuse to come in soon, and then what will we do?''

"He's come in here before and found nothing," Ola replied. "The Teronin forces can't reach the islands through the storm anyway, so we might as well continue as we are and give the girl as much time as possible. She isn't truly recovered from the killing thrusts yet, and there are bound to be new ones once the battle begins. I'll protect her as best I can, but . . ." She spread her hands. Mapa, as usual, kept his placid gaze carefully neutral.

On the eleventh afternoon, Ma'eva brought word that the Teronin war canoes, those hidden far to the north, had put to sea.

"They're skirting the storm's edge, following it north and west," he said. "There are many of them and they're moving fast, although not so fast as you and the girl did with your magic sail. The birds could hardly keep up—that's why I couldn't tell you sooner."

"That wasn't a magic sail, Ma'eva. It was just Tarawe's skirt," Iuti said. Ma'eva's look was disbelieving.

"Those Teronin canoes are trailing barbed nets, killing unwary seafolk along the way," Ma'eva said.

Iuti muttered a curse. "That must be at Pahulu's command. She gains her power from stealing the life force from others. She's probably ordered the Teronin to sail around to the southwest edge of the archipelago. That's where her own winds will be strongest, and she can use them to guide the fleet through the islands to Fanape."

Ma'eva nodded. He looked tired, something Iuti had never seen before. Sea mimics rarely remained interested in one thing long enough to become exhausted by doing it. She hated to continue her demands on him, but knew she must.

"Tell Risak to prepare the southern fleet for immediate sail," she said.

"There is a big canoe sailing with the others," Ma'eva said. "A new one with two hulls and much carving and colored paint. It would be beautiful if the faces in the carvings weren't so like the things that sorceress is dredging up from the deep. There is a thatched house on the platform between the hulls.''

"A ceremonial canoe," Iuti said. "Why would . . ."

"It joined the others yesterday from the inland waterway bordering Losan Island."

Iuti's stomach tightened. "The drummers," she breathed. She closed her eyes and remained still for a moment. There was no way they could have finished Kunan's war drums so quickly without magical help, but she had no doubt they were aboard that canoe. That meant Pahulu knew of their existence and planned to put them to her own use. Ma'eva caressed Iuti's cheek with a cool, wet hand. She opened her eyes.

"Tell Ser Risak about the drummers," she said. "Tell him not to join the others on the war canoes."

"Will you bring the girl?"

"Aye. I must. I don't want to take her back to that place, Ma'eva. I once promised to take her away from its evil."

"It's not the place that's evil," he reminded her.

"Well, of course, I'm going with you," Ho'ola said when Iuti returned with her news. "Here, take one of my capes. That one you've been using stinks of dead fish. Besides, it's soaked through. I'm only a healer, not a god. I won't be able to save you from the lung sickness in the middle of battle." Ho'ola tossed a heavy, deep-red cape onto Iuti's pile of quickly gathered supplies.

Iuti glared at her. "It's bad enough I have to include Tarawe and Ma'eva in this," she said. "I won't take—"

"Who's going to protect Tarawe while you're out swinging your sword, warrior woman?" Ola demanded. "The closer she gets to the deaths her storm is causing, the harder it's going to be for her to resist the killing thrusts. Do you think she's been doing it all on her own even here?"

That was exactly what Iuti had thought. She turned to see that Tarawe's surprise was as great as her own.

"Mapa, be sure there's a good supply of bushberry in my pack," Ola said. "You've lived alone too long, Iuti Mano. You think you can, and should, fight every battle alone. There are times when that won't work, and this is one of them. Tarawe, pull your skirt up from the back, between your legs. That's right. Now tuck it into your belt in front. It'll stay drier that way. Here, Mapa, let me show you how to . . ."

And thus, the packing was taken firmly out of Iuti's hands. Glowering, she stepped back to watch the healer finish the preparations. "Is he coming, too?" she asked when Mapa slung a travel cape around his own broad shoulders.

"Who did you think was going to take care of *me*?" Ho'ola replied.

They left by separate exits, not wishing to attract notice by traveling as a group or by cloaking themselves with magic. Mapa took Tarawe. Ho'ola and Iuti each traveled alone. Iuti tried to avoid splashing as she made her stealthy way through the flooded streets. She hunched over inside Ho'ola's cape, trying as best she could to keep her inner clothing dry. She was still irritated with Ola, but the frustration was blunted by the unexpected relief she felt at not having to face both Mano and Pahulu alone.

But if that old woman gets herself killed, she promised as she sidestepped what she knew to be a deep pothole, I'll follow her right into the nether world to tell her "I told you so!"

A gust of wind lifted the corner of Iuti's cape as she rounded the last corner leading to the dock. She scanned the deserted pier before moving on, mentally sorting the shapes and sizes of the rain-slicked shadows. Nothing looked like a human watcher. Nothing moved. She stepped out onto the dock.

"It's a cold night to be out walking," a soft voice said. It was a Teronin voice, the sorcerer's voice. A chill colder than the night crept up Iuti's back and she cursed silently. She had managed to avoid the sorcerer's curiosity for eleven days and now, on the one night when it was most important not to be seen, she had walked right into him.

She turned around, pretending to be startled, although she knew he probably wasn't behind her. A sorcerer's voice in the dark rarely pointed to his physical presence.

A shadow moved to her right. This time the voice came from there. "What are you doing out here, healer? I've not heard of anyone ill or injured on the docks."

Healer? Then Iuti remembered the cape. Of course, she thought. He's been lurking about trying to discover what Ho'ola is up to. He thinks I'm the healer! She turned again, feigning confusion. A pair of Teronin guards stood just beyond where she had seen the sorcerer move.

She felt the first tingle of a search spell and quickly called out, "I no be the healer. Who's hidin' there 'n the dark? I jus be goin' fishin' an' that be the truth. Th' healer be home 'n the dry." She turned again, relieved to feel the search spell stop before it reached the knife and the supply pack at her waist. They were not things a poor fisherwoman would carry.

A growled order brought one of the guards into the open. He approached Iuti carefully and when he reached her, he threw back her cape's hood. "I no be th' healer," she said again. The guard was one of those who had stopped her at the Lowtown bridge. He leaned close enough to see her face, then frowned and straightened.

"This ain't Ho'ola," he called. "It's just that stinking farm woman. She's always out here pulling in rotten fish. Where'd you get that cape, Grandma?"

The second guard moved into clear sight, but the sorcerer remained under cover. She could feel his disappointment. Now, if she could just avoid his anger and further curiosity. "That big one what takes care o' th' healer. He be givin' me the cape," she said. "Couldn't stand the stink on me old one, he say. It be generous n' I be grateful, Sar. Tha's why I come fer th' fishin' tonight. T' pay 'm back, Sar. Kin I offer ye . . ."

It was too much. She felt the tingle of the search spell again and the sorcerer's shock when he discovered Ho'ola's knife and the travel supplies folded into her waist pack. He shouted an order, and instantly she abandoned her disguise. She straightened, swinging the heel of one hand up into the slouching guard's face. At the same time, she cloaked herself in a warding spell to prevent the sorcerer from affecting her movements. The crack of the guard's skull on the stone wall behind him was loud in the darkness. He collapsed without further sound.

The mental touch of his death struck like a physical blow just as Iuti flung the dagger from her waist pouch into the second guard's heart. She blocked the second icy thrust and whirled to face the sorcerer. She flung an attack spell toward him, but it was too late. He had sealed himself inside a protective spell. That meant he was not a fighter, only a finder, after all. He still presented a danger, however.

The sorcerer's one good eye blazed as he glared at her through the flickering mist of his protective seal. His lips moved, then stopped. And then he smiled, because he thought he was safe. He thought he had only to wait until she moved far enough away, then open the seal and attack her from a distance. Or, if she didn't move, he could simply wait until the next Teronin patrol crossed the docks and found them. He looked warm and dry inside his self-made haven.

"You should have studied islander's magic, sorcerer," Iuti said. "If you had, you'd know that a simple shielding spell offers little protection if you end up locked within it." She muttered a spell of her own, then spat on her left palm and pressed it against the gelatinous mist surrounding the sorcerer. It didn't penetrate, but when she closed her fist and pulled, the mist stretched and followed. The astonished sorcerer pressed from the inside but could not reach out through the mist. He stumbled as Iuti yanked him forward.

Knowing he could hear her, although his own cries of outrage were sealed with him inside his self-made prison, she said, "It looks like I'm going to have to take you along, too. Unless you want to come out and face me now in an honest battle. No? I thought not. Your kind likes to spread terror only from a position of personal safety.''

She recognized the sorcerer's curse even though she couldn't hear it. She grinned in response and pulled him along as she kicked the two guards into the water and hurried to the end of the pier.

A pair of shadows met her. ''You travel in dangerous company, farm woman,'' one of the milis said.

Iuti offered him a smile in the darkness. ''So do you, sweet friends. Help me get this vermin into the boat, then go home to warmth and safety. There is much evil abroad tonight. I can taste it in the wind.''

The milis exchanged a quick look, then showed her the narrow stairway to the boat landing. ''I wonder how deep this bubble would sink if we just pushed it into the river?'' the female asked when the Teronin balked at climbing down the stairs.

''Deep enough,'' came Ho'ola's voice from below. ''I'll see to it if you don't get down here right now, Teronin scum.''

Iuti pushed from above, and finally the sorcerer descended. The bravado with which he had faced Iuti dissolved completely as he recognized Ho'ola. Here was a threat he knew enough about to dread openly. The healer ran a finger over the misty envelope, testing Iuti's holding spell.

''I see you finally learned how to do it right,'' she said. ''Too bad you had to show me tonight, though. This one's disappearance will be noted.'' She set a spell of her own around the cowering sorcerer and ordered him belowdeck into the fish hold.

''If not by the Teronin, then by Pahulu herself,'' Iuti agreed. ''He's one of hers, there's no doubt. We'll have to get rid of him as soon as possible.'' She called to the milis to release the bow and stern lines.

They did so, but then leapt lightly aboard before Iuti could push the fishing vessel away from the dock. ''Mano's teeth,'' Iuti muttered. ''Not you, too.'' The milis' painted faces curved into matching grins.

Iuti admitted to herself as they threaded their way

through the moored fishing vessels and roving Teronin patrol boats that having so many extra hands on board was a blessing. She and Tarawe would have been hard put to keep a close lookout and row at the same time. She had to admit, too, that it was much more comfortable sitting in the shelter of the boat's small cabin while Mapa and the milis did the work.

In the farthest reaches of the cabin, Ho'ola snored softly. The healer had muttered a spell and put herself to sleep almost as soon as they left the dock. Now she lay on the decking with one lined cheek pressed into the embroidered cushion Mapa had provided.

"Ser Iuti?" Tarawe said softly. She was huddled close to Iuti's side. When Iuti saw that she was shivering, she wrapped her own cape around Tarawe's so they could share their warmth.

When their looks met, Tarawe blinked. She glanced up at Iuti's hair, then at the scars on her cheek. "Will you teach me how to do that?" She nodded toward the sorcerer in the hold.

Iuti nodded. "It would be a good trick for you to know," she said. "Pahulu is an island-born witch, and if she gets the chance, she'll use it on you. It's probably most important for you to know how to get out of it, but to learn that, you have to know how to get in. I'll show you how to set a simple shielding spell as soon as we're away from the city. I wouldn't want you to accidentally release the Teronin while we are still within hailing distance of his comrades."

It was quiet for a time, save for the sounds of the storm and Ho'ola's heavy breathing. "Ser Iuti?" Tarawe said.

Despite her concern for silence, Iuti was pleased that Tarawe was acting more like herself again. "Aye?"

"Does it ever get any easier to kill?"

A chill crept along Iuti's arms. The deaths of the two Teronin lay like icy slivers at the back of her consciousness. She felt death more sharply now than she had when Mano was still with her. It surprised her that she hadn't noticed it before.

"If it ever becomes easy," she said, "then you have

entered the realm of true evil. Never let it become easy, Tarawe.''

Again a brief silence. ''Sometimes it's so hard I wonder if I can even survive it,'' came Tarawe's soft voice.

Iuti shifted so she could see Tarawe better. ''There is more killing ahead, Tarawe. When it comes, let Ho'ola help you. Don't try to absorb it alone.''

''Patrol off the port bow,'' the mili on lookout called softly. Mapa stopped the sweep oar and they drifted in silence, listening to the slightly irregular cadence of four dipping paddles. It must have been late in this patrol's watch, for they were being noisy and careless. The Teronin canoe passed near enough to cast a shadow through the darkness and rain. Tarawe remained silent for a long time after the canoe disappeared.

''I'll feel safer when I have my sword again,'' she murmured finally.

Iuti wished she felt the same.

☜ Chapter 16 ☞

THEY found the weapons cache at midnight. They might have missed it in the driving rain had Ma'eva not appeared just upriver. To get their attention, he jumped on deck in the form of a flying fish, then quickly back off again.

The city dwellers were merely startled by the flash and slap of silver scales, but Iuti and Tarawe knew immediately who it must be. Flying fish lived only in the open ocean. Iuti ordered the boat close to shore.

As quickly as they recognized the landmarks Ma'eva had described earlier, Tarawe was over the side and splashing up the riverbank. She led Iuti unerringly to the frond-covered overhang under which Risak had hidden their belongings. She waited impatiently while Iuti pulled the bundle into the open. Her right hand was rolled into a fist in her eagerness.

There is something wrong here, Iuti thought. Tarawe is a healer's child. A human attuned to both the sea and the air, and one never meant for killing. Why is she so eager to grasp a blade forged for war?

"Leave it sheathed," she said sharply as soon as the weapon was in Tarawe's hands. "Take these supplies back to the boat."

Tarawe seemed genuinely startled by Iuti's tone. She quickly gathered up an armload of Teronin clothing and hurried back to the fishing boat.

Iuti spoke briefly to Ma'eva, suggesting that he wait until the sorcerer was disposed of before revealing himself to the others. That disappointed him. He had been eager to meet the two humans with the brightly colored faces, but he dissolved back into the fish without argument.

Once aboard and under way again, Iuti and Tarawe changed back into trousers and tunics. Tarawe managed to make the switch without displaying an inch of skin, an act the scantily clad milis found remarkably humorous. They threw Tarawe winks and kisses and, until Iuti ordered them to stop, an impressive variety of suggestive gestures. Oblivious, Tarawe set to polishing the hilt of her sword.

Iuti laid her hands atop Tarawe's. "If you hope to survive the coming battle," she said, "you would do better to lay aside this weapon and improve your skill with the greater one Ho'ola has given you. We'll have many warriors capable of swinging swords, but only you have a chance at controlling the storm."

"What do you want me to do?" Tarawe asked.

Exasperated, Iuti pointed out at the rain. "Study the wind, girl. Practice moving it. See if you can turn it downstream in our favor, or at least steady. That would be a start."

"I already did that," Tarawe replied.

Iuti stared at her, then abruptly stuck her head out of the cabin to check the wind. It blew strong and steady, directly downstream. Mapa was using the sweep oar only for direction now. He no longer needed it to give them way.

I never even felt it change, Iuti thought. Then, as a test, she called, "Make it blow stronger."

"It's too strong now," Tarawe called back. "The shoreline trees are already being broken."

Iuti came back inside. She wiped rainwater from her eyes. "How do you know that?" The shore was all but invisible from the deck.

Tarawe touched her cheeks, then stared at her palms. Surprise lit her eyes and she smiled. "I can feel it!"

They reached the river mouth at dawn. Risak was waiting in a small scout canoe. He was clothed in knee-length brown trousers and a soldier's padded tunic. There was a Teronin sword belted to each hip, and another sheathed on his back. His hair was in a warrior's knot. As he climbed aboard, the milimilis whispered to each other but, surprisingly, made no comment aloud. Their studied gazes ran the length of Risak's lean body.

"Only three of the southern war canoes have been able to reach the open sea," Risak said. "The rest are still on the beach. The wind is blowing directly onshore, and the surf is so rough the canoes can't cross it into the safety of deep water."

There were two wind callers waiting with the fleet, he said, but even working together, they hadn't been able to turn the wind. As they approached the river mouth, the round-bottomed fishing boat began bobbing like a dried copra nut on the crisscrossing swells. It took Mapa and both milis to keep the outgoing tide from sweeping them into the breaking surf. Tarawe's wind and that from the oncoming storm fought for dominance over the small craft.

Iuti called Tarawe from the cabin. Tarawe strapped the sword to her back before stepping outside.

"Can you do anything with this wind?" Iuti called over the roar of wind and waves. "Can you calm it or at least turn it slightly offshore so the canoes can launch?"

Tarawe looked up and around for a moment, then cupped her hands. She muttered something into them. With a smooth twist of her right wrist, she scooped the wind into a turn and sent it blowing directly offshore. Or at least that was how it appeared to Iuti. She stared in astonishment.

Tarawe closed her left hand into a loose fist, turned it palm down, and opened it again. The raging surf settled—all at once. There was a hiss of collapsing waves, a swirl of dissolving seafoam, then nothing but a strong northerly current and the rippling swells of summer doldrums.

The sudden lack of wave-borne resistance caused the sweep oar to slam starboard, throwing Mapa and the milis to the deck. The eunuch's Lowtown curse of wonder was echoed by the whores. Without the roar of the surf, their voices carried clearly in the clean, brisk wind.

Iuti was so shaken that she sat down hard on the dripping gunwale. She met Risak's look. His lower lip was caught between his teeth.

Tarawe laughed. "I didn't know I could do that! I didn't know I could tell the water what to do, too!" She stared at her left palm and grew serious again. "I think I might have hurt some of the seafolk, though, by stopping the waves all at once. I should have done it more gradually."

"Only a few were injured." Ma'eva's voice came from behind Iuti. The milis jumped. "Far fewer than were being hurt before."

Iuti glanced back, but whatever form Ma'eva had taken had disappeared. Except for the small ripple where he had been, the water's surface was as smooth as glass. The calm stretched in a circle to a point just beyond where the outermost stormbreak had been. There it stopped abruptly, as if a transparent wall had been set between the southern fleet and the storm still raging outside.

"Tarawe," Iuti said. "Have you set a shield around us?" Waves dashed into ragged shards against the invisible wall. Rain slid in glimmering sheets down its sides.

Tarawe reached back to brush her fingertips along the hilt of her sword. "I used that spell you taught me on the way downriver," she said. "Only I made it bigger. Is that all right?" A single raindrop, a last errant reminder of the former deluge, splashed against her forehead. She touched it with her finger and brought it to her lips. "This rain tastes like old Pahulu back on Fanape."

A hail from one of the war canoes caught Iuti's attention. She motioned the canoe to come alongside. "Risak," she said. "There is a Teronin sorcerer down in the hold. Will you take him back to the shore? He's well locked inside his shield now, but if Ho'ola or I should be disabled, he might be able to break out. Be sure he's secured somewhere where that can't make a difference."

"I'll see to it," Risak said. He glanced at Tarawe. She

was leaning over the side, trying to reach the water with her hand. A single wavetip lifted just high enough to wet her fingers. She laughed and flicked the water into shimmering slivers.

Risak watched her for a moment, then joined the milis in helping pull the canoe alongside. Iuti left him to explain the sudden calm to the others and reentered the cabin to wake Ho'ola. The healer blinked her eyes open, took one look around at the open sea, and promptly retched into the bucket Mapa had ready.

"Auntie, I never realized you were such a land person," Iuti said. She wondered how anyone, especially a healer, could be seasick on this gently rolling sea. A glint of humor shone in the eunuch's dark eyes. It was clear he had been through this before.

Iuti bent forward to lay one hand on Ho'ola's forehead, the other on her stomach. She whispered a small charm her father had employed whenever he was forced to travel by sea. Then she sat back to watch the color return to Ola's cheeks. Mapa left to empty the bucket.

"Why didn't you do that earlier?" Ola groaned. "You must teach it to me immediately."

"We were traveling down a *river*, Auntie. It never occurred to me that you were spell-sleeping to avoid becoming ill. I thought you were just conserving your strength."

"Ha. Would that I could," Ola replied. "Keeping the death thrusts from Tarawe depletes my energy faster than a water leech sucks tainted blood."

"Are you still . . ."

"Of course I'm still absorbing them for her," Ola snapped. "The child just thinks she's doing it all on her own. She's a true innocent, Iuti Mano. She never should have been allowed to kill once without being guarded, much less a hundred and more times. The full force of her storm-kills would destroy her if it were to touch her mind all at once." Ola squeezed her eyes shut and rested her forehead in her hands.

Iuti muttered the seasickness charm again. "I'll teach

this to Mapa," she said. "You'd never be able to manage
it on your own just now."

Then she told Ola about Tarawe and the storm. "She
calmed it just like she calmed herself when we first faced
the demon drummers. All at once and with no seeming
effort. She said she used the shielding spell I taught her
while we were coming downriver, but she must have done
something else, as well. I know I couldn't set a shield so
large." She glanced up at the pounding waves outside.
"Nor one so strong."

"I'd better talk to her again about mixing up her
magic," Ola said. "By the gods, I wish I'd met that child
when she was just a babe. To think that such untamed
power has been allowed to lie fallow this long. We're
lucky that old sorceress on Fanape never realized her
potential."

"Tarawe's own mother was a healer," Iuti said. "How
could *she* not have noticed?"

"Perhaps she did," Ola replied. "It would explain why
she allowed Tarawe to watch her work but never acknowledged her openly as an apprentice. It might have
been the only way she had of protecting Tarawe from
being discovered by those who couldn't be trusted."

"Dangerous," Iuti muttered. She touched Ola's arm.
"Come," she said. "We need to change vessels. There's
a small privacy hut on the canoe we'll be using. After
you've talked to Tarawe, you can put yourself right back
to sleep."

Mapa had returned and when Ola struggled to rise,
he lifted her, pillow and all, into his strong arms. He
climbed over the side of the fishing boat and into the
canoe with a grace that belied his great size.

While the rest of the canoes were being launched, the
wind callers were brought to meet Tarawe. At first, neither of them believed that Tarawe was responsible for the
current island of calm surrounding them. They were sure
it must be Ho'ola or even Iuti Mano herself. One even
questioned Tarawe's part in creating the original storm.

Irritated, Tarawe flicked her fingers. A swirling air
eddy toppled the man right into the sea. After he was

aboard and dry again, both wind callers agreed to a more serious discussion of how they could help manipulate the wind to the fleet's best advantage.

The largest of the great war canoes carried forty paddlers, seated side by side along the deep, narrow hulls. The outrigger platforms were broad and curved so that they rode high out of the water. They were heaped now with warriors' travel food and gear. The outrigger floats had been reinforced and the sails doubled to withstand the force of the storm they must pass through.

The canoe that was to carry Iuti and her larger-than-planned entourage—the milimilis insisted on continuing the voyage—was half the size of the others. If Iuti had had her way, it would have been halved again. She preferred a vessel that was easily maneuverable even if most of its crew was lost.

She consulted with the various chieftains, impressing upon them the importance of stopping Pahulu and the Teronin at Fanape. Risak had already warned them about the drummers and about the seafolk's threat. When Iuti reminded the chieftains to save the oceanfolk's lives and environs whenever they could, they glanced nervously at the sea and nodded in silence.

Just as they were ready to set sail, Risak appeared on the scout canoe and formally asked permission to come aboard Iuti's vessel. Iuti frowned. She crossed her arms and denied him access.

"I mean you no disrespect, Ser," she said. "Your value in this struggle has been beyond measure thus far. But you cannot go with us on this voyage. You *must* not. The drummers are certain to join the battle, and you—" She stopped. She could not, she would not, speak of his disability before the others.

"No one knows better than I what the drummers can make me do, Ser," he said. "Neither do I intend disrespect, but there are those aboard this canoe who need watching, and despite both of our efforts otherwise, it seems my duty is to watch them."

He slid a thin knife from his belt and laid the blade against his own throat. "I assure you, Ser, the drums will not influence my allegiance long enough for it to do you any harm.''

Go back, friend Risak! Iuti wanted to cry. Go back to the safe shore. Let me sail into this evil knowing I've saved at least one good man. The knife at Risak's throat drew blood when the slight movement of his breathing brought it into contact with his skin. He balanced on the edge of the canoe as if he had been born there.

Iuti held his unwavering look for a moment more, then cursed silently and stepped back. Risak nodded very formal thanks and sheathed his blade. The southern crew, their eyes wide with curiosity, remained absolutely silent.

''Pull sail to the wind!'' Iuti called as soon as Risak was aboard. She raised her right hand and pointed with all of her fingers to the northwest. ''Steersman, follow my course.''

''Aye,'' came the quick reply. The great, triangular sail moved, and the call to the wind was sounded across the waiting fleet.

''Tarawe, do you see my direction?'' Iuti called over the snap of the sail and the sudden rush of seawater along the canoe's sides.

''I see it,'' the girl replied.

''Hold your wind to this course, steady and strong until I tell you to change or until it changes on its own. Can you do that?''

''Aye, Ser Iuti,'' Tarawe said. Only a hint of fear marred the eagerness in her tone. Tarawe's right hand lifted. The wind turned, and the voyage back to Fanape began.

❧ *Chapter 17* ❧

THE fleet moved through the great storm as if it weren't there. Tarawe held the wind steady, and only an occasional wash of rain swept across the calm waters. The swells still ran deep and swift, but the current was strong to the north. It, too, helped them on their way.

At midmorning, Ma'eva joined them. He leapt aboard as a flying fish again, but this time stayed to re-form as a man. The southern paddlers cried out in concern when the change began, and would have kicked the flapping, flickering fish back overboard if Iuti hadn't stopped them. She quickly urged the curious milis back to give the sea mimic room.

Ma'eva changed first into a shadowy squid wrapped around one of Iuti's ankles. Then, with obvious attention to his audience's astonishment, he shaped himself sensuously into his favorite human form. The milimilis cheered and called out their approval of his perfect, sea-damp shape. The paddlers stared as if not willing to believe what they had just seen.

Ma'eva grinned at them all and settled beside Iuti to tell her the news of the sea. The fleet sailed on, propelled by Tarawe's steady breeze.

"How can she be doing this?" Risak asked after the midday meal. Tarawe had fallen asleep inside the hut, and Risak was sitting with Iuti and Ma'eva on the front edge of the outrigger platform. The milis sat leaning together, just behind.

"How can a child who knew nothing but a stolen storm chant a handful of days ago," Risak asked, "control the

176

wind now as if she owned it? Look, it holds its course even while she sleeps."

"She reminds me of the great sponges at Kinai," one of the milis said. "She absorbs everything around her—"

"—and has but to squeeze herself a bit to give it back in her own way," finished the other. They both giggled.

"It's a rare thing to see such power partnered with such innocence," Iuti said.

"There are folk in the sea," Ma'eva said, "who carry strange powers that no one else can understand. They rarely retain their innocence for long."

Iuti knew he spoke of Mano Niuhi. She disliked comparing Tarawe to the shark, even though she knew that what Ma'eva said was true. Over the many generations since Mano had established bonds with her seafaring ancestors, the great shark had changed. The early stories portrayed him as a gentle, generous creature, simply curious to better understand the land folk who inhabited the edges of his domain. That he occasionally ate the injured or diseased among them was simply a matter of his nature.

But as time passed, and particularly since he had partnered with Iuti, he had grown cunning and cautious. His generosity extended only to those who served his needs. He had grown hungrier over the years and no longer waited for the injured or ill. Iuti forced her mind back.

"She'll make a fine lover someday," the female mili was saying. "Just think what she could do for a partner within a storm of her own making."

Her companion twisted his fingers in the sign of erotic agreement. "We must be sure to teach her the basics of our art. She's delightfully virginal under all that strength."

Ma'eva leaned forward, his eyes wide with interest. The milis motioned him closer.

"Mili, don't you dare," Iuti said.

Ma'eva blinked. "I'm interested only for your sake, friend Iuti," he said. "You're always telling me not to be afraid to learn new things." The milis sent him a pair of airborne kisses. He grinned and sat back again, winking at Iuti and running his perfect fingertips across his naked thighs.

"Mano's teeth," Iuti muttered. She wondered if there was anything new the milis could teach the sea mimic. She swallowed back a laugh and turned her attention to the sea. Risak ran his fingers over the necklace of Kunan's hair that Iuti had given him, and remained silent.

Some hours later, at Tarawe's request, Risak cleared a small space near the outer edge of the deck and began drilling her in the proper handling of her sword. He showed her the best stance and movements to use with a blade of its size, picking up from the point at which he had left off teaching her inside the drummers' prison.

Risak claimed to be instructing her in self-defense, but Iuti recognized the sword's killing field he was helping Tarawe construct. As uncomfortable as it made Iuti feel, she could think of no fair reason to ask him to stop.

Shortly after dawn the next day, Tarawe was standing alone on her small piece of deck, turning and thrusting with her unsheathed blade. She stopped occasionally to study the curling air movements her swinging metal caused. The wind in the sails continued steady, so the others had little to do but watch. At times, they chanted to the rhythm of her swaying turns. One of the milis whistled a Lowtown tune that turned Tarawe's practice into a dance.

Iuti, too, was watching Tarawe when the first hint of danger reached her. Ho'ola stirred and sat up abruptly. At the same time, Iuti felt a slight disturbance under the canoe. There was a rise in the sea that had nothing to do with the natural pattern of sea swells and crossing currents.

Iuti was on her feet and shouting a warning an instant before the water's surface shattered.

A great, roaring beast burst from the sea just behind the outrigger deck. It was black and gray, green as mold, and foul with slime. It was lined with all the worst colors of darkness. Dead and dying seaweed dangled from its rotting surface, and its breath stank of decayed seaflesh. Its gaping mouth dripped foaming white teeth.

Tarawe had just lowered her sword and turned away from the place where the creature appeared, but at Iuti's shout, she spun back. She brought her weapon around and up, an inexpert move, off the true arc a swordsman of Risak's skill would have used, but with enough force to slice the blade at a ragged angle across the rearing monster's face. The thing jerked back, then threw itself forward again. Without hesitation, Tarawe pierced it to the heart.

Its death cry split the air as Iuti threw herself atop Tarawe. She knocked her to the deck and held her tightly, protecting her in the only way she could from the collapsing monster. Its enormous weight was sure to crush them and the canoe into the sea.

But in the last instant, the monster's death cry changed to the roar of falling water. The hammering weight that slammed onto Iuti's back tasted of nothing more than a cold, shattered wave.

The steersman shouted. The sail master replied. The sail slapped and snapped, loose in the wind. Then the canoe steadied as the sail was brought under control again. Conflicting orders and calls of concern rattled across the fleet until Ho'ola's sharp voice lifted over the rest.

"It's gone," she cried. "It was only water to begin with, and I've changed it back into its natural form. Here, let me through. You. Tie down that covering. Do you think I want my belongings spilled into the sea? Help me over this, Mapa."

Iuti fought to regain her breath. She remained firmly in place over Tarawe until the entire collapsed monster had drained away. Finally she met Tarawe's wide-eyed stare. "Are you all right?" she asked.

"What *was* that?" Tarawe replied.

"One of Pahulu's creatures. A wave monster she dredged up from the sea bottom to search for me."

"It felt like it was attacking *me*," Tarawe said. She

made no attempt to remove herself from Iuti's protection, even after Ho'ola had knelt at their side.

"It sought the storm caller," Ma'eva said. He was huddled between the milimilis, Iuti saw. The whores looked pale even through their paint. "Pahulu just thinks she's looking for Iuti Mano. That will change now."

"Perhaps not," Ola said. She motioned Iuti to untangle herself from Tarawe. "The dying wave tasted Iuti before it did the girl, and Iuti was holding the killing sword by that time."

Iuti looked down at the sword in her hand. It was true. She must have pulled it away from Tarawe as they fell, an action done without conscious thought. She dropped the blade quickly.

"At worst," Ola went on, "the message the water carries back to Pahulu will be confused. We can hope she'll base her conclusions on her expectations and continue to believe Iuti is the one she seeks."

Iuti looked down at Tarawe. "Are you hurt?" she asked again.

"I think I ripped my pants," Tarawe said.

The first wave monster was not the last, nor was it the largest, or the most fierce. But its appearance had given the fleet warning. Those that attacked later met readied sorcerers and warriors eager for battle. Extra lookouts were set, some to watch out for their own crew mates, others to scan the seas surrounding the neighboring vessels.

By Iuti's earlier order, each vessel carried its own sorcerer. None could match Ho'ola's skills, but all were knowledgeable in the ways of war. Knowing the nature of the beasts was enough to give the sorcerers power over them. As quickly as Pahulu's creatures broke the water's surface, spells were cast to revert them to their natural form. More than one crew was doused, however, when their sorcerer didn't complete the dispersal spell before the monster had lifted overhead.

As the day progressed, the steady wind became more difficult for Tarawe to maintain. For a time, it was enough simply to draw the fleet closer together so her sphere of influence would not have to be so large. But eventually she was forced to admit that she couldn't control all of the violent gusts that intruded upon their path. It became more and more obvious that the storm raging outside was being deliberately manipulated against them.

"This wind is very angry," Tarawe said. "It doesn't like being turned and torn this way."

"Aye," Ma'eva agreed. "There is great upset in the sea, as well. I must go back to my kinfolk and do what I can to help them." He touched Iuti's knee, flicked a coy look at the milis, and slid back into the water. His dark form flickered the instant he touched the surface, and a flash of silver fled into the deep.

Ho'ola spent most of her time awake now, talking softly to Tarawe and occasionally arguing with her. The healer's exhaustion was beginning to show, and she turned frequently to the ever-attendant Mapa for a renewal of the seasickness charm.

"Remember," Iuti heard Ola say, "to control the winds of your original storm, you'll have to resay Pahulu's chant. If she can find you in time, that will give her direct access to your soul. Don't push me away when I come to your aid."

Tarawe didn't like that—Iuti could see it in her eyes. The girl didn't want to believe that Ho'ola was still protecting her from death's icy thrusts.

"She's as pigheaded a student as you always were," Ola muttered as she passed Iuti on her way back to the sleeping hut.

They passed the first of the easternmost atolls at noon, and at each of the following islands they passed during the long day, a small cadre of warriors was sent ashore to help the islanders hold their land against possible Teronin invasion.

As the afternoon wore on, the weather worsened. Tarawe became more and more distracted, and the other two wind callers were hard put to hold the wind steady on their course. When an unexpected, and uncontrollable, whirlwind snapped one of the canoe's masts, Iuti ordered all the sails furled. Paddles were slipped into the sea, and the precarious island of calm echoed with the steady travel chant of battle-ready warriors.

Ho'ola grew increasingly uncomfortable and retired with Mapa to the privacy of her hut. To Iuti's surprise, the milimilis seemed perfectly comfortable on the canoe despite the rougher seas, and their occasional forays into the hull to serve food and drink invariably resulted in a return to good cheer among the crew.

"They are a useful pair," Risak said, "even if a bit unlikely." Iuti smiled at the milis' antics and agreed. She was glad Ma'eva had returned to the sea.

At dusk, there came a time of near calm. Outside, the storm still raged, but within Tarawe's shield, the brisk northwest wind ran steady again. The paddlers called for a return to the sails, but Iuti signaled the sail masters to leave them furled. The sudden diminishment of Pahulu's attack disturbed her.

"We must be almost as near Fanape as the Teronin," she said. "Pahulu's attention is most likely split between calming the storm for her own fleet and making it worse for ours. We can't count on that lasting."

Suddenly Tarawe tensed. She unsheathed her blade and stood staring to the north.

"What is it?" Iuti asked. She could see nothing but the darkening sky and the storm outside.

Tarawe pointed. "It's there. My storm's heart. I can feel—" She winced and blinked. A shudder slid across her body.

"Ola!" Iuti called, but the healer was already clambering over the secured supply bundles to reach Tarawe's side.

"She shouldn't be doing that," Tarawe said. "She shouldn't be using my storm that way." She caught her breath and would have fallen if Iuti hadn't been there to catch her. Again a visible shudder of revulsion moved across her skin. Iuti felt it pass beneath her hands.

"She's using my wind to kill the dolphins!" Tarawe wailed.

"Let me help," Ola called softly. "Tarawe, let me take—"

"No!" Tarawe pushed her away. Suddenly she went rigid. Her eyes filled with pain, then, just as abruptly, flashed with rage. "Stop it!"

Iuti tried to hold her, but Tarawe pushed even her away. She shifted her sword to her left hand. "Get away from my wind! Get away from my storm!"

Tarawe's voice cracked across the rising wind. It was sharp and fury-filled. The sword sang as she swung it up. It flashed as lightning streaked the sky.

"Tarawe, no! Wait!" Iuti shouted. She could feel Ho'ola trying to pass the girl's guard, to stop her from responding to Pahulu's distant, blind attack.

"Tarawe, let me block—"

In her unreasoning fury, Tarawe interpreted Ola's attempts to help as an additional threat. She called out the shielding spell Iuti had taught her on the river. Not the exact spell—there were words included that Iuti didn't know—but it must have been close enough, because a glimmering mist began forming around her. Iuti forced her way inside to stop the shield from closing completely.

"These are my waters and my people!" Tarawe cried. "This is my wind and *my storm*! Take your evil stench away!" She cupped her right hand and lifted it high.

"No, Tarawe!" Iuti cried.

The wind howled as Tarawe began chanting Pahulu's song.

Chapter 18

As quickly as Iuti recognized the shielding spell Tarawe was attempting, she whispered a counterspell of her own. It allowed her to reach Tarawe physically, but even with Ola's help, she couldn't penetrate the solid wall of defense Tarawe dropped around her mind.

It took Iuti's full strength to pull Tarawe's cupped hand away from the sky. Ola stopped Pahulu's chant by stuffing a corner of her ever-present pillow into Tarawe's mouth.

"Stop it, Tarawe! Stop! You can only hurt yourself by attacking Pahulu from here," Iuti shouted across the screaming wind. Tarawe didn't hear, or paid no attention if she did. She struggled and fought with a strength far beyond her size and training.

The waves and the wind fought along with her. They twisted and swirled with her every move, and had the sail not been furled they would surely have capsized. As it was, the canoe shuddered at the pounding. The air and the water screamed with Tarawe's fury.

Tarawe spat out the pillow and screamed a curse. Before she could begin Pahulu's chant again, Iuti pressed a hand across her open mouth. Tarawe bit down hard, locking her teeth into Iuti's palm.

"The sword!" Iuti shouted.

Tarawe shook her head, ripping at Iuti's flesh.

Like Mano! Iuti thought.

"Risak, take her sword!"

It was like wrestling a gut-spitted shark. Again, the thought came unbidden. Iuti thrust it away. Tarawe

184

writhed and twisted and tried to tear herself free. With only one hand, Iuti could do no more than wrestle with her on the heaving deck. Over the shouts of the paddlers and the din of the storm, she heard the rasp of metal swords slipping free of their sheaths.

In a move only a master swordsman would have dared, Risak raked one of his blades along the edge of Tarawe's flailing weapon until the hilts locked. He thrust his second sword into the center of the melee and, with a quick twist, cracked the flat of its blade across Tarawe's clenched knuckles. Her sword flew free.

Instantly the fight ended. Tarawe collapsed under Iuti's hands. A shudder deeper than all those before racked her body. She coughed and gagged and caught at her breath. "Oh, Ser Iuti," she cried when she saw Iuti's torn hand. "I didn't mean to hurt you!"

"You'll hurt us all if you don't stop this new storm you've created," Iuti called. She wished she could be gentle, but the canoe was about to be lost. Already there were paddlers overboard, and she could feel by the twist of the deck that more than one outrigger lashing had come loose. The whole thing would break apart soon.

Tarawe blinked and stared around. Splintering wood shrieked and a cry of warning sounded as the high, decorative prow was torn away by a slamming wave.

"Stop the wind, Tarawe," Iuti cried. Ola was still trying to penetrate the solid seal that protected Tarawe's mind. She muttered and whispered, close to the girl's side, but her chanting was continually interrupted by wracking dry heaves.

Tarawe glanced toward her sword.

"No!" Iuti insisted. "You don't need the sword. Do it with your hands just like you've been doing all along. Stop the wind, Tarawe. Seal the rent that's been made in our protection before Pahulu finds her way inside."

Tarawe began to cry. Iuti started to shake her, but then saw that she had cupped her hands and was lifting them slowly. Tarawe sang a simple dispersal chant, the

one Ho'ola had taught her, while her tears dripped one
by one into her palms. Her lower lip trembled.

She glanced once again at the fallen sword, then
squeezed her eyes shut. She closed both fists and turned
her hands down. When her fingers opened, the sea and
the wind calmed, as quickly but much more smoothly
than they had at the Veke river mouth. A flutter of trembling fingers reset the isle of protection around the fleet,
and a lift of Tarawe's chin restored the wind, directly
on to Fanape.

Then Iuti treated her with tenderness. She licked the
fingers of her injured hand and slid them across Tarawe's tear-stained cheeks. Carefully she chanted a release spell for the mind shield Tarawe had set. She was
stopped by oddities in Tarawe's unpracticed use of the
warding spell, and by the changes the girl had made in
her panicked attempt to lock it from the inside. The
shield still withstood Iuti's attempts to enter, but it was
clearly not stopping the horror Tarawe had set it against.
Her face was contorted with pain.

"Help me, Ola," Iuti said.

Ola recovered long enough to rub a sweet-smelling
oil under Tarawe's nose. She muttered a charm, and
Tarawe's eyelids began to droop. Only after she was
deeply asleep did the invisible shield gave way. Tarawe's expression registered pain even after Ho'ola established a shield of her own around them both.

"Pahulu is using Tarawe's storm to kill again,"
Ho'ola said. "I sensed no direct attack against the girl.
That shield she set didn't stop the death thrusts, it only
stopped me from absorbing them for her. She'll kill herself if she does that when we face Pahulu directly. Her
mind is so raw now, it's a wonder she can make any of
her magic work. You must convince her of that, Iuti.
She won't listen to—"

Ola stiffened and looked up. She lifted one hand as
if to ward herself from a blow, then cupped the hand
around empty air and threw it toward the sea. Tarawe
twitched, then lay still. Ho'ola retched over the side of
the canoe.

Iuti nodded to Mapa. "Help her as best you can," she said. Mapa slid the pillow under Ola's knees and murmured the seasick charm once more. He stroked the sea-soaked hair from his mistress's ashen face.

The fallen paddlers had already been pulled from the sea. They and the others were hurriedly retying the loosened lashings and restowing tangled gear. Iuti glanced once more at Tarawe and ordered the sails lifted. The need for speed was now as great as the need for caution.

Finally she looked down at her right hand. Tarawe's teeth had left deep punctures in the center of her palm. On one side, a ragged strip of flesh had been torn away. My primary sword hand, she thought. I am blooded before I even reach Fanape.

The marks reminded her again of Mano. She searched the recesses of her mind but found no sign of the shark who had once shivered with pleasure at a battle just fought. She found only remembered pain and struggle, and images of the frenzied Tarawe and her sword.

No, Iuti thought. That is *not* Tarawe's sword. I selected the steel from which that blade was made. I spoke to it first when it came from the flames. I gave it its first taste of human blood. That sword is mine!

She stared at the blade. It looked harmless now, lying cold and alone on the debris-strewn deck. It was clearly a weapon involved in a war Iuti didn't understand. It had *wanted* Tarawe to draw Pahulu to the canoe. Iuti knew that without knowing how she knew. You are mine, she said to it silently, but I cannot bear to touch you!

"Risak," she said, "will you . . ."

"Shall I drop it overboard?" Risak asked.

Yes! she wanted to cry. She shook her head no. Without knowing how Tarawe and the sword were bound, she dared not destroy it. But she would be damned if she would let the girl touch it again.

Risak grunted. He removed the sheath from Tarawe's back and scooped up the sword without touching the blade. He wrapped it in a blanket and tied it into the bundle of his personal belongings.

Someone touched Iuti's arm. "Come away from the girl for a time," the male mili said. "The healer is with her. She's safe enough now."

His partner's soft, scented fingers cradled Iuti's injured hand. "Come. Let us help you with this, Ser. The others can clear away the mess."

Iuti cursed the gods who would give her such an injury just hours before she was to meet Pahulu and the Teronin. Then she blessed them for the unexpected gift of the milis' ministering hands. When the wound was cleaned and bandaged as best it could be, she set as strong a healing spell as she dared so near the enemy's stand.

More than half the night was gone by the time they reached Fanape. The island itself was a circle of semi-calm in the midst of the raging storm, a carefully constructed refuge for Pahulu and her adopted army. Iuti ordered the fleet to a halt just outside the breaking surf that edged the outer reef.

The canoes carrying the various war chiefs had just gathered near Iuti's vessel when a loud, screeching cry drew their startled looks upward. A ragged, storm-torn gull burst through the protective wall and tumbled helplessly toward them. It struggled to spread its wide wings, but only one worked properly. The other was bent in the middle and its tip dangled loosely.

The bird cried out again just as it was about to strike the water. Tarawe shifted in her sleep, and a sudden updraft lifted the gull high and near enough for Risak to reach out and catch it. He laid it carefully on the deck and motioned to Iuti. She joined him quickly.

The gull was the one Ma'eva had used. "Is he in there?" Risak asked.

"Surely not," she said, but stopped as Ma'eva's face began pulling away from the bird's. The southern warriors murmured in concern. None had ever seen a sea

mimic emerge from an air creature before. That the bird
was left behind when the change was complete seemed
to disturb them more than the change itself.

Ma'eva's first move when the separation was complete
was toward the water. Iuti assumed he was going back
to his own element, but he only hung his head over the
side and emptied his stomach. She was glad Ho'ola was
asleep beside Tarawe. Pahulu's attacks had ceased for a
time, and the healer was taking what rest she could.

"The others are here," Ma'eva said as soon as he was
able. "They came this afternoon in many, many canoes.
They are hiding on the island."

A chorus of southern curses sounded across the gathered canoes.

"Ma'eva," Iuti said. "Why did you come like this?
In the bird? Why didn't you come by sea?"

"I tried. All the seafolk have tried to enter this place
of refuge, but we can't get in. Only the birds are able to
break through the wind, so I—"

He turned suddenly, back to the gull. "Ayiii," he
cried. "You're hurt. You're injured. Oh, you stupid bird.
You shouldn't have let me kill you." He cradled the limp
gull in his arms. "I didn't mean to kill you."

"The gull isn't dead," Risak said. "Her wing is broken. In two places, I think. She'll need time to grow a
new set of feathers, but she'll survive." He met Iuti's
look. "If any of us do."

"I'll bet the girl set the shield so the wave monsters
couldn't attack us anymore," one of the milis said.

"We were just commenting on their disappearance,"
added the second.

It was true. There hadn't been a single sighting of Pahulu's watery creatures since Tarawe had redrawn her
protection around the fleet. Iuti had been sunk so deep
in her healing spell she hadn't even noticed.

"I wonder why she didn't do that earlier," Risak
mused.

Iuti glanced at Tarawe. "Probably because she didn't
know how until after she tried to shield herself from Pa-

hulu this afternoon. She used a warding spell like the one surrounding the fleet, but then tried to seal it from the inside with the locking spell I taught her this morning, along with some other things I don't yet understand. She probably learned something new in the doing.''

"It's a good thing she did it," Ma'eva said. Panic returned to his eyes. "Pahulu is sweeping the sea for all living creatures. She's using some to search for you and hoarding others to kill whenever she needs more power. Didn't you hear the flying dolphins scream today? Pahulu forced them to drive a school of their smaller cousins directly into the whirlpool at the storm's center.''

"By the gods," Iuti breathed. That must be what Tarawe had felt, the reason she had attacked Pahulu so suddenly and blindly. For one attuned to the sea, the death of one of the magical dolphins could cause far greater pain than the death of a simple human.

"The dolphins were torn into shreds while herding their own kin to their deaths," Ma'eva said, "so their souls were lost along with their bodies. And it hasn't ended. Pahulu knows you're here, Iuti Mano, and she knows now that she can anger you by using the storm to kill. She's trying to draw you outside this place." He looked up and around.

"What about the Teronin?" one of the war chiefs called out.

"They're all on the island," Ma'eva replied. "That big canoe is there, too. The one with the carvings and paint. They carried the whole thing to the island's center. Those strange, noisy humans were crawling all over it until it grew dark. Now they're hiding inside. The seafolk don't like their pounding.''

"We don't like it either," the war chief said. "We must surround the island and attack from all sides as soon as it's light.''

Ma'eva shook his head. "You'll never get across the reef. It's too shallow for these big canoes.''

The southerner laughed. "We don't need canoes to cross a reef. These warriors can run at full speed across the most treacherous of coral.''

"The coral is not the danger, human," the sea mimic said.

Ma'eva turned to Iuti. "Mano Niuhi himself guards that reef, friend Iuti. Not even Pahulu dares to step into the water. The reason she killed the dolphins was to gain enough strength to guard the Teronin while they came ashore. Even so, many were lost to Mano and his cousins. Half of them at least, but the sharks are still hungry. They call your name."

A murmur of concern sounded among the gathered warriors.

Iuti stared out toward the island. Lightning streaked the sky with garish colors and lit the islet with an evil grccn glow. The fringing reef lay black and deadly beyond the storm-torn surf. Iuti leaned overboard to touch the sea. She licked her salt-wetted fingers.

"I am here, brother," she muttered into her hand. She pictured Mano sliding sinuously through the bloodied waters. "We will settle our differences once and for all, here in this place. I promise you that. But first I will deal with Pahulu and the demon drummers. I will not leave *them* as my legacy."

"Ser?" It was Risak. He brushed her arm lightly.

Iuti washed her hand in the sea, then straightened. "We must attack immediately," she said.

"But the sharks . . ." one chieftain began.

"She's kin to the sharks," another said. "They're no danger to *us*."

"Wouldn't it be better to wait until dawn when we can see . . ." said yet another.

"If we wait until dawn, we'll be dead before we leave our canoes," Risak said. "The sharks will be no more than play toys compared to the drummers once they've welcomed the sun."

"Go back into the water, friend Ma'eva," Iuti said. "You've done all that can be done here. Call all of the seafolk who travel with us now to the outermost edge of the shield. When it opens, swim swiftly to the open sea."

"I would fight on the land with you if I could," Ma'eva said.

She touched his perfect cheek, tracked now with dry-ing tears. "I know. But you must not. Go now, so I'll know you're safe." She brushed her fingertips across his lips, then turned quickly away so he wouldn't see her fear for him in her eyes. She listened to his polite farewells to Risak and the others, to his last whispered blessing for the bird, and then to his laughter, and that of the crew, as he dove back into the sea.

The milimilis, she thought, and smiled. They couldn't let him go without making him laugh one more time.

Iuti motioned for Risak to join her and crossed to where Ho'ola and Tarawe lay. "Wake Ola," she told the ever-vigilant Mapa. "Tell her to take away the bird's pain, then to join us."

She woke Tarawe herself. She washed the sleep potion from Tarawe's face, then brushed the fingers of her in-jured hand across the girl's cheek. "We need you," she said when Tarawe's eyes opened.

Tarawe met Iuti's look. Remembrance and fear im-mediately touched her eyes. She sat up quickly. "What happened?" she asked. She rubbed a hand over her eyes. It did nothing to wipe away the exhaustion written there. She glanced around at the closely gathered canoes. Then her eyes swept the deck. Looking for that damnable weapon, Iuti thought. She was glad the sword was well hidden.

"We've reached Fanape," she said.

Tarawe's look turned abruptly toward the island. An occasional flicker of light showed, far inland. That would be the drummers staying well inside their firelit drum house. The girl shivered.

Iuti explained what Pahulu had done to the dolphins, and what the sorceress was still doing to the seafolk on and around the reef. "No," she said when Tarawe stiff-ened. "Save your anger. Striking out blindly will only harm those creatures more, and us, as well. I need for you to be calm now, Tarawe, as calm as you were the night we met the demon drummers. Can you do that? There is a greater danger that we must face."

Tarawe's eyes widened.

"Mano guards the reef," Iuti said.

Tarawe caught her breath.

"He has already destroyed half the Teronin army. The southerners think he won't attack us because he and I are kin, but that isn't so."

"He didn't kill you before," Tarawe said. "That night when we left. Maybe . . ."

"I don't know why he spared me then," Iuti said. "Of all the things that have happened, that is the one that makes least sense. But I know Mano won't spare me or any of us tonight. I have tasted his challenge in the sea."

"What can we do?" Tarawe asked.

Again Iuti glanced around, this time at the gathered fleet. The warriors had already begun their battle preparations. Some chanted in supplication to their gods. Others turned their looks inward, seeking the solace of inner silence. More than one had pulled a paint pot and feathered headdress from the stowed gear.

The milimilis mimicked the warriors. They wrapped themselves in brightly colored sashes and ribbons, items entirely unsuited to battle. They freshened the paint on each other's faces and used handsful of pins to fasten their hair into tightly curled masses. The warriors' concern about the sharks receded as they laughed at the whores' foolishness. They really are a gift from the gods, Iuti thought.

Only Risak and the chieftains kept their fixed attention on Iuti, awaiting her instructions for how to get their army ashore. Only Risak was within hearing of her voice.

Iuti glanced up as Ho'ola joined them. "Auntie," she said quietly. "About Mano . . ."

Ola lifted a hand in dismissal. "I know. You and he have parted company. I've known since you first stepped into my house. I could see it in your eyes, and read it in the scars on your cheek. How do you intend to get us past the brute?"

Iuti smiled at Ola's unfailing faith. "You exhibit remarkable trust in me, Auntie."

"Hmmph. Trust has nothing to do with it. I just want to get off this damn canoe."

"My shield can keep the sharks out," Tarawe said. "It's keeping them out now."

"Once we cross the outer edge of the reef, we can't use the shield," Iuti said. Ho'ola nodded her agreement, and Iuti explained, "Pahulu is an island-born witch. She might be able to lock us inside if we take it too close."

"I thought you could break that locking spell," Tarawe said.

"We couldn't even release the small shield you set this afternoon until after Ho'ola put you to sleep," Iuti said. "I doubt Pahulu will be so obliging as to nap during the battle for our benefit."

"That's what comes of mixing your magic," Ola added. Tarawe frowned but didn't look convinced.

"It's possible the changes you've made in the shielding spell would prevent Pahulu from trapping us inside it," Iuti said, "but we can't take that chance." She ran her hand, her injured hand, over her scarred cheek. She stared at her bandaged palm. "You and I are going to have to sing our way ashore."

"Sing!"

Iuti laid a finger on her lips. "We mustn't let the others know. They think they're safe from the sharks because of my kinship with Mano. If they learn of the true danger they face, the smell of their fear alone will be enough to draw Mano to them."

"Tarawe's *voice* will alert him to what you're doing," said Ola. "*She* can't sing the sharks' song."

Tarawe muttered something and settled into that quiet calm she had used with the drummers. Her eyes were bright with interest. Oh, you'd like that, wouldn't you, youngster? Iuti said silently. You'd like to learn how to call the masters of the sea.

"I'll take care of singing the sharks," Iuti said aloud. "I'll call them toward us and away from the rest of the fleet. Tarawe, your job will be to sing the water into a whirlpool around us, strong enough so the sharks can't break through. Do you think you can do that, Tarawe?"

Tarawe looked at her hands. The wind around them began circling slowly.

"Not the wind," Iuti said. "Just the water. You mustn't touch the wind until we're well inland. Pahulu will recognize you as the storm caller the instant you do, and we can't defend against her and the sharks at the same time."

Tarawe turned her left index finger in a circle. A small, swift vortex formed beside the canoe. She met Iuti's look again and grinned.

"The wind will carry the taste of Tarawe's spinning water to Pahulu," Ola said. "It will take a little longer, but not long enough to see us safely across the reef."

"What Pahulu will taste is the family of Mano," Iuti said. "She'll still think it's me, and any attack she makes will be weakened because I'm not the one she seeks. She'll still be fighting me blind, and I can withstand that for long enough to get us ashore."

She turned to Tarawe. "Do you remember when you were injured in the drummer's den?" she asked. "When I mixed our blood together before setting that healing spell on you?"

Tarawe nodded.

"Iuti Mano, you didn't!" Ho'ola exclaimed.

Iuti frowned her to silence. "I had no choice, Auntie. I'm a warrior, not a healer. I had no time to study her wound. I knew only that it was deep and dangerous. The taste of my blood is the least of our family's secrets I've given away during these last months. Be glad the deed is one that can serve us now."

Tarawe calmed her tiny whirlpool with a flick of her fingers. Her eyes were wide with curiosity again.

"That spell is a strong one," Iuti told her. "But it works only on women of my family line. By mixing the blood we'd both spilled in battle, I made you my kinsister."

Tarawe blinked. When her eyes opened again, a touch of fear showed there.

Iuti smiled. "I didn't turn you into a shark-woman, Tarawe. I only made you kin enough for the spell to work, and enough so that your taste might still fool Pahulu. It won't when you touch the wind, for that's her strongest element, but it might with the water. Will you try?''

Tarawe swallowed hard and nodded. Suddenly she stiffened. Ho'ola cursed and reached up to snatch at empty air. She threw whatever invisible thing she had caught overboard. The water rippled, then was still.

''Pahulu's started killing again,'' she said. ''I can help if you'll let me, Tarawe, but you have to leave your mind open to my touch. If you seal it like you did before, you're going to feel the stab of every death thrust your storm causes in the coming battle. There will be many, because Pahulu knows she can reach you that way. You would never survive it.''

Tarawe eyed her for a moment, glanced at the injured gull, then nodded again. Ola laid a hand on Tarawe's shoulder, and pain that Iuti hadn't realized was there disappeared from the girl's eyes.

Ola met Iuti's look. ''I'll have to be with her when you cross the reef. If it was calm I might be able to help her from the canoe, but this damnable seasickness . . .'' She shrugged.

''We three will go,'' Iuti said. She glanced up at Risak. He nodded his inclusion, as she had known he would. ''And Risak.''

''And Mapa,'' Ola said.

Iuti sighed and slid a cool look toward the milis. Would they insist on joining her for this part of the journey, as well? They waved and winked and, although Iuti was sure they couldn't have overheard, signaled that they intended staying at her side. She shook her head in wonder at their unaccountable loyalty, and scratched at her healing hand.

''Risak,'' she said. ''Call the other wind callers, and the sorcerers, as well. They'll need to know our plan. If they work together, they can confuse the winds around the fleet enough to keep Pahulu's attention at least partially turned that way while we cross the reef in separate places. Once the danger of the sharks is past, the battle can be fought on more equal terms.''

"Until the drummers wake," Risak said.

Iuti stared toward the island. "Aye, until the drummers wake. Come, let's even the odds before they do."

❧ Chapter 19 ❧

TARAWE stretched her protective shield as far as she could around the curve of Fanape's reef. A wave monster dashed itself against the invisible shield and collapsed. A whirlpool formed and sucked the monster away, re-formed it, and threw it back again with even greater force. The beast shattered on the unyielding wall.

More of the water beasts appeared and attacked. Ragged wind and thundering rain tore at the surrounding sea. Funnels of water lifted from the surface and wormed across the lightning-lit sky as Pahulu made one last effort to disable the southern fleet while it was still at sea. For her own safety and that of her Teronin lackeys, she dared not allow the full force of the storm to wash ashore, swamping the low-lying island as it had so many others.

When Iuti's canoe had reached the most distant point from the others, she motioned to Tarawe and the girl lifted all the southern vessels on great ocean swells, carrying them across the lip of the reef and onto the coral. They could hear Pahulu's fury in the wind, but they knew now that the storm could not prevent them from getting ashore.

As quickly as they were carried into the shallow water of the reef flat, Iuti and Tarawe leapt overboard into waist-deep water. Risak followed, then Ho'ola in Mapa's strong arms, and against Iuti's better judgment, the milimilis. Two southern paddlers stayed on the canoe to protect it as best they could from the storm that would strike as soon as Tarawe removed the protective shield.

The instant Iuti's feet touched the water, she started calling the sharks. "Come," she sang in the secret language of her family. "Come to your sister here in the cold sea."

Tarawe turned in a quick circle, leading the water in a tight spiral around them.

"Come to me, brothers," Iuti sang. "Share greetings with your kin." She and her companions edged forward across the sharp coral, being careful not to cut themselves and bloody the water. There was no use antagonizing the sharks any more than they had to.

"Come."

The water rippled all across the reef. A splash and many small, sudden movements in the storm-tossed shallows revealed that the sharks had heard Iuti's call. She sang the words again, and then again. It was a simple beckoning spell, designed to entice the sharks to her side. The ripples began to converge on the place where she and the others were standing.

"Drop the shield now," Ho'ola said with a quick touch to Tarawe's shoulder. Tarawe flicked her right hand. The air shimmered for an instant. Then they were struck by the full force of the storm and the bitter taste of Pahulu's rage. The wind shrieked across the water, dousing them with sea spray. It ripped at their clothing and hair.

Tarawe's whirlpool spun faster. Water was sucked away from their feet, leaving the coral bare in places, knee-deep in others. The dark, heavy presence of the sharks drew closer.

Across the reef, barely visible through the blinding rain, Iuti saw the southern army leap from the safety of their canoes.

The sharks hesitated at the vibrations of so many booted and sandaled feet splashing across the reef. Some turned back that way. But Iuti sang the beckoning spell once again, and her kinfolk turned their attention back to her call.

Iuti could smell Tarawe's fear. She could taste her own as Mano and the cousins swept toward them. She brushed her right hand across the ring of Kunan's hair that circled her neck. She had rolled her own hair back into a warrior's knot atop her head, and its heavy, solid weight made her feel like she was whole again.

Mano circled only once before turning directly for Iuti. She braced herself and saw Risak do the same, but the great shark swerved aside as he struck Tarawe's racing waters. Across the reef, the warriors splashed nearer and nearer to shore. The wind screamed and tore at them. It ripped at the water's surface, tearing it into icy spray. Even Risak had difficulty balancing against the powerful gusts. Iuti ducked away from a wavering, searching streamer of black.

"Come, brother!" she sang, forcing herself to continue moving forward slowly. She wanted to run with every bit of speed her legs could provide. "Come with your cousins to my side. Let us swim together on this fine stormy night."

Mano circled. He circled again. Around and around he swam, unable even with great thrusts of his powerful tail to break through their protective maelstrom. The small cousins mimicked Mano Niuhi's fury, providing him a frenzied wake.

Tarawe was pale, but she moved steadily forward with the help of the milis' surprisingly sure hands. An eel wormed from its hole and snatched at Iuti's heel. Pahulu had discovered their small group and set the reef creatures against them. Risak sliced the eel's head away, then stumbled as a giant clam shell snapped closed just a finger's breadth from his own foot. Iuti steadied him, before ducking again to avoid Pahulu's dark seekers writhing through the winds.

A southern battle cry echoed across the reef, announcing that the first of the fleet had reached the Fanape shore. Mano dashed himself against the spinning waters, enraged because he now understood what she had done, yet was unable to stop either her or her song.

Iuti continued singing until she was as certain as she could be through the heavy curtain of the storm that the last of the southerners had left the water. Then she grew silent and motioned the others forward more quickly.

Despite Iuti's silence, Mano circled and circled until the water was so shallow that he was forced to twist his great body off the coral and turn away. Many of the smaller cousins followed Iuti all the way to the shore; some even threw themselves onto the dry sand in their frenzied attempts to reach her.

Because of the thrashing sharks, the Teronin who had noticed Iuti's small group and run to meet them held back. Risak's swords flashed as he and Iuti dashed across the sand, and it was only an instant before Mano's club once again tasted Teronin blood. As planned, a squad of southerners quickly joined them to provide added protection for the storm caller and Ho'ola. They brought the other wind callers, as well, so that Tarawe's identity could be kept secret as long as possible.

The wind shrieked and moaned. As they moved into the trees, coconuts and wind-torn fronds swept in among them, striking southerner and Teronin alike. The wind callers did the best they could to deflect the deadly missiles from their own troops, but they glanced more and more hopefully at Tarawe. The girl kept to her word, however, to get as far inland as she could before lifting her own hand to the wind.

She carried a Teronin sword, one of Risak's three. Iuti had forbidden her to bring her own blade ashore. Tarawe fought cautiously, striking only when she had to protect herself or Ho'ola and Mapa. She made no effort to land killing blows.

She will never be the warrior she once aspired to be, Iuti thought. A man ran at her, his eyes wide with hatred. Iuti knocked him aside. She will never be able to harden her heart to this kind of killing.

Iuti slashed and battered her way through the Teronin line. Nor will I be the warrior I once was, she thought as she settled into her battle rhythm. She still moved with strength and precision. She could detect no diminishment of her purely physical skill in this first true battle without Mano's aid. Still, something had changed.

She swung her shield down to block a swinging blade, then up again quickly to put the Teronin sword she carried in her left hand to use. A slice of ice dug deeply into her soul while a stab of pain shot through her injured palm.

She turned toward a glint of metal, but Risak was already there, disarming and impaling the attacker without seeming to move. The man was not a true Teronin, Iuti saw. He was one of Pahulu's soul-dead recruits. His strangely pale eyes had been dead long before Risak's blade took his life.

The Teronin were forced farther and farther back. The heavy end of a coconut frond struck Iuti's shoulder, spoiling her rhythm. A Teronin sword slid into the gap and scraped like fire coral across her right thigh. She spat a swift pain spell, something she had rarely had to do when Mano fought with her, and shoved the Teronin from her path.

I feel it! she thought as she reestablished her rhythm. Without Mano I feel it all! The pain, the wrenching stretch of overextended muscles, the jarring blows of steel on steel—the shock of peering into the eyes of a man she was about to kill. And the icy touch of death.

A warrior too young to be holding a copra knife, much less a Teronin sword, threw himself at her. She struck him with the base of Mano's club, disabling him but leaving him alive. She could not remember how long it had been since she had offered such mercy. How could I have become so immune to the horror? she thought.

Iuti could feel Pahulu searching with the wind. She would be glad when she could face the sorceress directly and be done with this battle one way or the other. She glanced back. Ho'ola was walking now, one hand closed around Tarawe's right wrist. Tarawe's face was tight with pain. Mapa hovered over them both, while the milis fluttered around all three.

A Teronin warrior ran at one of the milis. He tripped and fell and did not move again. Those whores carry the luck of the gods, Iuti thought as the mili smiled and patted his carefully coiled hair before moving on.

Again Iuti's instant of inattention allowed a Teronin too near. A sword tip touched her shoulder.

"Mano's teeth!" she muttered, then cursed again in the Teronin's own tongue for her continued, unthinking dependence on the shark's vigilance. "I fight alone!" she screamed, and her voice pushed back the startled enemy almost as effectively as her sword.

Suddenly they broke through the Teronin line. "To Pahulu!" Iuti shouted. They ran along the narrow path leading to the village center. Wind slammed and spun through the trees, tearing at their clothing and hair. Iuti's tunic came loose at the waist. Her hair was suddenly torn from its knot.

"You have found me, witch!" Iuti called as the long, white strands tumbled and tangled around her face. She signaled Risak to move back, to stay behind her with the others. She would have preferred he return to the shoreline battle, or better yet to the distant canoes, but she knew he wouldn't leave.

"Do you fear for my safety or your own?" he asked without breaking stride.

"Both!" she returned. He would know any other answer was a lie. They both knew that if the drummers entered this battle before Pahulu was taken, Risak might well become more an enemy than an ally. As might I, Iuti thought.

Risak surprised her by grinning. His teeth glinted white in the storm-lit jungle. "Then it's best I stay where you can see me," he said. His voice dropped to a whisper. "Hold! There! Beyond the ragroot tree."

Iuti peered in the direction of his pointing sword.

"The large shadow," he said. "The green tinge."

"I see it. Ho'ola?"

Mapa quickly stepped off the path and pulled a handful of powderberries from a nearby bush. He tossed them toward the green glow while Ho'ola said a word. They watched as the berries continued uninterrupted in their flight. They landed with silent dusty puffs at the foot of the shadow.

"Illusion," Ola said. "An air construct set here to help Pahulu watch the path. She must be distracted, though. Otherwise, the thing would have moved by now. Come on, let's get by before she thinks to use its eyes again."

Risak hesitated when he came to a fork in the path.

"The village," Iuti said, pointing left. She had followed him only a few paces before Tarawe called out.

"She's this way, Ser." The girl was pointing down the lesser-used path.

"Of course," Iuti murmured. Pahulu would defend her power from the place most dangerous to Iuti Mano—the house where Iuti had lived during her brief stay on the island. The sorceress would have surrounded herself from the beginning with Iuti's belongings, using them to focus her evil intent on the one she believed to be her worst enemy.

Iuti motioned Risak back. He didn't even try to hide his relief that the battle against Pahulu would be fought outside the drummers' sight.

As they ran toward the small clearing, the wind found them again. This time it stuttered and stopped, then slammed with fury again. Pahulu had recognized Iuti's taste at last. Banana trees were ripped from the ground. Coconuts and half-ripe breadfruit flew through the air like stones. The southern wind callers set a counterwind swirling around their small group, much as Tarawe had done with the water earlier. It stopped some, but not all, of the flying debris. Mapa swept a spinning mass of rotting leaves from Ho'ola's path.

A sharp crack and the tearing cry of splintering wood sounded from ahead. "Look out!" Iuti shouted. A giant breadfruit tree toppled slowly toward them. It creaked and groaned as its wide, shallow roots were ripped from the ground. Suddenly the tree rushed down at them, like one of Pahulu's collapsed water monsters on the cold, dark sea.

Iuti reached for Tarawe, but one of the milis was between them. When it was clear they could not reach safety before the tree reached them, the mili threw herself atop Tarawe, offering the girl the scant protection of her own body.

Behind them, one of the wind callers screamed as the foremost branch smashed into his upraised arms. He, too, had taken one last chance to protect the girl. The crack of breaking bones was as loud as that of the breaking branches. Iuti threw herself flat.

Once again she was left waiting for Pahulu's crushing evil to strike, and once again it did not. Pieces of the tree fell. Small branches, torn leaves, and thick, pasty fruit crashed all around her, but the tree itself did not fall. With a great wrenching groan, it halted in its death plunge and hovered just a hand-span above them. Wind, like a solid block of stone, held it aloft.

"Go!"

It was Tarawe's voice, a mere whisper above the groaning tree. She had pulled herself free of the mili and rolled onto her back. She held her right hand raised. The wind sucked past her and up, pressing against the tree. Her hand was cupping slowly, trembling with the same cadence as the trembling leaves.

"Go," she said again. "Hurry!" She crawled slowly backward, the mili still protectively at her side, while the others scrambled free. As soon as the injured wind caller was pulled to safety, Tarawe closed her hand and the sucking wind stopped.

The tree crashed to the ground.

For an instant there was silence, broken only by the snap and crackling of branches being crushed under their own weight. Then the storm winds swirled around them again. Both fury and triumph sounded in their breathless cry. "I have found you, Storm Caller! You will not escape me again. Now you are mine!"

Again, the wind callers tried to protect Tarawe by ex-

erting their own small influence over Pahulu's winds, trying to confuse the sorceress once again. A sudden funnel
of wind swept the injured wind caller from his feet. He
was lifted into the air, his broken arms dangling. His
scream was sharp and shrill as he was battered first one
way, then the other by the whirling wind.

"No!" Tarawe cried, and moved to stop the maelstrom. But it was too late. The wind caller's limp body
was thrown against the upraised roots of the fallen breadfruit tree. His head cracked against the splintered wood.

Pahulu's wind immediately increased in power.

Tarawe fell back to her knees. Her face was twisted
with pain Ho'ola could only partially block, and with a
rage that Iuti recognized as suicidal. Tarawe's control had
reached its limit. She snapped a wrist in Pahulu's direction. In the distance, the sound of another broken tree
echoed through the storm. Again Pahulu's wind surged
with added power, and again Tarawe collapsed to the
ground.

Iuti grabbed her hands before she could try again.

"Why can't I hurt her?" Tarawe cried. "My storm is
stronger than hers. I can feel it!"

"She's not fighting with her storm, Tarawe!" Iuti had
to hold Tarawe tight to keep the girl from being swept
away. Pahulu's taunting laughter echoed across the
shrieking wind. The air had grown dark around them
with the massing of the sorceress's writhing, searching
tendrils.

"She's using *your* storm!" Iuti cried. "Every time you
strike at her, she'll use your winds to kill. She'll gain
more power while you suffer from the death thrusts. You
can't fight her that way."

"How then?" Tarawe was sobbing and gasping for air.
Ho'ola had crawled to her side, but it was clear that the
healer could absorb little more of Tarawe's pain. Even
Mapa's face was strained from the silent support he con-
tinuously offered his mistress.

"Stop the wind!" Ola said.

"Stop your storm," Iuti said in the same instant.

Tarawe shuddered. "My storm?" she whispered.

"Let it go," Iuti said, for it was clear the girl had come to love this wondrous storm she had created. "You can make another. At another time. In another place, where it can bring good to the world instead of all this evil. Let it go, Tarawe. Say the words to set your storm free."

Tarawe turned her look toward where they knew Pahulu to be. "Pahulu's words?" she said.

"Aye," Ho'ola agreed. "I know of no other way. We'll protect you as best we can."

Tarawe shuddered again. "And you will kill me if you see that I'm about to fail." She glanced at Risak. Ma'eva is right, Iuti thought. She'll have no innocence left when this is finished.

"You understood that danger before we came," Ola said. "You agreed that we can't allow Pahulu to strip you of your raw and untrained power."

Tarawe pushed to her feet. She turned her hand slightly and the wind around them calmed. "I won't let her take my power." She winced at another distant death, then her eyes grew steady again. "Come. I want her to know me before she dies."

Ola grabbed Tarawe's arm. "You must not kill her, Tarawe! There is no power in the world that could protect you from *that* death thrust. If you kill the sorceress, you will give yourself to her whole, and all the world along with you."

For just an instant, Tarawe looked like a child again, a lonely, frightened child. Then she pulled away. "I want her to know me," she said.

"I'll stay close to you," Iuti said as they began making their way through the tangle of the storm-torn jungle again. "Pahulu might still be slowed by her confusion as to which of us is the storm caller. It might give us needed time."

Tarawe glanced at her without slowing. "You couldn't kill me before when you thought it was necessary, warrior woman," she said. "What makes you think you can

do it now?'' She darted ahead to scoop up a handful of
pebbles. She stuffed them into her trousers pockets, then
waited for Iuti to catch up. She had returned to the deadly
calm she had used with the demon drummers.

"I am here!" Iuti shouted as soon as they reached the
small clearing surrounding her former home. She stepped
into the open, just ahead of Tarawe. The sides and most
of the roof thatch had been torn away from her small
sleeping hut; the platform on which it had been built was
almost bare, while the debris of her belongings lay scattered across the ground. Iuti smelled the sweet fragrance
of spilled candleberry oil and the foul stench of rotting
flesh.

Pahulu stood on the platform, her arms stretched high
as she called and dispersed the wind. She was surrounded on the ground by Teronin guards. Many among
them had the pale, vacant eyes of the soulless. Three
bodies, tangled in the ceremonial robes of wind callers,
lay in a heap beside the fire pit.

Pahulu spun toward Iuti as she called out. Confusion
flickered across her creased and lined face. It was clear
she did not recognize Iuti in her wild, white hair and her
Teronin garb.

"You wanted to meet the storm caller!" Iuti shouted.
"I have brought her."

Fury drove confusion from Pahulu's look. She snapped
her wrists in Iuti's direction, and a swirl of wind tore
across the clearing. Iuti set a warding spell but the whirlwind died before it reached them. Pahulu stepped back,
then threw another wind their way. She screamed in anger when the blast was turned away. The debris it had
lifted during its brief life fluttered and fell as it relaxed
into a harmless breeze.

"Is that the best you can do?" Iuti shouted.

Again Pahulu's attack was struck away. "How dare
you trifle with my power?" she demanded. "How dare
you—"

"Oh, be quiet, you old hag," Ho'ola called. She

stepped out from the trees, an arm's length away from Iuti. "Get down from there and take up a broom. You've made a mess of this place."

Pahulu glanced at Ola, then back at Iuti. Recognition lit her eyes at last. She grinned fiercely. "I recognize you now, Iuti Mano. Did you think you could fool me into thinking Ho'ola of Sandar is the one I seek? She's no wind caller. She's that sorriest excuse for a land-bound sorceress—a *healer*!" Pahulu laughed. The wind rippled at the sound.

"There's more work for a healer in this place than there is for you, breeze-twister," Ola returned.

Pahulu swung her hands up, lifting a wall of wind-borne sand and debris. It settled calmly before it reached Ho'ola.

"How—you can't control the wind. I know you can't!" Pahulu cried.

"I control it!" Iuti shouted. She motioned Risak to defend against the guards who had begun to widen their circle around Pahulu.

"Ha! I knew it was you all al—"

Pahulu was knocked from her feet by a blast of wind so focused it didn't even disturb the hut's remaining thatch.

"*I* am the wind caller!" Tarawe said. She strode to Ho'ola's side, shoulders back and chin lifted high. Her hands rested calmly at her sides. "It was *I* who called the storm."

Pahulu scrambled to her feet. She cursed and swore and paid no attention at all to Tarawe. "Enough of this play, Iuti Mano. I know how to reach you. Here! Taste another of your storm's killings."

A gust of wind swept up the heavy stone pestle that Iuti had used to pound breadfruit. It thudded against the back of one of Pahulu's own guard's heads. The dead-eyed warrior collapsed. Pahulu laughed and lifted her hand again.

"No!" Tarawe shouted. "Not again! Never again with *my* storm!"

She lifted both of her hands and began chanting Pahulu's wind song. Her voice lifted pure and strong over the din of the storm.

⬥ Chapter 20 ⬥

"Aaaghhh!" Pahulu's cry of fury startled even her own guards, all but those who were no longer capable of recognizing living emotion. "I see you now, Storm Caller! I feel you! I taste you on my wind! Begone!"

Pahulu did not use wind this time. She drove her evil magic straight toward Tarawe's soul. Iuti and the others were all driven back by its force.

All but Ho'ola. The healer lifted a hand and caught Pahulu's thrust in her palm. She closed her fist, and a shower of sparks and pale, glimmering dust drifted to the ground.

"Ha, sneeze-maker," Ho'ola called. "Now we play with magic *I* know. Toss us another one of those so I can show you what a land-bound *healer* can do."

Again Pahulu tried to attack the girl. Again Ho'ola caught and destroyed her attempt. Ola didn't return the attack, as Iuti knew well she could have. Instead, the healer refused Pahulu the renewed power that could be drawn from such an aggressive act. She simply neutralized each of the evil thrusts Pahulu sent her way, and gained power of her own in the doing. The exhaustion that had plagued her since they sailed aboard the river boat began to disappear from her expression.

"You're not so strong as you thought, are you?" Ho'ola called. "Whose magic have you been borrowing to create all this havoc? It's clearly not all your own."

Iuti met Risak's questioning look and nodded. While Ola kept Pahulu's attention, they crept to meet her guards. Three went down and a fourth was spinning away without a sword hand before the sorceress realized what they were doing.

"Kill them!" Pahulu screamed. "Show them no mercy! The man who takes Iuti Mano's life will be gifted with her *soul*!"

Iuti laughed her battle laugh, slipped under a Teronin's guard, and touched steel to the man's heart.

Suddenly Tarawe entered the fray, sending twists and gusts of air between the guards and Risak and Iuti. Iuti recognized the patterns of the killing fields Risak had taught the girl, although Tarawe used her winds now only to throw the Teronin off balance. She was wisely leaving the actual killing to Risak and Iuti. But she was a fool for intervening at all.

"Finish the chant, Tarawe!" Iuti shouted. "Leave these to us! Stop the storm!"

To Iuti's dismay, Tarawe laughed, loud and long, as she had the night she had challenged the demon drummers. Had Pahulu taken over her mind despite Ho'ola's aid?

"I don't need to chant this old witch's words to stop my storm," Tarawe called over the wind. "She's nothing but a simple wind mover. I can see that now." She laughed again.

"Watch me, witch!" she shouted. "Listen to the chant of a true *storm caller*!"

Iuti saw Ho'ola whisper frantically into Tarawe's ear. Even Mapa tried to restrain the girl, but it did no good. She laughed again and lifted her hands to the sky.

"*Go!*" she shouted. She closed her fists, turned them palm down, and opened them again.

And the storm went.

Just as it had at the river mouth, although not as abruptly. Flying debris tumbled gently to the ground. The slashing rain lost its sting and fell straight for just an instant before it thinned and stopped. The roar of the wind and the distant pounding of surf faded to the almost gentle sounds of a simple, blustery day. Far off in the jungle, one last great tree crashed to the ground, a final victim of the storm now so suddenly gone. Despite her victory, Tarawe winced at the sound.

Pahulu's winds still circled; they gusted and growled, but they were little more than breezes compared to the powerful winds that had kept them aloft before. A quiet like Iuti had not heard in days settled over Fanape. Even the Teronin warriors ceased their endless, shrill cries. All but the soul-dead recruits began falling back under Iuti and Risak's attack.

"You will die for this, youngster!" Pahulu screamed.

"Perhaps I will," Tarawe called back. "But not today, and not by your hand. See there, the southern warriors are winning. They come even now to help us rid the world of you."

It was true. A full squad of warriors had run into the clearing and were now fighting Pahulu's guard. Iuti began pulling back. It was time to move on. There was another job that needed doing, and she had to do it quickly if it could be done at all. Pale, dawn light was beginning to brush the cloud-cluttered sky.

Risak followed her away from the fighting guards.

"Stay here," she ordered.

He shook his head.

"I need you *here!*" she insisted, then tore her look from his to follow Tarawe's ringing laughter as it swept around the clearing. The girl had wrapped Pahulu in her own flying skirts. Ho'ola tossed another of the sorceress's glittering attacks to the ground.

The stone pestle flew up again, but before it could crack the intended southerner's skull, a gust of wind caught it and lowered it back to the sand. It rolled under the feet of an advancing Teronin and tripped him neatly.

Risak's brows lifted. "*They* don't need me here." Suddenly his eyes darkened. He stiffened and he turned his right ear to the jungle. Hurriedly he sheathed his swords and began untying the bag from his waist.

"It has begun," he said. "Come. The drummers sing to the rising sun."

Iuti heard nothing above the battle sounds and Pahulu's dying wind, but she didn't doubt Risak's word. There was no time to argue now. She left the increasingly impotent Pahulu to Ho'ola and Tarawe and pointed Risak toward the village.

As he ran, he pulled a package from his waist pouch. He licked his fingers before unwrapping what looked like a strand of hair from it. Stuffing the hair back into the pouch, he dropped the cloth covering, then shook out a handful of fringes made of cowrie shells and dried clatterberries. Strangely, they made no sound.

Risak stopped long enough to lace the fringes around his ankles and his wrists. "Many of the southerners carry these," he said with a grin. "We made them while we waited for you at the river mouth. It was Tarawe's idea to keep them silent until they were needed." He wrapped the last and most elaborate fringe around his forehead. The berries and shells bumped and tangled together without sound.

"She taught me the silencing spell back on the canoe, and I shared it with the others. I'll release the sound when the drums begin singing my song." He lifted a brow. "Or yours."

"Risak, my friend," Iuti said as they began running again. "You are a brave man, and a great fool." She grinned and saluted him as an equal.

"Aye," he replied.

"I could have no better partner fighting at my side."

He said nothing to that, he only ran his fingers across the braid of Kunan's hair that circled his neck.

The drums were louder now, although still nearly inaudible. Iuti heard them only because she knew they were there. The southern warriors had been warned against the drums' power, but this beat was insidious—even the most experienced among them might not notice before it was too late.

Iuti stopped Risak before he could burst into the clearing at village center.

"This way," she whispered. She drew him away from the path.

The ceremonial canoe had been placed at village center, near where Tarawe's uncle's house had once stood. Wind-torn remnants of the former island chief's home were strewn across the clearing. By passing behind what was left of the canoe house, Iuti and Risak were able to approach unseen to within twenty paces of the canoe.

There were drums scattered all around the canoe. According to Risak's account, at least half the men of Losan were milling about, waiting to begin beating on them. Some carried spears or carved clubs, just as they had back on Losan. Warriors' tools.

Kunan's drums—Iuti would have known them even if she had never seen the empty barrels—sat in a place of honor atop the outrigger platform. They were covered with a vine-draped, thatched roof. There was enough light now to make out Kunan's distinctive patterning on the major drumfaces.

The four dawn-callers sat intent over small, hollowed logs, beating a tattoo so softly and rapidly it hardly moved the air. One of the four sat directly in front of Iuti and Risak.

Risak shifted. Iuti laid a hand on his arm. If he was afraid, she couldn't feel it. He fingered the necklace of Kunan's hair.

"Kunan's are the important ones," she said. "The southerners are trained to resist the others."

Even as she spoke, a shout went up from the jungle. The clang of striking swords and the battle cries of victorious southern warriors suddenly burst into the clearing. A Teronin chief screamed an order at the drummers. The dawn-callers did not alter their rhythm. The rest of the drummers waited, poised over their drums.

Risak laughed softly. "They won't play the battle drums until the dawn has been fully welcomed. Come. Now is the time to attack." He reached out to pull the tangle of Iuti's hair close around her face.

"Leave your shield here," he said. "And keep that great club of yours sheathed. Act as if you're chasing

me, and they'll never look beyond the clothes you're
wearing. They'll think you're a Teronin and urge you
after me.''

Before Iuti could protest, he was on his feet and running. She shook her head and smiled after him, for it
was a good plan. She had thought of it herself, but had
not had time to speak it aloud.

"For Kunan!'' Risak roared.

He leapt in among the drummers and, with a single
stroke, severed both hands from the nearest dawn-
worshiping drummer.

The drums stilled for an instant, then a cry of horror
lifted. Another drummer tried to take his fallen col-
league's place, but Risak forced him away. Three bloodied fingers were left lying on the drum.

"Beat the damnable *battle* drums!'' a nearby Teronin
chief cried. His men were already engaged with the advancing southern warriors and were being pressed quickly
back.

Risak killed another of the dawn drummers, and yet
another. But then a flash of sunlight gilded the roof of
the drum house.

As if released from a spell, the drummers entered the
battle. The war drums, all but Kunan's, pounded deep
and sonorous, while shrill, screaming pipes split the air
like an infant's first wail.

The southerners hesitated, then pushed forward again.
Most had heard these sounds before and knew how to
block them from their conscious minds. Those who were
hearing them for the first time gritted their teeth and followed their comrades' lead. Many of them, Iuti saw as
she stepped from the shadows, were wearing silent
fringes like Risak's. Don't wait too long to give them
sound, she urged Risak silently.

She began running after the grinning swordsman. The
drummers did no more than glance at her before returning to their din. One swung his carved club, urging her
after Risak. She could easily have killed him, but she
passed him by. Up ahead, Risak took the hands of yet

another Losan warrior. Iuti felt no satisfaction at the sight of the drummers' blood, only grim determination that all of the blood-letting should end.

Suddenly one of the drummers recognized Risak. He shrieked, and the pounding rhythm changed instantly.

Risak tensed at the first beat of his blood song. Then he shook his head, and Iuti saw his lips move. A sudden discordant clatter and clicking disrupted the sensual beat. From all across the clearing, the release of Tarawe's silencing spell brought the tapping of shells and the hard, hollow thunk of rattling clatterberries. The demon drummers stared around in confusion.

Risak laughed aloud and again called Kunan's name. A drummer stumbled and fell over his own drum while Risak leapt ahead.

Iuti was stopped from following him by the Teronin chieftain. He had made his way in among the drummers, and it was clear *he* was not deceived by her disguise. They parried sword strikes, ducked and turned, and parried again. Behind him Iuti could see drummers scrambling into place around Kunan's drums. She struck again at the Teronin. Again she was blocked and pushed back.

She saw Risak reach the canoe. He yanked a drummer down from the edge of the outrigger and leapt up with both swords swinging, but then he stopped abruptly. He twisted and cried out, while the drummers cheered. Risak was tangled in a hanging waryvine wall.

The drummers immediately began pummeling him as if he were one of their drums. They jabbed him with sharp, ornate sticks and slapped at him with their carved clubs. Because he was on the outrigger, they could strike only at his legs and back, but their attack was brutally effective.

He chanted loudly, trying to employ Tarawe's spell to charm open the net, but he shuddered and hesitated, growing ever more helpless under the drummers' beating. As his movements slowed, the disrupting sound of his headdress and arm and ankle fringes lessened, the dreaded effects of his personal song began to take hold. He cried out in a long, heart-tearing wail.

Iuti finally found a way through the Teronin's guard. As her blade drank of his life's blood, she caught a flash of color near Risak. Sunlight on ceremonial paint, she thought. But when she looked back, she almost stumbled in her surprise. The milimilis had joined Risak at the net.

One of the drummers ran close to strike Risak's legs, but the milimili female intervened. She flicked a hand in the drummer's direction, and he stopped, twitched, and fell like a stone. The whore reached up to pat her hair.

When her hand came away, something silver glinted at her fingertips. She snapped it toward another drummer who had come close. That one, too, fell shivering to the ground. The rest of the drummers backed away.

Poisoned hairpins, Iuti thought with an unexpected return to good humor. A privileged whore's weapon, as useful here as in the trouble-filled brothels of Lowtown. Iuti's laughter returned her to calm.

Then, abruptly, all calm ended.

All at once, with a force that drove even Iuti back, Kunan's drums began to sing. Only the smaller drums at first. The great Father Drum still sat silent at the center of the canoe house. Still, the air trembled with the strength of the great warrior's call.

Iuti felt her own strength waver. Her feet slipped on the bloodied ground. Her legs cramped with each sudden move. Her right hand burned, and her arms began to feel like lead.

A Teronin cheer lifted as, all across the clearing, the southerners began falling back. Their clatterberry fringes offered no protection at all from Kunan's drums.

Iuti bit the inside of her cheek and tried to focus on the pain to keep her mind off the drums, all the while marveling at Kunan's power. She could barely move against it. She was surrounded now by Teronin as well as demon drummers, but only the Teronin realized she was not one of their own. The drummers concentrated on controlling the faltering southern army. At the far edge of the clearing, a few grim-faced southerners fought doggedly on, but the battle tide had clearly turned.

A single, booming throb brought all movement to a halt.

Even the drummers themselves paused at the sudden, heart-stopping voice of the Father Drum. A second throbbing note sounded, and quickly, furiously, they began beating the rest again. The Father Drum spoke a third time, and a Teronin near Iuti cried out and fell to his knees. A southerner, a paddler from Iuti's own canoe, threw down his sword and covered his ears with his blood-soaked hands.

They play now to destroy us all! Iuti thought as she watched southerner and Teronin alike fall helpless to the great drum's song. None could resist Kunan's cry. Iuti felt his power trembling deep within her.

She stumbled and caught herself. She stared up again at the great drum. It rested on its side, a drummer standing at each end. They swung in unison, their movements mirrored images of each other, their contact with the drumfaces an almost undetectable instant apart.

"Listen for my heartbeat," Kunan had said.

"I hear," Iuti whispered.

The drum sounded again in its vibrating doubled beat.

"I hear you, Kunan!"

Iuti thrilled suddenly to Kunan's booming welcome. An eagerness greater than any she had ever known, an energy greater than that she had known with Mano Niuhi, poured into her leaden limbs. She began walking forward again.

"Truly, brother, I gain strength from your voice," she shouted.

The drummers stared at her in confusion. She alone was moving against the power of the war drums. She alone was striding toward their god. She swept them from her path. She knocked them aside when they didn't move away quickly enough; she killed those who tried to stop her. She leapt without hesitation across their fallen bodies.

They didn't know who, or what, she was. But it took them only an instant to realize she must be stopped. The drum sounds changed, and amid much confusion, the Teronin began fighting again. They ran toward Iuti, but she had already reached the outrigger platform. The wide-eyed milis motioned that the net was open. They had removed Risak from the entangling vines and remained to guard him as Iuti lifted herself into the drum house.

The drummers screamed in outrage and growing panic as she passed easily through what they had thought was an impenetrable barrier. One grabbed her ankle. She kicked him easily away. Another threw a drumstick, which she deflected with the Teronin sword she still carried. The drummers on the outrigger beat madly at Kunan's drums, trying to steal her strength, not recognizing yet that their efforts only added to it.

A Teronin jumped onto the outrigger opposite Iuti and immediately caught himself in the waryvine wall. A southerner struggled to his knees and threw a knife into the Teronin's back. Behind her, Iuti heard the milis warn the Teronin away from Risak. One, at least, chose not to heed their warning. A heavy thud heralded his collapse.

Kunan's heart-wrenching call continued without pause. A naked drummer stood at each end of the mighty Father Drum, striking the patterned drumheads with carved clubs. Each stroke was made with a full swing of the body. The resonance resulting from the doubled beat rent the air as if it were a living thing. If Kunan had not been speaking directly to her, Iuti would never have noticed the simple trick by which the drummers amplified his sound.

The drummers' leader—Iuti recognized him by his patterned skin—stepped out from behind the great drum. He glared at her and lifted a freshly carved spear in warning.

She yanked it from his hands, met his look, and cracked the thin shaft across her knee.

He stared at the broken spear, then back up at Iuti. She pushed her hair back from her face.

"Yes," she said softly as his eyes turned dark with

recognition and with immediate terror. "It is I. Your Mother Drum. I've come for my mate."

She tossed the spear down and reached over her shoulder to tear away the back of her tunic, so that all the drummers would know who she was. Behind her, a drummer screamed. He pushed away from his drum, a fine resonant drum stretched over with leather from Kunan's thighs.

The leader shrieked at the panicked drummer and ordered him back to his post, but the drum's beat, when it resumed, held little of Kunan's power. The drummer's hands were too unsteady. The sound carried only the strength of an ordinary drum. That slight change brought movement back to the battered southern line.

"Tell them to stop," Iuti said.

The drummer understood her—he had heard her make the demand often enough back on Losan. They all had. A few slowed their beat. More strength returned to the southern line. The Teronin were torn between the drama on the canoe and the renewed attack from the jungle. Those southern warriors who could move took good advantage of the Teronin's divided attention.

The Father Drum sang on. Iuti motioned the drummers' leader aside so she could approach the intricately carved instrument. He hesitated, but then cunning touched his dark eyes. A hush fell over the drum house as he stepped away from her path

Iuti could almost feel the Losan drummers holding their breaths. She could taste their desperate desire for her approval. And then she smiled again, as she realized it was not the drummers she felt and tasted. It was their drum sound. They had begun playing her song so softly she hadn't even noticed.

"So you still want me for your Mother Drum," she murmured. She ran her injured hand along the side of Kunan's great body. The drummers at each end struck their beat, and a tremor shivered through Iuti's loins. Kunan's voice was deep and throbbing with temptation. She pulled her hand away. Kunan's power still tugged at her soul.

"We would be a pair, wouldn't we, brother Kunan?" she said. "We would make a powerful pair, you and I."

She walked around to the opposite side of the drum and touched it again—a light, feather touch.

"Ah, yes, Kunan Iliawe. Together, you and I could rule the world."

Kunan sang another sonorous note. It slid like buttered sweetfish down the back of Iuti's tongue. She had never known a sound so rich, so entirely compelling. She laid both hands on the drum and trembled at its touch.

"If we were joined, Kunan," she whispered, "we would never again have to deal with petty conflicts between north and south, between land folk and those of the sea. The drummers would think they controlled us, but they would be no more than our pawns. We would never again have to sing alone, Kunan."

If we were joined, she thought, I would never have to grieve for the loss of my brother Mano Niuhi or explain to my family how that loss came to be. By the gods, Kunan. With you at my side, I would never again have to sing alone.

The drummers had grown silent, all but those who played Iuti's song, hers and Kunan's, for they were the same song now. She had finished her circle of the drum.

She dropped the Teronin sword and motioned for the drummer at Kunan's face to give her his club.

"Ser Iuti, you must not!" Risak's voice reached her through her fierce desire.

The drummer grinned in triumph and thrust his carved club into her hand. She felt the sharp tingle of a strong warding spell, then another and another, as sorcerers among the southern troops tried to stop her with their spells. She laughed and brushed their simple magic away.

"No!" Risak cried again as she stepped to the face of the drum. But then he grew quiet, forced to stillness by a quick shiver of his own blood song.

Kunan waited.

The great drum grew silent, waiting with the rest for Iuti to sound the beat that would make them one. The drummer at Kunan's back readied for the resonant double strike that would seal their union.

Iuti walked slowly to the face of the Father Drum. She stared at the great circular pattern for a moment, then abruptly swung the club down and back. The Losan drummers began a high, shrill wail of joy.

⚔ Chapter 21 ⚔

"LET us be joined, Kunan!" Iuti shouted over the drummers' cry of triumph and the southerners' ragged call of protest. They had broken through the Teronin line at last, but none would reach the drum house before she struck the drum.

"Be free, Kunan Iliawe!" Iuti cried.

Without changing the swinging arc of her body, she dropped the drummer's blunt club behind her and slid Mano's weapon from its place on her back. She slashed the tooth-studded war club down across the face of the Father Drum. The thick, scarred leather split like an overripe breadfruit, and the drummer's echoing strike on Kunan's back thudded into flat silence.

Iuti slashed the drum again, and then again until the beautifully patterned skin was torn into ribboned shreds. Deep red droplets oozed from the torn leather and ran in thin rivulets across the ruined skin. Ignoring the shrill cries of the drummers and the roar of victory from the southern army, Iuti reached out to touch the glistening crimson. She lifted the warm, viscous fluid to her lips.

Kunan Iliawe's blood, she thought. The great warrior's soul was finally and fully free. Iuti waited for the icy touch of death, but felt only warmth flooding her soul.

Before the drummers could recover from their startled horror, Iuti moved to slash the back side of the great drum. Then she turned and smashed Mano's club down onto the drum that had been Kunan's thighs. It shattered like a gull's egg falling on hard stone.

The drummers finally tried to stop her. One hit her right hand with his club; she laughed away the pain and split the drum that had been Kunan's hands. Another jumped up from behind and jabbed a sharp stick into her back. She laughed again.

"Do you think I can't heal so paltry a wound?" she called. "I'll heal it so perfectly there won't even be a scar to mar the Mother Drum's eye."

A third attacking drummer spun away after being struck by a perfectly aimed stone. Iuti knew without looking who had thrown the small pebble. "You see?" she said to the bloodied drummer. "She *is* my most dangerous weapon."

Methodically Iuti crushed each of the drums into splinters. She tore Kunan's strong leather to useless shreds. Those drummers who tried to stop her died along with their drums, while the rest wept and wailed and finally slipped outside the waryvine net to hide with the others under the canoe.

In the end, only the Father Drum's great barrel remained unbroken. Iuti stood facing its beautifully carved side. She brushed a hand along its rim, feeling for one last time Kunan's compelling call.

"Farewell, friend Kunan," she said. "Fair winds. Watch for me in the land of warriors' dreams, for I will meet you there one day."

She shattered the Father Drum with a single, steady blow.

Iuti was alone in the drum house when she finally looked up and around. The southerners were fighting strongly now, sure of their victory with Pahulu's magic gone and the power of the demon drums broken. One by one, the remaining Teronin fighters gave way, or gave up, or died.

Iuti climbed down from the outrigger platform and crossed to what remained of the canoe house. Risak was there, still attended by the milimilis. His left leg was broken below the knee, and his back and both legs were torn and bruised from the beating he had taken while trapped in the waryvine net. He lay now in a spell-induced stupor.

"How did you know to come here to his aid?" Iuti asked the milis. She noted with appreciation that they were keeping Risak's tattoos carefully covered.

The female mili lifted a painted brow. "When we first saw this warrior at the river mouth, we knew he had a wound only we could heal," she said. "We've been watching him closely from the beginning."

"After Ho'ola and the girl locked the old wind witch away, we followed you here," said the male. "You run very fast for an old woman, Ser." He giggled and turned his attention back to his partner. She whispered something while glancing slyly at Iuti, and he laughed again.

Ho'ola had already set Risak's leg. Having pronounced the milis capable of caring for the rest of his wounds, she was about to move on to the other injured southerners. Iuti knew Ola would care for the Teronin, as well, and even the drummers if they would allow it, but not until after her work among the southerners was finished.

"The whores brought us all safely through the jungle," Ola said. "They distracted the Teronin with their antics. Then, if they came near, downed them with those dreadful hairpins they carry. The poison they use is one even I don't know."

The female mili rolled a curl back into her hair and mouthed a kiss to a passing southerner.

Ola shook her head and handed her bag of potions up to Mapa. She struggled to her feet under his guiding hand.

"I didn't feel your touch in the warding spells the southern sorcerers sent my way," Iuti said. "Did you trust me that much?"

"Would my spell have made a difference?" Ola asked.

Iuti smiled and shook her head. "Still, I thank you for not burdening me with it, Auntie. Where is Tarawe?"

Ola looked around, as if surprised the girl wasn't at her side. "She was with me a moment ago. She helped the milis bring Risak here. By the gods, I think the drummers dreaded Tarawe stalking through their midst as much as they did you crushing their drums."

"Aye," Iuti said. "I expect they did."

"We left Pahulu trapped inside one of her own spells and guarded by a full squad of warriors," Ola said. "Perhaps Tarawe went back to check on her."

Iuti's right palm itched. She rubbed it against her blood-smeared trousers. The cut on her thigh, the one she had taken at the battle's start, had already begun to heal, and she had taken no other injury of consequence. She scratched her hand again, nodded to Ho'ola and the milis, and left in search of the girl.

She cut through the jungle, since the path was as storm-damaged now as the rest of the island. She knew Tarawe wouldn't be so foolish as to present Pahulu with the opportunity of escape, but it made her uneasy not knowing where the girl was.

This is her home, Iuti reminded herself. She lived here most of her life. She's probably sitting alone somewhere, grieving for the family and friends she's lost. Iuti doubted that thought as quickly as it crossed her mind. Tarawe had left no one on Fanape for whom to grieve.

At the clearing, Pahulu screamed in silent rage inside the flickering mist Tarawe and Ho'ola had sealed around her. She fought the gently giving inner surface to no avail. Despair had made her eyes go pale, but when she saw Iuti, they darkened again in hatred, and fear.

Iuti watched her for a moment, waiting for the surge of satisfaction that the sight of a captured enemy always brought. She waited for the urge to kill the sorceress, even though she knew she would not. But nothing came. She felt only revulsion for the woman who had used her powers in so evil a way, and relief that she would never use them so again.

I will never be the warrior I once was, Iuti remembered thinking during the heat of battle. Strangely, the realization brought her no pain. She turned away to continue searching for Tarawe.

As she stepped onto the path that led to her favorite fishing site, her hand itched again. She looked down. The wound on her palm, the ragged gash Tarawe's teeth had caused, was fiery red. Iuti closed her hand into a fist, wishing for the cool touch of a metal sword's hilt.

She stopped suddenly and shook her hand open. "What am I thinking?" she muttered. "I have no wish to take up another weapon. I wish only to be finished with killing." The itching diminished, but the redness remained. She frowned and began walking again, hurrying now, because she was more and more certain that something was wrong. Tarawe wouldn't hide from her. Not now. Not here on this isle. She glanced down at her hand again.

When she reached the beach, she found the sand scuffed by many booted footprints, both southern and Teronin. A single line of prints, made by small, bare feet, crossed over the rest. Iuti followed them to where a thicket of powderberry bushes extended almost to the high-water line. There, she discovered the furrowed lines made by a small canoe being dragged across the sand.

With a feeling of dread, Iuti lifted her look to the sea.

"By the very gods!" she breathed.

Tarawe was poling a canoe, a small one meant only for shallow water use, across the reef.

Iuti called to her, but Tarawe seemed not to hear. She had reached the breaking waves at the edge of the reef. She lifted her left hand and the waves flattened as if they had never existed. Tarawe paddled the canoe smoothly onto the open sea.

What is she doing? Iuti wondered. What can she be thinking to enter Mano Niuhi's waters alone in such a small vessel?

"Tarawe, come back!" she called.

She heard Tarawe's distant hail to one of the southern war canoes. The two men aboard paddled quickly toward her, shouting questions. A victory signal had already been sent from shore, but they would be eager for news of the recent battle. One of them pointed at something in the water.

Sharks, Iuti thought, judging by how carefully he stayed back from the gunwale. Tarawe seemed unconcerned by Mano's presence, thinking herself safe, no doubt, inside one of her private shields. She motioned toward something on the deck.

"Ah, no," Iuti muttered.

The canoe was the one they had traveled on, and she recognized the blanket-wrapped bundle the men aboard passed to Tarawe. As the girl's hands touched the package, Iuti's right palm blazed into fiery pain.

The sword! Iuti thought. That damnable sword!

Tarawe laid the bundle across her lap. A quick motion of her hand sent the great war canoe and its startled crew drifting swiftly away.

Iuti looked up and out across the water. "Mano," she whispered. "Has it been you all along? Has it been you causing all this horror?"

She remembered now that on the night Tarawe had called the storm, the girl had washed her blade in the sea. True, they had been well away from Fanape by then, but Mano could easily have tasted the newly formed battle bond between Tarawe and her. If revenge was what he sought, he would have known he could control Iuti's movements by controlling those of the girl's.

"Did you slide a piece of your soul into the sword that night, brother?" she asked. "Did you take that moment of companionship between the girl and me to create the opportunity for your revenge?"

But why, she thought, did he not simply kill me that night, when I was so completely at his mercy? Why did he attack the false Pahulu and allow me to swim in his waters unharmed?

The drummers! she thought. And the Teronin, and the true Pahulu.

By the very gods! Mano had allowed her to live so she could bring about this day's battle. This horrible day's bloody feeding ground. He had used Tarawe as bait, and led them both along the dangerous path that would bring the battle back here.

And Pahulu? she wondered. Had Mano been using her, as well? Was that how a simple wind caller had come to hold such power over the creatures of the sea? She remembered that as soon as Ho'ola had touched Pahulu's magic directly, she had accused the sorceress of using borrowed power.

"Did you make Pahulu your kinswoman, too?" she

asked. "Is that why she insisted on believing I was the one she sought when so much evidence should have told her otherwise? Did you use us both to bring about this one last feeding frenzy?"

Iuti stared at Tarawe, sitting silent now, motionless on the small canoe. The bundle containing Iuti's sword rested on her lap. And now you wish to use the girl, Iuti thought. But first, you must kill me. Mano knew she wouldn't continue the killing as before, blindly allowing him to feed on the horrors of her work. Nor could he trick her again into helping create new battlefields. No, he planned to kill her here, today, and then take Tarawe and her raw, untamed power for his own. With Tarawe at his side, he would never be hungry again. The war among the humans, perhaps even among the seafolk, would go on until the end of time.

Iuti reached up to retie the warrior's knot in her tangled hair. She slid her shield back onto her arm and pulled the tooth-studded club from her back. She stepped into the water.

"Did you like the taste of your own kin's death?" she asked the distant shark. She knew he was listening. She could feel his presence in the cool water that swirled about her ankles. "Did it disturb you when Tarawe's accidental storm grew out of control and none of your pawns could stop it? Did it please you that the seafolk and even your own cousins suffered because of it? Ah, brother Mano, you have swum into the deep side of evil."

She trod the reef carefully, not wishing to fall on the sharp coral. There would be injury enough soon.

When she reached waist-deep water near the edge of the reef, she stopped. The tide was low and the surf calm. The only reminder of Tarawe's storm was the broken coral on which Iuti stood, and occasional floating debris. She could see Tarawe clearly now. The girl had stopped paddling and was letting the canoe drift slowly with the current. She was very near the place where Iuti and the shark had fought on her first day at Fanape.

Tarawe unwrapped the sword with fumbling hands and

dropped the blanket onto the outrigger. One corner slipped overboard to trail in the water. She struggled for a moment, then stiffened and pointed the sword's tip toward the island. She acted as if she was unaware of Iuti's presence at the reef's edge.

Tarawe lifted the sword in her right hand and swept her left in a backhanded arc. Iuti braced for a gust of wind. She remembered too late that Tarawe used her left hand to control the water. A rippling, racing current swept her off her feet and she fell heavily onto the jagged coral. As she pushed herself upright, bleeding from a dozen deep cuts, she cursed Mano's duplicity.

A shadow appeared beneath the canoe.

"Come and kill me if that's what you intend!" Iuti shouted. "Face me openly, and let us finish this thing!" She ran her fingers over the necklace of Kunan's hair.

"Come, brother Mano! Let us mix our blood and share one last meal," she called. "But be warned! I won't take just your body this time, although I'll do my best to take that, too. When I die, kinsman—as I surely will—I will take your soul with me to the land of warriors' dreams."

Mano's great gray fin shattered the sea's surface. Iuti dove through the breaking surf.

Mano remained near the canoe, drawing her into deep water and away from any protection the reef might offer. He wanted her in the exact place where they had fought before. She knew the site by its smell and its taste and the shapes of its currents. Mano began circling in the manner of his kind.

An unexpected, unnatural current tumbled Iuti in the water. She righted herself. Unless Tarawe put down the sword, she was going to have to fight the girl as well as the shark.

Mano circled.

Iuti saw no sign of the small cousins. Tarawe was probably keeping them away, so that Mano could enjoy his revenge alone.

"We've always been solitary fighters, you and I," Iuti

sang to the beat of her family's shark song. "I learned today that is not always the best way."

A wave lifted beside Iuti and slammed down into churning foam. It pressed Iuti deep beneath the surface. As she strained to reach the air again, she sent a strong release spell Tarawe's way. As quickly as she sucked in a new breath, she followed the spell with another, stronger charm, this one using knowledge she had gained while breaching Tarawe's self-protection the afternoon before. Could only a single day have passed since then?

From atop a swell, she saw Tarawe shake her head in confusion and slowly lower the sword. "Drop the blade!" Iuti shouted. "Tarawe, drop the blade!"

Tarawe stared at the sword. A look of revulsion crossed her face.

"Drop it!" Iuti yelled.

But Mano's control of the sword was strong, and by making Tarawe her kinswoman, Iuti had unwittingly made the shark's bond with her stronger. The flashing tip quivered. Tarawe's expression grew grim again, and the sword lifted skyward. Iuti could feel Mano's silent laughter through the sea.

The water near her churned into a froth—a perfect cover for Mano's attack. Iuti used one of Tarawe's tricks and mixed an attack call with the release spell she had cast earlier. She put all the strength she had into forcing an opening through Tarawe's shell, and this time it worked.

Tarawe shuddered and cried out. She threw the sword from her. It stuck in the coir wrappings at the farthest edge of the outrigger, and instantly, the water calmed.

"Stay there!"Iuti shouted. "Don't touch it again! Not even to throw it overboard."

Tarawe backed as far away from the blade as the tiny canoe allowed.

"Now!" Iuti shouted. "Now, Mano. It is just you and I. Let us be finished with it."

The water next to Iuti boiled as Mano Niuhi rose to the surface and swept by. He did not touch her with his teeth; he only scraped his grinding skin across her shoul-

der and arm. She twisted her shield toward him and felt
the knife-edged teeth sink deep. The force of his own
movement tore a ragged gash along his side.

Their blood mingled in swirling eddies.

Mano struck again, and again. Each time, he swerved
away without closing his great jaws around her. He
slammed into her legs and arms, he slid like fire coral
across her back. "Scrape away the Mother Drum's eye,"
she sang, and twisted the war club around so that it
scraped across Mano's own back.

There was a brief pause. Mano circled. When he came
at her again, it was directly. He had finished playing. Iuti
swung the club at his onrushing body, using both her
own and Kunan's strength. On land, it would have been
more than a killing blow. In the water, it struck Mano
with only enough force to make him turn again. His great
jaws closed around the club and ripped it from Iuti's
grasp.

The shark thrashed in fury as his own teeth, tightly
laced to the fire-hardened wood, caught in the soft parts
of his mouth. He shook his head, twisting and turning as
he tried to shake the club loose.

Iuti caught a glimpse of the canoe where Tarawe was
still huddled at the end farthest from the sword. She was
moving her left hand in a slow circle. To keep the small
cousins away, Iuti thought. Tarawe could not stop Mano
Niuhi, but she could make sure that he at least had to
fight alone.

He struck again.

Iuti used the shield to protect herself this time, but it,
too, was quickly ripped away.

"So this is how it ends," Iuti sang. She was not ready
to die, but she knew that she must. She knew that she
would. Mano's misused power must be removed from the
sea. She wrapped her injured hand tightly around Kunan's hair. It offered no further strength, but it gave her
courage.

Mano raced for the kill. Even knowing it was useless,
Iuti lifted her arms to protect her face. She whispered
the words that would bind Mano's soul to the last beat of

her heart. The water swirled. She braced herself for the impact.

A flash of gray crossed her vision and she was thrust suddenly from Mano's path. The searing agony of knife-edged skin scraped along her entire right side.

Shark! The recognition was like a mockery. One of the small cousins had come to steal Mano Niuhi's revenge.

Iuti fought her bloody way to the surface, coughing, gagging, praying for an end to this horror. The water near her swirled again, but the thrashing turmoil turned away. Iuti swallowed a mouthful of blood-slimed water and choked as she saw the shark that had postponed her death.

It wasn't one of the small cousins. It was a great gray shark, as long and as sleek as Mano Niuhi himself. The two huge creatures twisted like twins as they thrashed through the sea. Except for the injuries caused by Mano's own weapons, the two sharks were identical. The new-comer turned on Mano and forced him away—

—and suddenly Iuti understood.

"Ah, no," she cried. "Ah, Ma'eva, no!"

She tried to swim toward the battling sharks, but something had been broken in that last collision. She could barely lift her right arm. Her side felt as if a knife had been run through it. Broken ribs, she thought, and some-thing else, deep inside.

Still, she tried. Ma'eva was in deadly danger. This was not a ride-along form he had taken, like the gull. This was a true sea change. He was as much a shark at this moment as Mano himself, and any injury he took would be his own. It would remain with him even if he changed forms again.

Mano Niuhi smashed his powerful tail into Ma'eva's side. Ma'eva rolled and righted himself and returned to the attack.

"Let it go!" Iuti cried. "Ma'eva, let it go. Let him kill me. There's no need for you to die, too."

Ma'eva continued his defense, slashing with razor-sharp teeth and battering with his powerful tail. He rammed Mano Niuhi with his broad, sensitive snout, forcing Mano away from Iuti again. But Ma'eva could not win. Iuti knew he could not.

Mano fought not only with the power of his kind, but with the memories of his ageless ancestors. Worse, he fought with the cunning and precision of his adopted kinswoman. Iuti recognized the patterns and rhythms of her own legendary battle technique in Mano's moves. Ma'eva was thrust back, and back again. He weakened, but he refused to be driven away.

Iuti held her right arm tightly to her side and began paddling toward the canoe. There was a great splash as Mano and Ma'eva lifted entirely out of the water and crashed back again. Mano's teeth locked into Ma'eva's right side. He tore a ragged chunk of flesh away. Ma'eva faltered.

Suddenly the canoe was beside Iuti. Tarawe reached down to help Iuti aboard. "No!" Iuti said. "I can't leave. I'll take the sword. Then you go back—" She stopped, unable to catch her breath against the pain in her side.

"But Mano will kill—"

Iuti motioned her to silence. She made her way to the outrigger struts and wrenched the sword free of the bindings. Its weight was almost more than she could carry. Then, suddenly, smoothly, the burden became more bearable, as if the water itself were buoying the heavy metal. Iuti glanced up at Tarawe and saw that it was. A swift, steady current carried Iuti back to where Mano and Ma'eva fought.

Ma'eva was almost finished. His skin was torn, shredded like Kunan's drums. His great tail moved at an awkward, painful-looking angle. His blacker-than-black eyes had gone dull. Iuti saw the telltale flicker of a sea mimic attempting a form change, but the change did not come. Ma'eva didn't have enough strength left to change into some smaller, swifter creature that might be able to get away.

Iuti began to sing.

"Come to me, brother," she sang. "Come to your sister here in the cold sea."

Mano hesitated in his frenzy the instant the song began.

"Come," Iuti sang.

Mano bumped Ma'eva from his path and swam slowly toward Iuti. She could taste his triumphant laughter through the sea.

"Come."

He came, gliding leisurely, for he knew she was finished. Behind him, a current buoyed Ma'eva and carried him away. Mano's great jaws opened. Rows and rows of teeth glinted in the sunlight. He circled once, then broke for the kill.

Iuti lifted the blade in her one good hand.

Perhaps Mano didn't recognize the sword, or maybe he thought it couldn't kill him a second time. He opened his bloody jaws wide and swam directly into Iuti's carefully aimed stroke.

"Fair seas, brother," Iuti gasped as she thrust the cold metal deep into Mano Niuhi's mouth. She twisted the blade until it reached and ripped through his gills, then she plunged its tip into the great shark's brain. Mano thrashed once. His teeth ripped the skin from Iuti's arm as she was knocked back and away.

Then, suddenly, Mano Niuhi went limp. His torn body turned slowly around the killing blade as it began drifting down, and down. Iuti Mano shuddered with the killing cold as her brother and her sword disappeared together into the deep.

☙ *Chapter 22* ☙

When Iuti looked up, she saw that Tarawe had brought Ma'eva to the side of the canoe. She was keeping the great, gray shark moving slowly, so the sea would continue flowing through his gills and he wouldn't drown. Tears glimmered on her cheeks.

"He's dying, Ser Iuti," she said. "I don't know how to heal a shark. Why doesn't he turn back into a man, or a bird?"

Iuti took hold of the canoe's side. "He can't change at all. He hasn't the strength." She reached up to pull the warrior's knot from her hair.

"What are you doing?" Tarawe asked as Iuti pulled away a single strand and wrapped it around one of Ma'eva's pectoral fins. Once, twice, three times—and the magic number four.

"Come to me, friend mimic," Iuti whispered. "Come back to the form you held when last you were bound to my will."

It had been a small thing, that impulse that had caused her to set an extended binding spell on Ma'eva the night the storm was called. It was a game they had played since they were children, each trying to trick the other, just because they were such close friends and it gave them both pleasure.

It was such a very small thing, but . . .

A flicker of movement crept along the great shark's body. Tarawe caught her breath. The shark's ebony eyes began to narrow. Its body shortened and its massive, broken tail split into the emerging shape of two human legs.

There was a deep, ragged gash in the right thigh. The left leg was clearly broken below the knee.

The pectorals stretched and thinned into arms and hands and fingers and nails, all torn and scratched and bloody. Not until the last did the wide jaw narrow and flatten into the face of a man.

"Help me," Iuti said. "The canoe won't hold all of us, but we can rest him across the outrigger. I'll follow you ashore."

Together, they lifted Ma'eva's mangled body aboard. "You can come, too," Tarawe said then. "My water won't let the canoe sink."

Iuti blinked up at her. She laid her head on her arm, rested both on the edge of the canoe. "I keep forgetting I don't have to do everything alone," she said. She smiled ruefully before shaking her head at Tarawe's offer. "I'm better off staying in the water. My ribs are broken, and if I try climbing up there, you'll have two unconscious warriors on your hands. If you'll just paddle slowly . . ."

Tarawe huffed. "I need no paddle. Shall I send a message on the wind for Ho'ola to meet us on the beach?"

Iuti nodded. It was all she could manage, that and silent thanks.

A turn of Tarawe's wrists sent a questing breeze landward and brought a gentle current up from beneath the canoe. The water, warmer now, buoyed the vessel and Iuti together and swept them with all gentleness toward the shore.

Iuti and Ma'eva remained in deep, healing sleep for five days. During that time, the last of the Teronin were searched out and subdued. Without Pahulu's magic and the power of the Losan drums, few of them chose to resist. Only the soul-dead fought on until they were killed.

Once the others realized the war was truly at an end, they were as eager as the southerners to lay aside their weapons and return to their mainland homes. Biers of storm debris were assembled to burn the dead, and for a time, the heavy pall of many souls searching for the land of warriors' dreams settled over the island. Then a sweet ocean breeze spun the billowing smoke into thick columns and carried it neatly into the sky.

By the time Ho'ola allowed Iuti to wake, islanders intent on resettlement had begun to arrive from atolls destroyed by the storm. There were breadfruit and coconut trees still standing on Fanape, and the taro crop had not been damaged by salt water, as on their home islands. Pahulu had never allowed the waves to wash that far inland.

Because the sharks had feasted so well near Fanape's shores, the reef would remain dangerous for many generations. But it was only a natural danger now—a cautious fisherwoman could set her nets among the colorful corals without undue fear. The island would never be a rich place. It never had been before, but it offered a clean and peaceful life for those who chose to treat it well.

"What of Pahulu?" Iuti asked after Risak and Ho'ola had told her the rest.

They were sitting in Iuti's old sleeping hut, which Mapa and the milis had rebuilt to house her and Risak and the still-sleeping Ma'eva. Iuti's body ached with every move; her side where her ribs had been broken still burned with each breath. But she could feel herself healing. She was grateful for her aunt's powerful spells and potions.

"Pahulu has been stripped of her power," Risak said. He was still wearing the necklace of Kunan's hair, and his fingers played across the dark strands as he spoke. "Even her wind magic is gone—not even the smallest breeze moves to her touch."

"The southern sorcerers will escort her home," Ho'ola said. "Her disgrace will serve as an example to others of her clan who might be tempted to use their birthright to grasp at unearned power."

Iuti followed Ola's look toward Tarawe. The girl sat just outside the hut, feeding bits of pounded breadfruit to the injured gull. If the acquisition of power had affected Tarawe adversely, it didn't show in her gentle handling of the bird.

"She has the touch of a true healer," Ola said.

Risak laughed. "She almost had that gull flying awhile ago. It was as clumsy as if Ma'eva were still riding inside, but it almost made it back into the air. Tarawe won't give up until she has it there."

"I think she might be hoping to establish a bond with the gull," Ola said. "She claims no other family god, and she's wise enough to know she'll need strong protection from now on."

Ola sighed and leaned back against a support pole. Mapa adjusted her cushion. "I offered to take her back to Sandar as my apprentice, but she refused. Hmmph. She claims to prefer the open air and the sea."

There was a flash of color as the milimilis appeared through the trees. Between them, they carried a stringer of reef fish as brightly patterned as themselves.

"I hope they didn't use some Lowtown poison to catch those," Ho'ola muttered.

"Ho. Good," the male mili called. "Our mighty warrior has awakened."

"How could she not," his partner replied, "after what we did to her there in the dark last night? Are you hungry, warrior woman?"

"Sleeping warriors who respond to our touch as sweetly as you did usually are," added the male. He winked and lifted a coy shoulder.

Iuti stared at them, then at Ola, who grinned and shrugged. Risak hid a laugh behind his hand. Risak had already told Iuti that he and the milis were going to travel together back to his home in the mountains. The whores had promised to stay with him there, he said, until the hurt he had taken among the drummers had healed. It seemed a strange solution. But, Iuti thought as she watched the milis mince across the clearing, I suppose if anyone can make Risak whole again, it's this deadly, darling pair.

The milis dropped their catch beside Tarawe, who quickly tugged a redfish free to feed to the bird.

"When will you wake the sea mimic?" the male mili asked as he perched on the edge of the raised floor beside

Ho'ola. He reached out to tuck a strand of Ola's hair behind her ear.

"We'd offer to do it for you," said the female, "but that old farm woman warned us not to teach him anything new." The milis slapped each other's knees and burst into giggles.

"Mano's teeth," Iuti muttered. But she lifted a questioning look to Ola. She, too, was eager to see how Ma'eva fared. The healer glanced toward Ma'eva's still form.

"I don't suppose I'll get any peace until he's awake, too," Ola grumbled. "And then I won't get any peace at all. Here, Mapa, help me move. My joints have grown as hard as coral in this sea-soaked air. Risak, move that great sword out my way."

"Be careful," Iuti said as the healer began washing the sleeping potion from beneath Ma'eva's nose. "Wake him slowly. He'll be confused, and he might try to revert to some more natural form."

Ma'eva's body flickered as Ola worked, but to Iuti's relief, the binding spell held. The sea-blue eyes he finally blinked open were entirely human. Ma'eva stared up at Iuti for a moment, blinked again, then grinned. His perfect smile was not quite so perfect with three of his teeth missing.

"Friend Iuti," he said. "You're still alive."

"Aye," she replied. "As are you, friend mimic."

The milis applauded in delight. They kissed first Iuti, one on each cheek, then Ma'eva before helping him sit upright. Ma'eva looked confused when he saw his body until he noticed the hair wrapped around his wrist. Then he smiled again.

"Ah, unfair, Iuti Mano," he said. "You've tricked me again. I knew you liked this body. How long do you intend keeping me captive this time?"

She grinned. "Until you're well. I don't want you changing into something these injuries might kill, not after Ho'ola worked so hard to keep this man-form alive."

Ma'eva brushed the light covering from his waist and

ran his fingertips over his thighs. He feigned dismay and slid a rueful glance toward the milimilis. "It's a pity you couldn't have called me back to a more colorful form," he said.

That made Iuti laugh again. "You don't need a form change to look like a Lowtown whore, Ma'eva. I'm sure our friends here will loan you face paint and ribbons . . ." The milis immediately voiced agreement and began pulling scarves and ribbons from the folds of their fluttering garments.

"You already look like Risak's twin," Ola said, "sitting there with your broken legs and yellowing bruises."

Ma'eva lifted his chin at that, but winced and stopped before the move was complete. Ola comforted him with a touch. A look of concern crossed Ma'eva's features.

"The gull," he said. "Is she . . ."

"She's fine," Tarawe said. She had approached so quietly that Iuti hadn't even noticed. Tarawe handed the gull carefully, almost shyly, to Ma'eva. "She says you can fly with her again when you're both well and after you've paid—" She glanced at Iuti and stopped.

Ma'eva, too, glanced at Iuti, then quickly away. Concern of a different sort touched his eyes.

Iuti frowned. She wasn't surprised that the bird had spoken to Tarawe. It seemed almost inevitable after what they had both been through. But . . . "What is it? Do you need help paying your debt to the birds, Ma'eva? You know you have only to ask and I . . ."

Ma'eva hid his face in the bird's tattered feathers.

Iuti turned back to Tarawe. The girl grinned and pressed her lips tightly closed.

"The sea mimic is *blushing*!" one of the milis whispered in astonishment.

"Ho'oma'eva," Iuti said sternly. "*What* did you promise those birds?"

He looked up at her with one eye. It was circled with a fading purple bruise. "The Great Pearl," he said in a very small voice.

Iuti's mouth fell open. "What!"

"I had to promise them something of value, Iuti

Mano," Ma'eva said, lifting his face again. "Gulls don't take riders for free, not when they come from the water."

Iuti settled her hands on her hips, trying hard not to laugh. "Just how do you plan to harvest that great stone?" she asked.

A slow smile crept across Ma'eva's face. "Well . . . *you* just offered to help . . ." His toothless grin brought Iuti a warmth she had thought could never reach her again.

"It was you, wasn't it?" she asked. "It was you who killed the sorceress the night Tarawe called her storm. Mano Niuhi didn't take his revenge that night because he wasn't even there."

"He was nearby," Ma'eva said.

"I thought I told you never to mimic the sharks."

"I thought I heard you say you didn't want to die in that place," he said.

"Ho, *you* are the trickster, Ma'eva," Iuti said.

She turned to Tarawe. "I suppose you want to help us harvest that silly pearl."

Tarawe's eyes were bright with excitement. "Well, I do owe the birds a debt of my own," she said.

A sweet-smelling breeze brushed through the hut. It lifted the gull's few remaining feathers and sent a tiny gecko wriggling across the thatch behind Ma'eva's head. Iuti reached out to lift the small creature onto her finger. It stared at her with shining black eyes—and for the first time since coming to Fanape, Iuti Mano knew a moment of true peace.

About the Author

Carol Severance is a Hawaii-based writer with a special interest in Pacific Island peoples and their environments. After growing up in Denver, she served with the Peace Corps and later assisted in anthropological fieldwork in the remote coral atolls of Truk, Micronesia. She currently lives in Hilo, where she has worked as an artist, a journalist, and a playwright. She shares her home with a scholarly fisherman, a surfer, and an undetermined number of geckos.